Jules Verne

The *La Chasse au météore*

Meteor Hunt

The First English Translation of Verne's Original Manuscript ⇒ Translated and edited by Frederick Paul Walter & Walter James Miller

UNIVERSITY OF NEBRASKA PRESS ⇒ LINCOLN

Publication of this book was made possible by a grant
from The Florence Gould Foundation

Library of Congress Cataloging-in-Publication Data
Verne, Jules, 1828–1905.
[Chasse au météore. English]
The meteor hunt = La chasse au météore : the first
English translation of Verne's original manuscript /
Jules Verne ; translated and edited by Frederick Paul
Walter and Walter James Miller.
    p.   cm.   — (Bison frontiers of imagination)
Includes bibliographical references.
ISBN-13: 978-0-8032-4677-5 (cloth : alk. paper)
ISBN-10: 0-8032-4677-3 (cloth : alk. paper)
ISBN-13: 978-0-8032-9634-3 (pbk. : alk. paper)
ISBN-10: 0-8032-9634-7 (pbk. : alk. paper)
I. Walter, Frederick Paul. II. Miller, Walter James,
1918—   III. Title. IV. Series.
PQ2469.C4E5 2006   843'.8 — dc22
2006008025

Designed & set in Monotype Fournier by A. Shahan.

BISON FRONTIERS OF IMAGINATION

CONTENTS

FOREWORD

You're looking at the first-ever English version of *The Meteor Hunt*
just as Jules Verne left it to us on his death in 1905. It's a delightful
satirical novel, a valid extrapolation of the science of his day, replete
with typical Verne comments on American mores and human greed.
It's not to be confused with the fraudulent pastiche, a version that's
literally a semiforgery, perpetrated by Verne's own son Michel but
published *in his father's name* in 1908. That grotesque distortion of the
real Jules Verne's real novel was translated into English the following
year as *The Chase of the Golden Meteor*.

For seven decades, in both France and the Anglophone world,
Michel's version was assumed to be the master's original work. But
scholars of the Société Jules Verne finally uncovered the sordid details of a conspiracy to deceive the public. In 1886 they issued for the
record a limited edition of Verne's own *La Chasse au météore*. Since
1994 French readers have enjoyed commercial editions. Now the English-speaking world can also appreciate its own version of *The Meteor
Hunt* by "the real Jules Verne."

Unfortunately, that phrase "the real Jules Verne" is all too familiar to savvy Anglophone devotees of the founder of science fiction.
For a century and a half, they've been subjected to phony, adulter-
ated, incomplete translations of the Great Romancer's other novels.
As Brian Taves, Library of Congress expert on Verne, tells us, WJM
"first vividly exposed" these crimes in his 1965 essay "Jules Verne in

America." He "elaborated on these problems in [his] *Annotated Jules Verne* series, and other scholars have since followed his lead."

Actually, *scores* of scholars, whole troops! This edition of *The Meteor Hunt* is a small albeit important part of a massive effort to give Anglophone readers the world over "the real Verne." Thanks to publishers like the University of Nebraska Press, Wesleyan University Press, the United States Naval Institute Press, Prometheus Books, and Oxford University Press, this historic project should be completed in the first quarter of the twenty-first century . . . six generations after the first criminally slapdash versions of Verne appeared in English.

But several commercial publishers still reissue the old frauds! So editors and translators of post-1965 versions take pains, in annotations and other commentaries, to explain the differences between their genuine articles and the old counterfeits. And of course Verne's stories deserve and evoke critical commentaries on literary and scientific grounds alone. Hence this edition will provide you with all such buffet services, to be sampled or ignored as you see fit.

If you've been provoked by these opening remarks to learn more about the *Meteor Hunt* scandal and about the Verne translation mess in general, you'll find more details in this foreword. This curtain raiser (to augment rather than mix the metaphor) also supplies you with general background information about Verne and his oeuvre, the origins of *Meteor*, and our policies and priorities in translating it.

While you're reading our English equivalent of the rediscovered book, words tagged with an asterisk may prompt you to consult our notes on the text (e.g., "because she was female*" on p. 5).

And we hope, after you enjoy *The Meteor Hunt* proper, that you'll want to compare your own reactions with ours. We discuss Verne's style, plotting, characterization, and themes in greater detail in our afterword.

BOLTS FROM THE BLUE

The Meteor Hunt poses this question: *What might happen if a large body from outer space hits the earth and it proves to be gold?* Verne had first considered this possibility in his original ending for *Hector Servadac* (1877). In that novel a comet grazes our planet and carries off Gibraltar, a slice of Algeria, and the sea in between. Some Frenchmen, Spaniards, Englishmen, and an Italian girl spend two years on a journey through the solar system. In spite of their diverse backgrounds, most of them get along well with each other, except with the Englishmen, whom they regard as too aloof. As the comet in its new orbit heads back to earth, it shoots off a splinter of itself. The main characters use a balloon to escape the coming collision, landing back in Captain Servadac's French military post in Algeria. But the English remain on the splinter, which is captured by the moon's gravity and becomes a "satellite of a satellite"!

The comet proper sinks into the squishy bottom of the Caspian Sea. Chemists analyze its protruding parts and find that it's composed almost one third of gold, with a total value of 245 sextillion francs (49 sextillion dollars). Hurray—this now increases tremendously the world's supply of gold on hand. But wait—this also *de*creases its value! Gold now becomes worth "exactly nothing, deserving, more than ever before, to be dubbed 'a vile metal.'"

But Verne's publisher, Pierre Hetzel, couldn't accept this "ruin of the capitalists," as Dr. Olivier Dumas, president of the Société Jules Verne, has termed it. Hetzel forced Verne to rewrite chapter 20, the ending, so that in the published book the title character now lamely "realizes" that his solar journey must have been just a "dream." As Dumas sees it, Verne got his revenge by waiting until Hetzel died before writing *La Chasse au météore*. Dumas published the original chapter 20 and discussed it in his society's *Bulletin* in 1985.

In addition to revealing the source of the scientific idea behind *The Meteor Hunt*, *Servadac* foreshadows two social and economic questions that also figure in *Meteor*: To what degree do nations create distinctive national characteristics in their respective citizens, and why does humanity venerate an essentially useless substance, gold, as a monetary standard? The artificial—no, as Verne sees it, the *fictitious*—value we accord to gold excites Verne's disgust from his first novels to his last.

It was in his amazingly productive seventies that Verne wrote *La Chasse*, his second try at problems caused by an invading body from outer space. But this time he confined all the human action to Mother Earth. Two amateur astronomers, Dr. Hudelson and Mr. Forsyth, neighbors and at first friendly rivals, both discover, independently but apparently at the same time, a new meteor orbiting over their home state of Virginia. They now become bitter enemies—each wants the meteor to be named after *him alone*. The competition heats up to the point where Jenny, Hudelson's daughter, and Forsyth's nephew, the young lawyer Francis Gordon, fret that they might not be able to marry as planned.

In his superbly constructed story, Verne includes a strong contrapuntal subplot: the adventures of an aristocratic couple who have a lot to learn, the hard way, about love and marriage. Conflicting views about what the woman-man relationship is and should be spice up all strands of the plot. As usual, in the middle-class level of Verne's world, servants provide provocative interaction. Mrs. Mitz, Forsythe's housekeeper, supplies him with stiff and badly needed loyal opposition. The bachelor Judge Proth also has a domestic manager, Kate, who raises serious philosophical questions about the nature of property. And a sassy, nosy, and perspicacious teenager, Loo, makes bright assessments of the situation that differ from the judge's but are equally arresting. Large groups—from crowds of commonfolk to meetings of world diplomats—give Verne plenty of opportunities to test out popular stereotypes about nationalities. Throughout, his masterful dialogue reminds us of his long experience with the theater.

Like many professional authors, Verne was as much a rewriter as a writer. He finished a second or third draft in 1904 and put it aside for a final checkup whenever the publisher might call for it. When he died a year later, he had a total of six recently drafted novels ready for final editing. In the case of *The Meteor Hunt*, we now know that all that really remained to be done was to crosscheck dates, addresses, and names; correct a few blurs in Verne's scribble; and delete a few commas and capital letters.

A SON'S CHICANERY

For decades the Verne family insisted that this was *all* that Verne's son Michel *did* do, back in 1908: he just *edited* those posthumous works—"guided them into print"—for Hetzel's son Jules, now the publisher. Many serious and respected books—like Jean Chesneaux's *The Social and Political Ideas of Jules Verne* and Jean Jules-Verne's biography of his grandfather—based their accounts of Verne's later intellectual development on this simple assumption: *the posthumous works were authentic.*

But in 1978, the Italian scholar Count Piero Gondolo della Riva, visiting the home of Hetzel's descendants, discovered several of Verne's original, hitherto unknown manuscripts—including that for *The Meteor Hunt*, along with a telltale list of changes to *Meteor* to be made by Michel! Comparison of Verne's original version with that published by Michel in 1908 revealed that the son had actually made *thousands of major and minor changes*, many more than were on the list.

To Verne's seventeen chapters Michel added four more. He created a dominant new character, Zephyrin Xirdal, who in effect takes over the action and the outcome. To succeed in this, Xirdal invents a "neuter-helicoidal current" and "atomic howitzers." Gregory A. Benford, science professor at the University of California, Irvine, flatly calls these inventions "wholly imaginary physics." Verne's original *La Chasse* extrapolates only from the known and accepted science of his day. Michel violated one of his father's basic principles in his "hard science" works: scientific integrity.

Michel also muted Verne's fascinating discussions of American mores and of marriage in general. He changed poor Mrs. Mitz into an American Mrs. Malaprop. For his own thematic purposes, Michel deletes one of Loo's most significant efforts—an attempt to reconcile the rival astronomers. He deleted, too, a coy section in which his father anticipates the postmodernist technique of self-reflective narration.

In Dumas' view, Michel "destroys the moral of the story," which Dumas sees as the overwhelming influence of the god Chance on human affairs. Michel certainly tampers with several main themes. In the eyes of most critics, Verne's smooth, graceful narrative is lost in Michel's lumpy expansion. (FPW has penned a fuller account of Michel's "rewrites," which you'll be ready for only after you've finished Verne's work proper: you'll find it in an appendix at the rear.)

One of the many ironies here is that both the author's son and the publisher's son were motivated, in "improving" Verne's original, by the hope of selling more books and making more money, while *The Meteor Hunt* itself is a strong indictment of human greed. It has been clear since the late 1970s that Michel transformed substantively all the works published posthumously under his father's byline—even, as Taves points it up, "originating two of the books himself."

Michel's basic cynicism was exposed by the German scholar Volker Dehs when he found, in the Bibliothèque National, a letter from Michel to Hetzel *fils* in which Michel actually *gloats* that there had been "no question from anybody about the *authenticity* of these posthumous works . . . [Rather one critic] praises a portion of the novel of which *there is not a trace, not even a rough draft* in the handwritten manuscript (the Xirdal character and the ending)" [italics ours]. So Dumas reports in his preface to the 1986 edition. And, as he mused in 1989, "The novels that Jules Verne left were a sacred trust." To which Herbert R. Lottman, in his "exploratory biography," adds, " His son should not have touched them; in doing so, even at the publisher's request, he committed a literary crime. In distorting his father's work, he changed its spirit." But is this forgery only a *literary* crime?

Unwittingly, as one of Michel's victims, the London publisher Grant Richards bought the rights to produce, in 1909, an English translation (by Frederick Lawton) of Michel's version under the title *The Chase of the Golden Meteor* and—of course!—"by Jules Verne"! The two sons' handiwork was really paying off. Not only had they deceived the British publisher and his translator, but, unhappily, Bison Books was also misled into reissuing this version in 1998.

Taves was outraged. The following summer he poured forth his fury in a long diatribe in *Extrapolation*, one of our leading journals about science fiction. His first sentence set the tone: "It's happened again." And he expertly reviewed Verne's tragic publication history. But the parent press of the Bison imprint, the University of Nebraska Press, is now more than atoning for that mistake. Nebraska has gained the right to publish new translations of several of the posthumous works, including (as you can see in your own hands) the real *Meteor Hunt*.

And we can now understand the strange dilemma that the UC Irvine physicist Gregory A. Benford was grappling with when he wrote the introduction for the Bison edition. In first reviewing Verne's overall history, he of course praised Verne's record for using mainly hard science. Yet, as we have seen, Benford still had to admit that the inventions in *The Chase* are just "wholly imaginary." How could he possibly have resolved the telltale contradiction? Not knowing the true story, Benford joined Chesneaux and many others as a sufferer from Michel's irresponsibility.

A HISTORY OF WRONGDOING

Discoveries in Europe about fraudulent editions of late Verne were matched by discoveries in America about phony editions of the *early* Verne.

In 1963 WJM started work on a new edition of "the standard translation" of *20,000 Leagues under the Sea*. This was the 1872 version by Mercier Lewis, one of the pseudonyms of the Rev. Lewis Page Mercier, MA from Oxford. WJM's suspicions were aroused when he read, in the second chapter, that Professor Aronnax "had just returned from a scientific research in the disagreeable territory of Nebraska." Checking the French, WJM found that Verne had simply said *les mauvaises terres*, the badlands! This gaffe was just the beginning. WJM uncovered hundreds of sophomoric misinterpretations (like confusion of *dix* with *six*, or ten with six, channels with canals, and wrench with key), ghastly scientific errors (Captain Nemo says his steel is 0.7 to 0.8 the density of water!), and so many omissions that WJM figured the English reader could have known, at best, only seventy-seven percent of Verne's novel. Many of the cuts seemed politically or religiously motivated: Lewis left out a famous passage about Nemo's political heroes, his denunciation of British imperialism, and the professor's talk about Darwin. The net result: "the standard translation" (still published by at least five houses) features a haphazard storyline, shallow characterization, an intellectual depth of near zero—a book, as one critic put it, "fit only for boys." But even most boys know that the specific gravity of steel is a good deal greater than that of water: actually 7.8!

While working on a new complete version, WJM made other, maybe even more ironic discoveries. In 1961 *Galaxy* magazine had run an article that sneered at Verne for creating steel so light that chunks of it would float, for not giving specifications for his batteries, and for additional foolish blunders. Like other American critics, the article's author, T. L. Thomas, blamed Verne himself for his *translator's* errors! Even such a science fiction expert as Damon Knight had been deceived until WJM's editor at Washington Square Press asked Knight to evaluate WJM's work.

Then WJM discovered that Bantam Books had issued a new and complete version by Anthony Bonner, but he found that when in doubt, Bonner had relied on Lewis's translation—for example, on the density of steel. And although, when consulting Lewis, Bonner must certainly have sensed the cleric's chicanery, Bonner said nothing at all about it in his introduction because he wrote no introduction. He neither exposed Lewis nor claimed a rightful first for himself. (Bonner's own mistake in following Lewis remained uncorrected for four decades until FPW helped Bantam issue an improved version.) So WJM added "Jules Verne in America: A Translator's Preface" to his 1965 edition (and Knight supplied an afterword); this edition, as Taves sees it, started the rescue mission.

With one exception, it was finally confirmed that all of Verne's major novels had been similarly violated in the huge late-nineteenth-century rush to sell him to the Anglophone world. For example, when translating *The Mysterious Island*, W. H. G. Kingston rewrote Nemo's deathbed speech to make it less offensive to English imperialists; and the American teacher Edward Roth added many of his own ideas to his version of *From the Earth to the Moon*. The one novel to escape such cynical treatment was *Around the World in Eighty Days*. Why? By then (1874) Verne had become so world-famous that as each chapter appeared in a French magazine serialization, foreign correspondents cabled home a summary. Naturally, when the time came to translate the finished book, nothing could be left out.

After 1965 "whole troops," as we remarked above, joined in a campaign to rehabilitate Jules Verne in the English-speaking world. As "completely restored and annotated" editions began to roll off the presses, Verne became more highly regarded in the academic and literary worlds. Stanford Luce, Arthur Evans, and William Butcher were among the first Anglophone scholars to write their dissertations on the founder of science fiction. Two American universities, as well as the nonprofit Naval Institute Press, have taken the lead with whole series of new versions. There is even now a *Jules Verne Encyclopedia* by Brian Taves and Stephen Michaluk; Jean-Michel Margot, president of the North American Jules Verne Society, resurrected one of Verne's barely known plays, *Journey through the Impossible*, now out in Edward Baxter's translation.

Thanks to scholars and publishers like these, Anglophone readers now know the genuine Verne as a fascinating writer for adults; they now know him not only as a prophet of science but also as a prophet of social and political developments.

For Verne foresaw not only our present concern with the consequences of comets or meteorites hitting the earth, but also the environmental and endangered-species crises and the possibility of crossing the poles by sailing under them, of producing self-renewing energy, of establishing underwater towns, mines, farms, and labs, and of escaping gravity by using gun tubes instead of forty-times-more-expensive-rocketry.

But he also foresaw, in *The Meteor Hunt*, our new concerns with the concept of "world property" (as manifest in the Antarctica Treaty), and in other works the emergence of new attitudes about gender and androgyny, the collapse of colonialism, the industrialization of China, the smoldering of French separatism in Canada, the rise of the American Goliath, and the prostitution of science by new power elites: private financiers and military-industrial complexes.

As you can see, "the real Jules Verne" could never separate the scientific from the social and political, as had his early English translators.

UNLUCKY IN LOVE

One situation in *The Meteor Hunt* reflects an agonizing period of Verne's own life, an agony that he suffered variations of over and over again. In *Meteor* he gives it a happy ending, once and for all. A review of Verne's biography will prepare you to appreciate this parallel—and others—between his life and this novel.

Sophie Allotte de la Fuye Verne gave birth to Jules in the seaport town of Nantes on the river Loire in 1828. She and her husband, Pierre, a maritime lawyer, would have four more children: another son the following year and then three girls. Although Jules enjoyed all his family, it was his brother Paul and his parents who most influenced him.

In his mind, his mother's forebears stood for the romantic way of life: they were adventurers, seafarers, soldiers, and wanderers. He saw his mother herself as a personification of the muses. Her imagination, he would write later, "is faster than a tornado . . . so curious when compared with how my own mind works."

To Jules, his father, descended from attorneys and judges, rather represented the logical side of life. In his country home near Chantenay, Pierre Verne trained a telescope on a church clock so he could better regulate his strict family and professional affairs. It was said that he knew the exact number of steps it took him to walk from his home to his office. But behind this façade of pure reason stood a pietistic man who practiced self-flagellation. That the telescope was focused on a church takes on double significance.

Pierre decided that his first son would carry on the family tradition, become a lawyer, and take over his father's practice. Jules envied his brother Paul, free to choose his own career on the high seas. Later Jules would rely heavily on Paul's naval training. In his teens Jules managed to juggle paternal logic with maternal imagination. He served as a law clerk in his father's office while (often secretly, in a bookstore) indulging his fantasy by writing poems and verse dramas. When it was time to go to law school in Paris, he dutifully attended lectures, passed his exams, and earned his law degree. But he spent all his free time enjoying the theater and penning comedies and historical dramas, earning the respect of Alexandre Dumas, who later would produce Verne's first comedy.

After six years of this double life in Paris, Jules finally wrote to his father about his true intentions. Only in his letters to his mother would he confide his deepest difficulties in pursuing a literary rather than a legal career. He suffered long detours—managing a theater, collaborating on operettas, writing mediocre fiction—before he found for himself the perfect balance between logic and imagination. He had to invent it himself: science fiction.

Five Weeks in a Balloon launched that new genre in 1863. This was the first of a series of sixty-five novels titled *Extraordinary Voyages* and subtitled *Worlds Known and Unknown* (paternal knowledge and maternal imagination?).

But in the other of humanity's two main searches in life—for love—Jules never found enduring success. When he and his cousin Caroline Tronson were in their late teens, he proposed to her and was humiliated by her laughing rejection. Then he fell in love with Herminie Arnault-Grossetière, to whom he dedicated at least thirty poems. For a while she returned his love but then married a man of property. Later he was so infatuated with Laurence Janmar that he sent his father to ask for her hand. Her father is reported to have mentioned Jules's weak financial prospects; actually, Janmar had concealed from Jules that she was practically engaged to a businessman. And there was a woman named Heloise.

Jules's failures had little to do with attractiveness (or maybe even with his personality). He was broad-shouldered and narrow-waisted, with beautiful teeth, a shock of hair like a red-gold flame, and an honest penetrating gaze from a handsome face. But his artistic manners, bold humor, and worse yet, his unsettled financial status probably disqualified him in favor of well-established, proper, middle-class suitors he described to his mother as "white hair mixed with black, the half-century married to the quarter-century."

It seems that the most agonizing rejection of all was Herminie's, leading to what Christian Chelebourg has convincingly called Verne's "Herminie complex." Apparently Verne's situation with her became traumatically symbolic of all his early experiences with women. After you've finished *The Meteor Hunt*, you can read in the afterword more about the parallel between the Herminie affair and our present novel.

Frequently humbled in love, sexually desperate at age twenty-nine, Verne now seemed willing to make compromises and take another of those long detours we mentioned above. He became enamored of Honorine Anne Hebé née du Fraysne de Viane, a widow with two girls. She had dainty dancing feet, laughing eyes, a good soprano voice, and a clear complexion. Her brother made easy money on the stock exchange. This shocked Pierre, especially when Jules asked for money to buy himself a seat on the Bourse to support a family of four. Jules made his request more urgent by hinting that he was at an age when legal sex became an urgent necessity and he hated to seek alternatives to marriage. In 1857 he and Honorine exchanged vows. He began a frantic gamble on being able to write in the early hours before going to work as a stockbroker.

His passion for Honorine withered fast, faster than his factitious interest in stocks. She seemed to him indifferent, if not harmful, to his literary ambitions; they had no intellectual interests in common. He went on long trips—Scotland, Scandinavia—even getting home late for the birth of his only child, Michel, in August 1861. She complained that he was no sooner home on his yacht (the *Saint-Michel*, on which he wrote many books) than he was planning to set out again on the next tide. In the presence of their grandson Jean she accused him of spending more time in the railroad station than in the house. But to be fair, we have no real account of her side of the story; we have long been waiting for a sympathetic biography of Honorine.

She finally appealed to Hetzel to help her save the marriage. For Jules had at last found true love in the arms of a lady in Asniéres with whom he could enjoy the intellectual life as well. She was one reason Verne frequently asked Hetzel to summon him to Paris "to read proofs." But alas, his lover died. The grandson, now a judge using the name of Jean Jules-Verne, insisted in his biography of his grandfather that Jules's relationship with her was strictly platonic. But years later Eunice McCauley represented WJM on a visit to Jules-Verne, telling him about WJM's work in progress. Eunice asked the judge about his description of Jules's relationship with the lady in Asniéres. The biographer's wife told Eunice that "he has no proof that it was platonic." Most other biographers, however—from the first, who hinted at a "unique siren," to the latest—write as if the only question is what the siren's name was. A Madame Duchene? Or Duchesne? Estelle Henim? Herminie come back?

In any event, we tend to see the novelist's many frustrations in sexual relations as explaining his ambivalent attitude toward women and middle-class mores, expressed so often in his writing—leading him at times to cynicism and misogyny, at times to acknowledgment of the possibility of mutual love (both to be found in *Meteor*), and even sometimes to a happy vision of ideal androgyny (as in *The Mighty Orinoco*). We mean the word *androgyny* in its most modern sense, as influenced by Jungian and feminist thinking. Here it refers to the belief that, contrary to patriarchal dogma, there are no innately feminine or masculine traits. Rather, persons of both genders potentially share most human characteristics. We shall expand on this in our endnotes, as Verne prompts us.

A READER-FRIENDLY TRANSLATION

In France the name Jules Verne has long been a household word; his fiction first appeared in the popular periodicals, and for many decades his new books were favorites for holiday gift-giving. Even with their scientific detail, sly satire, and psychological undercurrents, Verne's novels are targeted directly to the general public.

We've kept that reality in mind while composing this first-ever English translation of his own original *The Meteor Hunt*. Based on the 2002 Archipel reissue of the 1986 Société Jules Verne edition, our text aims not only for accuracy and fidelity, it aims also for a reader-friendly style. *Meteor* can be classed as a comic novel, and since its characters hail mainly from the United States, we've used American colloquialisms to approximate the humor, tone, and effect of the original French. In the same vein we've converted Verne's francs to dollars and his metric figures to U.S. weights and measures. In every case we supply Verne's original figures in our endnotes.

Verne's handling of personal names can also seem awkward to Anglophone readers, for example, his inconsistent attributions of "Miss" and "Mrs." to the millionairess Arcadia Walker, or his odd overuse of full names in some character identifications. We follow the standard English of her time and call the lady Miss Walker when she's single and Mrs. Stanfort when she's married. As for the repetitious use of full names, for the sake of naturalness and variety we occasionally abbreviate them to first or last name only.

Though Verne's novel is coherent and richly detailed, the manuscript (as we noted earlier) contains minor discrepancies, fluffs, and lacunae. These call for editorial decisions, and while preparing his 1986 edition, Dr. Dumas made a substantial number—and, while rendering the English version, we've made a few more. Each of these decisions is indicated in our endnotes. For students and scholars especially, we've drawn up an annotated bibliography of writings that have guided us and may guide you to go beyond our presentation here.

Finally, we want warmly to acknowledge the generous help of Jean-Michel Margot, who supplied us with valuable documents from his Verne collection, the largest in the Western world; Brian Taves and Colleen Cahill of the Library of Congress; Mary T. Hume and Barbara Bryant for their patience and encouragement; and Gary Dunham, our indulgent editor at the University of Nebraska Press. WJM's contribution to this edition of *The Meteor Hunt* was made possible in part by a grant from the Artists Fund of the New York Foundation for the Arts/Ruttenberg Foundation.

Frederick Paul Walter
Adult Services Librarian, Albuquerque/
Bernalillo County Library System

Walter James Miller
Emeritus Professor of English, School
of Continuing and Professional Studies,
New York University

THE METEOR HUNT

☞ 1. In which justice of the peace John Proth performs one of his most pleasant professional duties before going back to his gardening

The complications of the following story take place in a town that's located, we may as well admit, in Virginia, U.S.A. With your kind permission, dear reader, we'll dub this town Whaston, and we'll add that it occupies the east side, or right bank, of the Potomac River; but it strikes us as pointless to be more specific than that, so if you want to look for this community on even the best American maps, frankly, you're wasting your time.

One morning, on March 27 in the year of our story, any Whastonian crossing Exeter Street would have been surprised to see a smartly dressed horseman riding slowly up and down the road, then finally halting at Constitution Square near the center of town.

This horseman had to be under thirty years of age. In appearance he was your characteristic hardheaded Yankee.* He was taller than most, with a fine healthy complexion, auburn hair, brown beard, regular features, and no mustache. A big overcoat covered him down to the knees and spread over his horse's rump. He handled his high-spirited steed with skill and firmness. Everything about him indicated a man of action, a man of decision, and also a man who does the first thing that pops into his head. He would never fluctuate between hope and fear, the hallmark of a wishy-washy personality. Besides, any observer would have noted that his casual attitude did a poor job of hiding his natural impatience.

But what was his business that day in a town where nobody knew him, where nobody could recall ever having seen him before? Did he plan on staying a while? In any case he didn't seem interested in looking for a hotel. But if he had been, there were plenty of choices. In this respect Whaston was an exemplary locale, and no other U.S. city could offer travelers a warmer welcome, better service, finer food, or all the amenities at such consistently reasonable prices.

But this stranger didn't seem inclined to dawdle in Whaston. The ingratiating smiles of the hotel managers were definitely wasted on him.

And there was plenty of chattering back and forth between the customers and staff of the various hotels, who'd started filling up their respective doorways since the stranger's arrival in Constitution Square:

"Which way'd he come?"

"Down Exeter Street."

"And where's he from?"

"I'd guess from out Wilcox way."

"He's been riding around the square for the last half hour."

"Is he waiting for somebody?"

"Seems like it, and he's mighty impatient too."

"He keeps looking up Exeter Street."

"That's the way the other party will come, most likely."

"And who's this 'other party'? A guy or a gal?"

"Well good grief, he's all spiffed up."

"So he's got a date?"

"Yep, but not the kind of date you think."

"Then what kind?"

"Three or four times now, that stranger has stopped in front of John Proth's door."

"So, since Proth's the justice of the peace in Whaston . . ."

"It means this guy's bringing him a case to settle."

"And his opponent hasn't shown up yet."

"Right. And Judge Proth will fix things in a flash."

"He knows his stuff."

"And he's a decent fellow besides."

This may well have been the real reason why the horseman had arrived in Whaston. In fact, several times he'd stopped in front of John Proth's home without dismounting. He looked at its front door, he looked at the windows, he looked at the sign on which four words were legible: *Justice of the Peace*. Then he stood still as if waiting for somebody to show up on the doorstep. And this was the last time the hotel loiterers would see him pull up his horse, which, like its master, was champing at the bit.

Just then the door opened wide and a man appeared at the top of the little staircase going down to the front walk.

As soon as the stranger spotted this man, he tipped his hat and said:

"Judge Proth, I presume?"

"None other," replied the justice of the peace, bowing in return.

"I've got a simple question for you, and all you have to do is answer yes or no."

"Go on, sir."

"Did anybody drop by this morning asking for Seth Stanfort?"

"Not that I know of."

"Thanks."

And with that the horseman tipped his hat a second time, gave a flick of the reins, and headed at a jogtrot toward Exeter Street.

By this point it was the prevailing view that this outsider must have had business to conduct with Judge Proth. Based on the question he'd just asked, he himself was Seth Stanfort and was the first party to arrive for some prearranged appointment. And since it seemed likely that the time of this appointment had now come and gone, was he about to ride off and not come back?

Not surprisingly, since we're in America, home of the world's champion gamblers,* a round of betting started on the likelihood of the stranger's returning versus his leaving town for good. The hotel staffers and busybodies hanging around the square slapped down amounts ranging from fifty cents to five or six hundred dollars, which, being men of honor, the losers would faithfully pay up and the winners dutifully collect.

As for Judge Proth, he watched the rider head off in the direction of Wilcox. He was a philosopher and a sage, this magistrate, with at least fifty years of the said philosophy and sagacity under his belt—since he was born just half a century earlier with, you might say, both virtues already intact. What's more, he led the untroubled existence of a bachelor.* A native of Whaston, he'd rarely been out of town since his early youth. In the eyes of the citizenry, he was a man without ambition, and the folks in his jurisdiction were fond of him. He had an overriding sense of fairness. He was always tolerant of the foibles and passing frailties of others. To settle the cases that came before him, to make friends out of the foes who showed up in his humble courtroom, to patch up problems, to get things running smoothly again, to make the human interactions inherent in any social order as flawless as possible—this, as he saw it, was his mission as justice of the peace, and no magistrate was ever worthier of being called, literally, the best man for the job.

John Proth had no financial worries. If he worked at his calling, it was because he liked the work itself, and he had no urge to move up in his profession. He wanted a quiet life for himself and for everybody. He thought of his fellow man as a lifetime neighbor with whom he needed to coexist peacefully. His motto was early to bed and early to rise. He read a few big-name authors from Europe and America. Otherwise he stuck to the fair and balanced reporting of his town paper, the *Whaston Press*, in which local news took precedence over national politics. Every day he walked an hour or two around his neighborhood, and during his walks he tipped his hat so many times, he had to buy a new one on a quarterly basis. Beyond these strolls and the time he dedicated to his work, the judge relaxed in his peaceful, cozy home and tended the flowers in his garden, which repaid his efforts with a delightful array of fresh colors and sweet smells.

This quick description gives a fair idea of what made John Proth tick, so you can understand that the judge didn't worry much about the question the stranger had just asked him. Maybe if the horseman hadn't spoken to the master of the house but instead had questioned his elderly housekeeper Kate, she would have proven more helpful. Kate would have made a few reasonable demands on this Stanfort fellow, at the very least asking him just what she was supposed to say if another horseman — or horsewoman — should inquire after him. And Kate wouldn't have been shy about asking if the stranger planned on coming back to the judge's home later that day.

Mr. John Proth was totally free of any such such nosiness, any such need to know, traits more understandable in his housekeeper, first because she was elderly, mainly because she was female.* No, Proth hadn't even noticed the excitement out in the square that the stranger's arrival, presence, and subsequent departure had caused, and after shutting his front door again, he went to the garden to water his roses, irises, geraniums, and mignonettes.

Not following his example, the busybodies stayed on watch.

Meanwhile the horseman had ridden to the crest of Exeter Street, which overlooked the west side of town. Reaching the Wilcox subdivision, which this street joined to downtown Whaston, he brought his horse to a halt, but just as he'd done in Constitution Square, he stayed put in the saddle. From that vantage point he could see for a good mile around, and he could follow the winding road that went down to Steel, a village three miles away on the other side of the Potomac, whose church steeples stood out against the horizon. His eyes scanned this route, but it was no use. He definitely didn't find what he was looking for. And his movements were so impatient that they kept agitating his horse, and he had to rein it in repeatedly.

Ten minutes went by, then the horseman resumed his jogtrot back down Exeter Street, returning to the square for the fifth time.

"After all, it's still early," he kept telling himself while checking his watch. "We agreed we'd get together at ten oh seven, and it's barely nine thirty. She's coming from Steel, I came from Brial, they're both the same distance from Whaston, and the ride only takes twenty-five minutes. The road's in good shape and we're having a dry spell, so I doubt that the bridge is out. There won't be any problems or anything in the way. So if she's late, it has to be because she doesn't take this as seriously as I do. But punctuality means being right on time and not showing up too early. So I'm really the one who's at fault, since I got here a lot sooner than I would have if I'd planned better. All the same, the man's supposed to arrive first, out of respect if for no other reason!"

The stranger gave himself this talking-to the whole time he was coming back down Exeter Street, and he finished up his soliloquy just as his horse stepped onto the macadam of Constitution Square.

Obviously those who'd put money on the stranger returning down Exeter Street. had won their bets. So while the horseman rode past the hotels, the winners grinned and the losers shrugged.

At which point the town clock struck ten. The stranger brought his horse to a stop, pulled out his pocket watch, ticked off the ten strokes, and verified that the clock and his timepiece were in perfect agreement.

Only seven minutes to go till the appointment. And eight till it had come and gone.

Seth Stanfort went back by the entrance to Exeter Street, and neither he nor his horse could keep calm.

A number of passersby were hustling along the street. Stanfort completely ignored the ones heading uphill. He kept a sharp eye on those coming down, watching them the instant they appeared at the other end. It was far enough away for a pedestrian to need about ten minutes to cover the distance down to Constitution Square; but a galloping horse or a speeding automobile could do it in three.

Our rider, however, had no interest in the foot traffic. He didn't give it the slightest glance, and his closest friend might have walked under his nose unrecognized. The party he was waiting for could be coming only by horse or car.

But would she keep the appointment? There were only three minutes to go, just enough time to make it down Exeter Street—but no vehicle had turned the corner at the top of the hill, not even a bicycle or a motorbike, let alone an automobile, which could have gone like sixty and made it to the appointment with time to spare.

Seth Stanfort took a last look up Exeter Street. There were flickers of lightning in his eyes, and he muttered to himself with stiff-necked stubbornness: "If she isn't here by ten oh seven, the wedding's off."*

As if in answer to this statement, there was a clatter of hoof beats at the crest of the hill. Riding a magnificent horse was a young female who handled her steed with ease and firmness. The passersby jumped aside, and the road was clear down to the square.

Stanfort obviously knew the woman. He put on his best poker face. He didn't say a word, didn't move a muscle. After turning his horse, he calmly headed over and waited in front of Judge Proth's home.

The local curiosity seekers were on pins and needles again, and this time they inched closer; but the stranger didn't know they existed.

In a few seconds the woman had reached the square. White with foam, her steed pulled up a few steps from the judge's front door.

The stranger doffed his hat and said: "Good morning, Miss Walker."

"And good morning to you, Mr. Stanfort," Arcadia Walker answered, nodding graciously.

And believe you me, the eyes of Whaston were glued to the two newcomers. And the onlookers spoke among themselves: "If they've come with a case for Judge Proth, he'll work it out so they both win!"

"Yessiree, or he isn't the sharp fellow we think he is!"

"And if the two of 'em are single, the best deal would be to have 'em get married!"

So their tongues wagged back and forth. But Mr. Stanfort and Miss Walker evidently couldn't have cared less.

Stanfort was about to climb off his horse and knock on the judge's front door, but just then it opened on its own.

Mr. Proth reappeared, and this time his old housekeeper Kate stood right behind him.

In front of his house the horses had been pawing the ground so noisily, the judge had left his garden, and the housekeeper her kitchen, to come out and see what was going on.

Staying in the saddle, Stanfort spoke to the magistrate: "You're the justice of the peace?" he asked.

"That's right."

"I'm Seth Stanfort from Boston, Massachusetts."

"Pleased to meet you, Mr. Stanfort."

"And this is Miss Arcadia Walker from Trenton, New Jersey."

"It's a great honor, Miss Walker."

After looking the man over, Proth shifted his attention to the woman.

Miss Arcadia Walker was a delightful young lady. Twenty-four years old. Light blue eyes. Dark brown hair. Smooth complexion barely affected by the open air. Teeth flawlessly white and even. Taller than average. Ravishing figure. Bearing exceptionally lithe, agile, and elegant. In her riding togs she was completely at ease on her horse, which kept prancing around in reaction to Seth Stanfort's steed. She held the reins in stylishly gloved fingers, and any expert would have spotted her for a top-notch rider. Everything about her had that "certain something" characteristic of the upper classes in the United States — the American aristocracy you might say, if such a description didn't conflict with the democratic values of folks in the New World.

Miss Arcadia Walker hailed from New Jersey, had only distant relatives, made up her own mind, had her own money, boasted an adventurous nature typical of young Americans, did whatever she pleased, had already spent several years abroad in the European hot spots, and was up on the latest trends in Paris, London, Berlin, Vienna, and Rome. And thanks to what she'd seen and heard during her ongoing travels, she could talk to the French, British, Germans, and Italians in their own lingo. She was a cultured young woman whose education, thanks to her late tutor, had been exceptionally thorough. She'd even developed a good head for business, and she handled her money with unusual shrewdness.*

Most of what we've said of Miss Arcadia Walker can also be said symmetrically—that's the exact word—of Mr. Seth Stanfort.* Likewise independent, rich, fond of traveling, going everywhere, he spent little time in his hometown of Boston. In the winter he visited Europe's leading cities, where he repeatedly ran into a fellow American, the adventurous Miss Walker. In the summer he came back to the land of his birth, to those seaside resorts where he could mingle with upper-crust Yankees. There he would bump into Miss Walker again. Common interests soon brought these two dashing young people together, so the gossips—and that includes the ones in Constitution Square—decided they were perfect for each other: both were keen on traveling and would chase off to any place where political or military developments made the news. So, not surprisingly, the notion came to Mr. Stanfort and Miss Walker to join forces, since they wouldn't have to change their habits in any way. Figuratively speaking, they would no longer be two ships convoying side by side, but a single top-quality vessel so well rigged and so seaworthy, it could sail any ocean on earth.

So it wasn't some thorny legal dispute that had brought Mr. Seth Stanfort and Miss Arcadia Walker before the justice of the peace in this town. No, after handling all the legal formalities before the proper authorities in Massachusetts and New Jersey, they'd made an appointment in Whaston for today, March 27,* at 10:07, to take what wiser heads say is the most important step in a person's life.

Mr. Stanfort and Miss Walker having been introduced to the judge as you've seen, Proth's next move was to ask his two visitors what they needed from him.

"I want to marry Miss Arcadia Walker," the man answered.

"And I want to marry Mr. Seth Stanfort," the woman added.

The magistrate bowed to the couple and said: "Mr. Stanfort, Miss Walker—I'm at your service."

They bowed back.

"And when would you like me to schedule the ceremony?" Judge Proth continued.

"Right now, if you're available," Stanfort stated.

"Because as soon as I'm Mrs. Stanfort, we'll be leaving town," Miss Walker said.

Proth's face expressed how sorry he was, and all Whaston too, that their community couldn't get better acquainted with this delightful couple currently honoring the town with their presence. Then he added: "I'm completely at your disposal."

And he stepped back to welcome them inside.

But then Stanfort said: "Do Miss Walker and I have to dismount?"

"Not at all," Proth stated. "It's just as simple to marry you on horseback as on the ground."

It would be hard to find a more easygoing magistrate, even in the eccentric country of America.

"One question," Judge Proth continued. "Have you dealt with all the legal formalities?"

"We have," Stanfort answered.*

And he produced two marriage licenses, duly made out by court clerks in Boston and Trenton after payment of the required fees.*

Proth took the paperwork, put on his gold-rimmed pince-nez glasses, and carefully scanned the documents, which had been properly endorsed and stamped. Then he said: "Everything's in order, and I can now give you a marriage certificate."

Not surprisingly, the local busybodies had increased in number and were crowding around the couple, eager to witness this high-class wedding whose circumstances would have been outlandish anywhere else on the planet. Yet the two participants weren't just unconcerned, they were unaware.

From his doorstep Judge Proth spoke in a voice everybody could hear: "Do you, Seth Stanfort, take Arcadia Walker to be your lawfully wedded wife?"

"I do."

"And do you, Arcadia Walker, take Seth Stanfort to be your lawfully wedded husband?"

"I do."

The magistrate drew back for a second or two, as poised and intent as a photographer waiting for the right instant to snap a picture. Then he proceeded: "Seth Stanfort of Boston and Arcadia Walker of Trenton, by the power vested in me, I now pronounce you man and wife."

The two newlyweds drew close and held hands, to seal their union.

Then Stanfort took a five-hundred-dollar bill out of his wallet and handed it over, saying: "For your services."

And the new Mrs. Stanfort held out another such bill, saying: "For charity."

They both nodded to the judge, who bowed back, then they flicked their reins and rode quickly off in the direction of Wilcox.

And like the philosophical fellow he is, John Proth said to himself: "America's such an amazing place—it's almost as easy to get married as to get divorced!"*

2. Which welcomes the reader into the home of Mr. Dean Forsyth, whose household includes his nephew Francis Gordon and his housekeeper Mrs. Mitz

"Mrs. Mitz . . . Mrs. Mitz!"

"Yes, Mr. Francis?"

"What's going on with Uncle Dean?"

"I ain't sure, Mr. Francis."

"Think he's sick?"

"Not that I know of, but if he keeps this up, he's gonna be!"

These questions and answers flew back and forth between a young fellow of twenty-three and an old lady of sixty-five, both in the dining room of a home on Elizabeth Street, in this same town of Whaston that had just witnessed an exceptionally eccentric American-style wedding.

This house on Elizabeth Street was the property of Mr. Dean Forsyth. He was fifty-five years old and looked it—big shaggy head, beady eyes behind thick-lensed glasses, stooping shoulders, heavy neck always encircled by a double-layered necktie that climbed to his chin, rumpled baggy frock coat, loose vest with the bottom buttons always undone, pants too short and barely coming down to his clodhoppers, fez perched on the rear part of his grizzled head, face lined with a thousand wrinkles and tipped with your standard North American goatee.

This was the man whom his nephew Francis Gordon and his housekeeper Mrs. Mitz were discussing on the afternoon of April 3.*

Losing both parents at an early age, Francis had been raised by Dean Forsyth, his uncle on his mother's side. Though he had a bequest coming to him from his uncle, Francis wanted to make his own way in the world, and Forsyth had agreed. So young Gordon had enrolled in a humanities program at the renowned institution of Harvard.* He had graduated a lawyer and opened a practice in Whaston, where he became the staunch defender of widows, orphans, and homesteads. He knew his case law backwards and forwards, and he had an easy, eloquent courtroom manner. Young and old, his colleagues respected him to a man, and he didn't have an enemy in the world. He was a good-looking fellow with handsome brown hair and dark eyes, well-shaped hands, humor without sarcasm, natural friendliness, and skill at the various sports popular with Yankee gentlemen. And since he was one of the town's most eligible young men, he'd fallen appropriately in love with delightful Jenny Hudelson, the daughter of Dr. Hudelson and his wife Flora, née Clarish.

But at this juncture we aren't quite ready for young Miss Jenny. It isn't time for her to take the stage, and we'll be better off meeting her in her own family surroundings. It won't be long now, but you can't be too careful in telling this kind of tale.

Getting back to Francis Gordon, we'll add that he lived in the house on Elizabeth Street and most likely wouldn't be moving out till he and Jenny Hudelson got married. But once again we'll hold off on Miss Jenny and concentrate instead on the old housekeeper, Mrs. Mitz, bosom buddy of her employer's nephew, whom she loved like a son—or grandson rather, since grammas are usually the most doting elders of all.

Mrs. Mitz was your model housekeeper, a member of a dying breed, the descendant of an extinct species of servant* that's as loyal as a dog and as housebound as a cat. As you might imagine, Mrs. Mitz didn't mince words with Mr. Forsyth, and when he was in the wrong, she let him know it. If he disagreed, he had only one option: head for his study and bolt the door.

In any case Forsyth didn't mind being off by himself. He could depend on another person of some note, an individual who also hid from the scolding, lecturing tongue of Mrs. Mitz.

This was a little fellow nicknamed Omicron, whose moniker might well have been Omega if he hadn't been such a pipsqueak. He hadn't grown a notch since he was fifteen, at which point he'd stood only four feet six inches high. His real name was Tom Whiff,* and he'd been a hired hand in the Forsyth home right from the time he'd stopped growing; and since he was now over fifty, this means he'd been working for Francis's uncle some thirty-five years.

But it's important to understand how Omicron's role had changed over time: he'd evolved into Forsyth's assistant, helping him in his work with an intensity that easily matched his employer's.

And what exactly *was* this work of Dean Forsyth's?

He was an enthusiast, a man with great wild-eyed dreams, as you'll see for yourself.

And what was his specific line of work? Doctor, lawyer, scientist, author, artist, businessman, like plenty of other folks in the land of the free?

Not in so many words, but he did dabble in science—the particular science of astronomy, though he steered clear of the higher mathematics of heavenly bodies. Instead he was exclusively interested in discovering new stars and planets. Almost nothing that happened on the surface of the globe had any appeal for him, and he spent his life in the infinite reaches of outer space. But since they didn't serve meals there, he had to come down to earth at least twice a day. And on this particular morning, he was keeping everybody waiting at the dining room table, which made old Mrs. Mitz fret and fume.

"Ain't he coming?" she repeated.

"Omicron's with him, right?" Francis asked.

"Where his master is, he's never far off," the housekeeper answered, then added in her inimitable fashion: "But I ain't got the legs to climb up to their hangout and see."

The hangout in question was an actual watchtower, an authentic observation deck whose top floor was some twenty feet above the roof of the house. The floor underneath was a circular room with four windows that faced the four points of the compass. Inside, some optical instruments were pivoting on their bases—binoculars and telescopes of pretty considerable range—and if their lenses weren't hopelessly worn down, it wasn't the fault of their users. A more pressing worry was the possibility that Forsyth and Omicron might wind up ruining their eyes from constantly rubbing them against the eyepieces of their instruments.

This was the room where the two of them spent the better part of their days and nights, relieving each other, it's true, between going to bed and getting up at dawn. They peered, they examined, they searched all over the galaxy. They were forever hoping to make some discovery that could be named after Dean Forsyth. Any time the skies were clear, they were at it again; but on the thirty-seventh parallel, which intersects the state of Virginia, the skies didn't always behave. They featured all the cirrus, nimbus, and cumulus clouds anybody could want, and definitely more than the master and his assistant did. So the two of them kept up a running crossfire of threats and cusswords against those inconsiderate winds that insisted on draping curtains of vapor across the firmament.

And during all the endless, aggravating hours when nothing was visible, our amateur astronomer would scratch his scruffy head and say over and over: "For all I know, some new star could be within reach of my lens right now! This could be my big chance to find a second moon circling the earth, or some junior satellite orbiting the moon! Maybe there's a stray meteor out there, some shooting star* or asteroid going by right behind that damned cloud cover!"

"Absolutely," Omicron answered. "And just this morning, boss, there was an opening in the clouds, and I thought I spotted . . ."

"I spotted it too, Omicron . . ."

"We both did, boss, both of us . . ."

"I definitely saw it first," Forsyth insisted.

"No argument," Omicron agreed, giving an approving nod. "And I'm almost certain that it was . . . that it had to be . . ."

"I could have sworn," Forsyth insisted, "that it was a meteor heading from the northeast to the southwest."

"Yes, boss, practically in the same direction as the sun."

"To all appearances, Omicron . . ."

"Right."

"It went by at seven thirty-seven and twenty seconds."

"Twenty seconds," Omicron repeated. "That's what the clock said."

"And it hasn't come back since!" Forsyth snarled, shaking his fist at the sky.

"No, boss, and up in the west-southwest, nothing but clouds, clouds, clouds! I doubt if we'll see a square inch of blue the whole day!"

"It's deliberate!" Forsyth replied. "It's a plot aimed specifically at me!"

"Me too!" Omicron muttered. He saw himself as full partner in his boss's enterprises.

Needless to say, all the other citizens of Whaston had their own grounds for complaint whenever cloudy skies afflicted the town. Whether or not the sun shines, it's still everybody's business.

And you can imagine the vileness of Dean Forsyth's mood when a fog settled over the area, a forty-eight-hour fog no less. Even under cloudy skies it was still possible to spot some asteroid or other as it skimmed the surface of the planet earth; but in one of these thick fogs with less than a ten-yard visibility, the strongest telescopes and latest-model binoculars couldn't see across the room. And even though Whaston is watered by the limpid waves of the Potomac rather than the muddy currents of the Thames, this type of London peasouper is plenty common in these parts.

But let's get down to cases. When the skies had been clear early that morning, just what had Forsyth and his servant seen—or thought they'd seen? It was a shooting star with a long tail and it was moving so fast they couldn't gauge its brightness. What's more, as we've already heard, this meteor was heading from the northeast to the southwest. But since it had to be moving at a well-defined distance from the earth, it should have been possible to train a telescope on it for a good while—if that ill-timed fog hadn't gotten so thoroughly in the way.

And since then, naturally, this bad luck did nothing but provoke complaints. Would that shooting star put in another appearance on Whaston's horizon? Would they be able to figure out its components, determine its mass, its weight, its makeup? Would some other astronomer have better luck and find it somewhere else in the sky? Since Dean Forsyth had seen it in his telescope for only a short time, would he still qualify to name this discovery after himself? Or would all the glory go later on to one of those experts in Europe or America who spend their whole lives studying meteors, professionals who can scour the skies top to bottom from their observatories?

The two men went back to the windows facing east. They didn't say a word. Forsyth scanned the vast horizon bounded on one side by the jagged outline of the Serbor Hills and over which the wind was picking up, busily driving piles of gray clouds that left only a few skimpy openings here and there. Given his subnormal height, Omicron had to stand on tiptoe to get a better view. Forsyth folded his arms tightly over his chest, fists clenched. The other man beat a nervous tattoo on the windowsill. A few squawking birds fluttered past, as if jeering at Forsyth and his assistant for being earthbound humans! Oh, if only they could soar into the skies along with those birds—couldn't they fly through that cloud layer and maybe see that asteroid again, as it continued on its way in the bright sunlight?

Just then there was a knock at the door.

Wrapped up in their thoughts, Dean Forsyth and Omicron didn't hear it.

The door opened and Francis Gordon stood on the threshold.

Forsyth and Omicron didn't even turn around.

Francis went over to his uncle and tapped him on the arm.

Forsyth seemed to come back from some place not of this earth but out in space, where his imagination had taken him in hot pursuit of the meteor. "What?" he asked.

"Uncle, lunch is waiting."

"Oh is it?" Forsyth put in. "Well, so are we."

"You? What do you mean?"

"We're waiting for the sun to come back out," Omicron explained, and his master nodded in agreement.

"But I don't believe you've invited the sun to lunch, uncle, so we can dig in without him."

It was hard to dispute this. Since Old Sol was staying away all day, why couldn't Forsyth unbend and have lunch along with the rest of the planet?

"Uncle," Francis continued, "Mrs. Mitz is getting her dander up, and I'm afraid she . . ."

This was a compelling argument and it yanked Forsyth from fantasyland back into reality. He knew and feared his housekeeper's temper, and this summons from her called for instant obedience. "What time is it?" he asked.

"Eleven forty-six," Francis replied.

And 11:46 is what the clock said too, whereas Forsyth and his nephew usually sat down to lunch at eleven o'clock on the dot.

Normally his assistant Omicron would have eaten along with them. But that day Forsyth expressly ordered him to stay behind on the observation deck in case the sun came out again.

Forsyth and Gordon headed for the stairs and descended to the ground floor.

Where Mrs. Mitz was. She glared at her boss, who hung his head.

"What happened to Omicron?" she demanded.

"He's busy upstairs," Francis answered. "We'll have to do without him this morning."

"Whatever," Mrs. Mitz replied.

Lunch got under way, and their mouths ate but didn't talk. Mrs. Mitz usually kept up a constant chatter while bringing in each course and exchanging the plates, but that day her teeth stayed clenched. The silence was heavy, the tension unrelenting.

Trying to put an end to this, Francis said: "Well, uncle, did you get in a decent morning's work?"

"Yes and no," Forsyth answered. "The weather didn't cooperate."

"You're on the verge of some big discovery out in space?"

"I think so, Francis. However, I can't be certain without seeing it again."

"But is it worth stewing about all week?" Mrs. Mitz inquired caustically. "You spend your whole life in your tower and you get up in the wee hours—yes, I heard you three times last night—"

"Actually, my dear Mrs. Mitz—"

"Then, when you drop from exhaustion," the old housekeeper went on, "when your health goes bad, when you catch your death of cold, when you're stuck in bed for weeks on end, are your stars gonna come down and cure you, is the doctor gonna prescribe you a bottle of 'em to take instead of pills?"

Whenever the conversation descended to this level, Forsyth knew it was hopeless to talk back. He hated Mrs. Mitz's reprimands, but he didn't want to set her off by arguing with her; he meekly returned to his meal and promptly tried to eat from his glass and drink from his plate.

Francis Gordon made an attempt to keep the conversation going, but he was talking to the walls. His uncle wore a dreary expression and seemed to be shutting him out. But when all else fails, people talk about the weather, whether today's or tomorrow's. It's an inexhaustible topic that always works, and in fact the weather was exactly the issue that had Forsyth on tenterhooks. So at a particular moment when the cloud cover had left the dining room even darker, he raised his head, looked out the window, wearily put down his fork, and exclaimed: "How long is that damned sky going to stay cloudy? Why can't it rain and get it over with?"

"I'll say," Mrs. Mitz stated. "We've had a dry spell for three whole weeks, so the ground could sure use it."

"The ground!" Forsyth muttered, so scornfully that his old housekeeper was off and running again.

"That's right, the ground! It's as good a place as that sky you keep your head stuck in, even at lunchtime!"

"Okay, okay, Mrs. Mitz," Francis said, trying to soothe her.

"Besides," she kept on in the same tone of voice, "if it ain't allowed to rain the first week of April,* when the heck can it?"

"She's right, uncle," Francis continued. "This is early April, it's the start of spring, and that's the way things are. But spring weather isn't always bad! When the cold lets up, there are dry spells with clear skies, just like in midsummer. So conditions will get better and you can go back to work. Be patient, uncle."

"Patient!" Forsyth responded, his face as dismal as the sky. "How can I be patient at a time like this! What if it goes so far away that we can't see it? What if it never shows up on the horizon again?"

"It?" Mrs. Mitz exclaimed. "What's this 'it' you're yammering about?"

Just then Omicron's voice rang out: "Boss, boss!"

"What?" Forsyth exclaimed, leaping from his chair and heading for the door.

And sure enough, a ray of sunshine had come through the window, highlighting the glasses, bottles, and pitchers on the table.

"It's the sun . . . the sun!" Forsyth repeated, dashing up the stairs.

"Off he goes again!" Mrs. Mitz said, sinking down on a chair. "Is that right, I ask you? He spends all day and all night in the chilly springtime air. He could come down with a cold, congestion, bronchitis—and all because of his falling stars! Does he think he can catch one and stick it in a glass case?"

Old Mrs. Mitz went on and on, though her employer couldn't hear her and wouldn't have listened if he could.

Panting from his dash up the stairs, Dean Forsyth headed for the observation deck. The wind had picked up from the southwest and driven the clouds eastward. Directly overhead a wide patch of blue was showing through. A good part of the sky where they'd seen the meteor was now clear, allowing their instruments to follow its path without any interference. Sunlight bathed the room.

"Well," Forsyth asked, "what's going on?"

"The sun's out," Omicron answered, "but not for long, because the clouds are already back in the west."

"There's no time to lose!" Forsyth exclaimed, aiming his telescope while his assistant did the same with his spyglass.

For some forty minutes they maneuvered their instruments with intense dedication. How patiently they adjusted their sights to keep the target in focus! How painstakingly they probed every nook and cranny in that corner of the firmament! It was exactly the same ascension and declination where their shooting star had appeared the time before . . . they were sure of its coordinates.

They didn't see a thing. That whole patch of blue, that magnificent field for wandering meteors, was completely empty. There wasn't a speck. Not the shadow of an asteroid, not the tiniest hint.

"Nothing!" Forsyth put in, rubbing eyes that were now red to the lids.

"Nothing!" Omicron whimpered.

Then it started to cloud over again.

As far as the sky was concerned, and the whole day as well, that was that. The cloud cover was soon a filthy gray mass, then it started to drizzle. To their utter despair, Forsyth and his assistant had to give up any further attempts at skywatching.

Then Omicron said: "But sir, aren't we positive we saw it?"

"How could we be more positive!" Forsyth exclaimed, raising his hands to high heaven. Then, in a tone that was equal parts worry and jealousy, he added: "I only hope Stanley Hudelson didn't see it too!"*

3. Whose subject is Dr. Stanley Hudelson, his wife Mrs. Flora Hudelson, and his two daughters Miss Jenny and Miss Loo

And likewise Dr. Stanley Hudelson was saying to himself: "If only Dean Forsyth didn't see it too!"

He was a physician, though he didn't practice medicine in Whaston; instead he chose to devote all his time and talent to the exalted discipline of astronomy.

In any case Dr. Hudelson was well off, with both his own money and the dowry of his wife, Mrs. Flora Hudelson, née Clarish. Thanks to his shrewd handling of this fortune, his future was secure and so were his two daughters, Jenny and Loo.

This stargazing doctor was forty-seven years old, his wife forty, his elder daughter eighteen, and his younger fourteen.

The Hudelsons were old friends of the Forsyths, yet there was a definite rivalry between the doctor and Francis's uncle. It wasn't just that they argued about the various stars and planets, since what's out in space belongs to everybody, even those who weren't its original discoverers; but they often wrangled over the various atmospheric phenomena they'd observed.

The only thing that might have made things worse and led to moments of real nastiness would have been the presence of a Mrs. Forsyth. But as we've already seen, no such lady existed—Forsyth was a bachelor, and he'd never had any thoughts of marriage, not in his wildest dreams. Since he didn't have a wife to rush to his defense and complicate matters, there was every likelihood that squabbles between the two amateur astronomers could be patched up quickly.

True, in the second family there was still Mrs. Flora Hudelson. But as a woman, mother, and housewife, she was the soul of good-natured sweetness, incapable of being at odds with anybody, and never given to gossip or backbiting, unlike many otherwise reputable ladies in America and Europe. She was a model partner and her specialty was calming her husband down when he came home in a huff after some shouting match with his old pal Forsyth.

Mrs. Hudelson, it should be noted, was completely accepting of Dr. Hudelson's obsession with astronomy—she didn't mind if he spent his whole life in outer space, so long as he came back down to earth when she asked him to. But unlike old Mrs. Mitz who brutalized her master, she put up with her husband's foibles, waiting for him at mealtimes or on social occasions; she never scolded him and even managed to keep his food warm; she tolerated his absentmindedness when he was caught up in his work; she worried about it along with him, and she knew when to dole out words of encouragement if he seemed bothered by some discovery and was literally lost in space.

Everybody should have such a wife, not just astronomers.*

Their elder daughter, the lovely Jenny, gave promise of following in her mother's footsteps, of taking the same path through life. If Francis Gordon married Jenny Hudelson, he had a decent shot at becoming the happiest of men. Without slighting other American girls, we can honestly say you won't find a more attractive, charming, and gifted young lady anywhere in the United States. She was a sweet-natured, blue-eyed, clear-skinned blonde with delicate hands, dainty feet, a lovely figure, unassuming elegance, and goodness as well as good sense. So Francis adored her as much as she adored him. Besides, Forsyth's nephew was both a friend and a favorite of the Hudelson household. All of which had soon evolved into a proposal of marriage, an offer that was wholeheartedly accepted. The two young people were genuinely compatible. Jenny's domestic talents would create a comfortable home. Francis would provide financial security, since he was due to take over his uncle's fortune someday. But we don't need to bother with these inheritance prospects. It wasn't just that their future was secure—their current circumstances already had all the ingredients for happiness.

So Francis Gordon had become Jenny Hudelson's fiancé and vice versa; the wedding was supposed to take place in the near future, Father O'Garth presiding, at St. Andrew's, the biggest church in that blissful town of Whaston.

And the nuptials, rest assured, would be well attended, because both families were held in the highest regard. You can also rest assured that the happiest, liveliest, and least inhibited individual that day would be the maid of honor, Jenny's baby sister, darling little Loo.[1] This young lady hadn't quite turned fifteen, so she could get away with anything. She was everybody's favorite, everybody's pampered pet. Loo had a trait the personality experts say is standard for her type: she couldn't hold still for a second. She was a mischief maker, a sassy little thing who even dared to joke about "dad's planets." But nobody cared, everybody forgave her, Dr. Hudelson was the first one to chuckle, and the only punishment he administered was a kiss on her teenaged cheek.

Deep down Dr. Hudelson was a decent fellow but he was also bullheaded and temperamental. Aside from Loo, whose kidding he shrugged off, everybody else held his fads and eccentricities in awe. Addicted to skywatching, consumed by his quest for new phenomena, jealously guarding the discoveries he made (or claimed he made), he viewed his friend Dean Forsyth as a competitor and got into endless feuds with him over this or that meteor. They were two hunters out in the same meadow arguing about who shot what. Many a time clouds gathered and storms were on the horizon, but gentle Mrs. Hudelson usually managed to brighten up the skies. And she was capably assisted by her two daughters and Francis Gordon. Besides, once the wed-

1. *Author's Note*: Short for Louise.

ding of Francis and Jenny had brought the two families even closer together, these occasional storms would be less of a problem—and who knows, maybe the two hobbyists would team up and carry out their cosmic research as partners! After a day of hunting together in the vast reaches of outer space, maybe they would be willing to divvy up the spoils.

We can't resist mentioning that while he was studying the skies, Dr. Stanley Hudelson was also deeply interested in statistics—especially the branch of statistics that measures crime rates, whose fluctuations, according to authorities in the field, coincide with changes in the temperature and the weather. Dr. Hudelson put great energy into diagramming these correlations on a graph. He did everything he could to keep his crime chart up to standard. He shared his personal insights in a regular correspondence with Mr. Linnoy, Director of Weather Services for the State of Illinois. And there was no contradicting him, when, backed by that expert in Chicago, the doctor would allege that "crime rates go hand in hand with rising temperatures, if not on a daily basis, then at least on a monthly or a seasonal basis." According to this view of things, there would be a slight surge in criminal activity during fair weather, and a slight decline during foul weather. The cooler temperatures typical of the winter months, and the heavy rains characteristic of springtime, seemed to correspond to a decrease in crimes against person and property. What's more, the numbers positively plummet when the wind shifts to the northeast. Finally, it seemed that the three graphic curves charting insanity, suicide, and crime overlapped each other pretty closely under the same seasonal and temperature conditions.

Yes, Dr. Hudelson was completely sold on these interesting theories.* Consequently, to cope with criminal activity and the danger of being victimized by it, he advised taking the greatest precautions during those months when it was "criminally hot." So Loo smirked that she would lock herself in whenever it got warm, whenever it got dry, and whenever the wind blew the wrong way.

Dr. Hudelson's home was as well kept and comfortable as any in Whaston. Located halfway down Morris Street at No. 27, this lovely mansion was a landmark, its front yard and back garden adorned with leafy trees and green lawns. It was a two-story home with seven windows in front. Towering over the left side of its peaked roof was a sort of square turret, some thirty feet high and topped by a deck with railings around it. A flagpole stood in one corner and on Sundays and holidays displayed the American flag with its fifty-one stars.*

The upper room of this turret was consecrated to the task of stargazing. There the doctor manned his instruments, and on clear nights he took his binoculars and telescopes out onto the deck, where he could freely inspect the dome of the skies. There too, despite Mrs. Hudelson's warnings, he came down with the world's juiciest coughs.

"Daddy will end up infecting the galaxy," Miss Loo rattled on. "The whole universe will have runny noses."

But the doctor paid no attention and sometimes went out in temperatures below twenty degrees Fahrenheit* during those major winter freezes when the skies are at their clearest.

From the watchtower of his Morris Street home, incidentally, you can easily see the observation deck of the house on Elizabeth Street. No monuments stood in between them, no trees stuck their leafy branches in the way. The two dwellings were half a mile apart. With a respectable pair of binoculars and with no need for a long-range telescope, you can readily see people in the opposite tower or deck. Needless to say, Dean Forsyth had other things to do besides gaping at Stanley Hudelson, and Hudelson wasn't about to waste his time gawking back at Forsyth. They'd set their sights much higher and had no concern for earthly things. But it was natural enough that Francis Gordon would look for Jenny Hudelson up in her tower, and with the help of their field glasses they often spoke to each other with their eyes. And what's the matter with that?

Of course it would have been simple enough to run a telephone or telegraph line from one house to the other. A wire stretching between the turrets of their two lookout posts would have allowed Francis and Jenny to indulge in some delightful communing. And no doubt little Miss Loo would have frequently joined in, turning a duet into a trio. But Forsyth and Dr. Hudelson didn't want to be disturbed during their skywatching, had no time for idle chitchat, and there weren't any plans to install a phone line. But when the lovers were legally wed, wasn't it possible this amenity might be added? After the matrimonial bond, an electric one could bring the two families even closer.

That day Francis was just paying his usual afternoon visit to Mrs. Hudelson and her daughters. Admittedly he had the run of the house and he got a warm welcome in the downstairs living room. If he wasn't quite Jenny's husband as yet, Loo insisted he was already her brother, and when her teenaged mind was made up, that was that.

To nobody's surprise Dr. Hudelson stayed cooped up in his tower. He'd been there* since 4 a.m. Like Forsyth, he'd come down late for lunch, then he'd dashed furiously back up to his observation deck the instant the sun broke through the noontime clouds, again like Forsyth. Obviously he and his colleague were equally obsessed, and he wasn't likely to come back down very soon.

But if he didn't, it would be impossible to decide a certain pressing matter that was the whole point of this gathering.

"My, my," Loo exclaimed as young Gordon came through the living room door. "Here comes Francis, faithful old Francis! I wonder what he wants! It's like he never leaves!"

Grinning, Francis first took Jenny's outstretched hand, then greeted Mrs. Hudelson. Afterward, in response to Loo, he got her to blush by planting a noisy kiss on her cheek.

Then the two lovers sat down and started to talk, and they seemed simply to pick up where they'd left off the day before. It was as if they'd never been apart, and, in their thoughts at least, they really hadn't. In fact Miss Loo maintained that Faithful Old Francis never actually went away, that he pretended to go out the front door, snuck

27

in again at the back, and hid out of sight in some cubbyhole.

That day they talked about what they always talked about while waiting for their union to be finalized. Jenny listened to Francis with a relaxed seriousness that only added to her charm. They looked into each other's eyes and laid plans they fully expected to carry out in the near future. How could they have known that these plans would be drastically delayed? Hadn't both families consented to their marriage? Besides, Francis had just found a lovely house on Lambeth Street that offered all the amenities including a lush, year-round garden. It was on the west side of town, had a view over the Potomac, and wasn't too far from Morris Street. Consequently Mrs. Hudelson promised to go inspect this house the next day, and if the future occupant found it satisfactory, they would lease it the same week. Loo was to accompany her mother and sister on this tour of inspection. The girl insisted that her advice was essential, that she positively had to be involved in setting up the new household. So they agreed that she could come along and dispense her wisdom.

Suddenly Loo got up from her sofa, ran to the window, and exclaimed: "Hey, what about Mr. Forsyth? Isn't he due today?"

"Uncle will come by at about four o'clock," Francis answered.

"If we're going to settle this matter," Mrs. Hudelson commented, "we absolutely need him here."

"He knows that and he won't forget."

"If he does," Loo intoned, raising a small but threatening fist, "he'll have me to deal with and his days will be numbered."

"What about Dr. Hudelson?" Francis asked. "He needs to be here just as much as my uncle."

"Dad's in the tower," Jenny said, "and he'll come when we call."

"Leave him to me," Loo replied. "He's three stories up, but I'll have him down in no time."

Both Forsyth and Dr. Hudelson simply had to be present. After all, wasn't it a question of finalizing the date of the ceremony? The wedding was supposed to take place as soon as possible—provided, however, that the maid of honor had time for the manufacture and purchase of an appropriately gorgeous gown; for the first time in her life, sassy little Loo would be wearing the floor-length gown of a young woman.

And bearing this in mind, Francis quipped: "So what happens if the notorious gown isn't ready in time?"

"I'll demand that the wedding be rescheduled!" declared Miss Loo imperially.

And this decree was followed by an outburst of giggles that was raucous enough to reach Dr. Hudelson up in his watchtower.

Their conversation continued, the clock ticked away, and Forsyth still didn't show up. Loo leaned out the window to see if he was at the front door. He wasn't. And even when Mrs. Hudelson, Loo, Jenny, and Francis crossed the courtyard and went out into the road, they didn't see a sign of the man anywhere on Morris Street.

All they could do was go back to the living room and practice patience, a virtue Loo hadn't gotten around to cultivating.

"Uncle promised me he'd be here," Francis kept saying, "but for several days now, I'm not sure what's been going on with him . . ."

"You don't think Mr. Forsyth is sick, do you?" Jenny asked.

"No, he's all involved in something, God knows what. You can't coax ten words out of him from morning to night! What could have gotten into him?"

"Moon madness!" Loo snorted.

"Why, it's been the same with my husband," Mrs. Hudelson said. "This whole week he's seemed more distracted than ever. Wild horses couldn't drag him away from his lookout tower! Something unusual must be happening out in the solar system."

"Ye gods, I'm ready to believe it, the way my uncle's been carrying on!" Francis replied. "He doesn't go out, doesn't sleep, barely eats, keeps us waiting at mealtime . . ."

"That must thrill Mrs. Mitz," Loo commented.

"She was furious," Francis stated, "but it went in one ear and out the other! My uncle used to hate it when she harangued him, but now he doesn't even notice."

"It's no different with dad," Jenny said with a grin. "My sister seems to have lost all her influence over him . . . and God knows she used to have plenty!"

"Say it isn't so, Miss Loo!" Francis said, also grinning.

"Yeah, she's right," the girl answered. "But just you wait! With Mrs. Mitz and me on the case, my dad and your uncle will shape up real quick."

"Anyhow," Jenny continued, "what are the two of them so worked up about?"

"Some precious planet they've mislaid!" Loo snapped. "And they'd better find it in time for the wedding."

"We're joking around," Mrs. Hudelson said, "and meanwhile Mr. Forsyth still hasn't arrived."

"It's almost four-thirty," Jenny added.

"If uncle isn't here in five minutes," Francis stated, "I'll run home and—"

The doorbell rang just then.

"It's Mr. Forsyth," Loo announced. "Listen to him—he just keeps leaning on the bell, but he doesn't even realize it 'cause his mind's a million miles away!" Loo doesn't miss much.

It was Dean Forsyth all right, and when he came into the living room, Loo told him: "You're late, late, late! You deserve a good talking-to!"

"Hello, Mrs. Hudelson," Forsyth said, shaking her hand. "Hello, dear Jenny," he added, giving the young lady a hug. "And hello to you," he finished up, pinching Loo on the cheek.

Forsyth went through these civilities absent-mindedly, because as the saying goes, he "had his head in the clouds."

"You know, uncle," Francis continued, "when you didn't get here on time, I thought you'd forgotten our meeting."

"Yes . . . nearly . . . it's all my fault, Mrs. Hudelson, please accept my apologies. Luckily Mrs. Mitz reminded me in the nick of time."

"Good for her!" Loo declared.

"Go easy on me, my dear! I've got important things on my mind. I'm on the verge of a really intriguing discovery . . ."

"Aha! Just like dad, I'd say!" Jenny commented.

"What!" Forsyth exclaimed, leaping up as if the seat cushion in his armchair had just poked him with a loose spring. "Are you saying that Dr. Hudelson—"

"We're not saying anything at all, my dear Mr. Forsyth," Mrs. Hudelson put in quickly, justifiably worried that the old rivalry would flare up again between her husband and Francis's uncle. "Loo, go get your father," she added.

Light as a bird, the girl flew up to the top of the tower, and if she took the stairs instead of fluttering out the window, she must have been saving her plumage for better things.

A minute later Dr. Stanley Hudelson came into the living room with a worried expression, bloodshot eyes, and cheeks so flushed, he looked like he was about to have a stroke.

He and Forsyth exchanged a routine handshake. But clearly they were looking askance at each other, eyes furtive, faces lined with distrust.

In any event the two families were as one on the purpose of the meeting, which was to set a date for the wedding, or in the lingo of astronomy, to determine the conjunction of those two heavenly bodies, Francis and Jenny. So this was the only item on the agenda.

But it turned out there really wasn't much to discuss, because everybody agreed that the ceremony should take place as soon as possible.

As for Forsyth and Dr. Hudelson, they were completely oblivious. Were their minds out in the cosmos hunting for their lost asteroid? Was each man wondering if the other was on the verge of finding it again?

But anyhow they raised no objections to the young people's getting married in the near future. It was then April 3,* and the rest of the participants picked May 31 as the day of the wedding. An ideal date, you might think.

"But it all depends on one thing," Loo commented.

"What's that?" Francis asked.

"Whether the wind's blowing from the northeast."

"So what difference does that make?"

"Because, as dad says, criminals are less active in that kind of wind. After all, it would be a really bad sign if you got married during a crime wave!"

4. How two letters, one sent to the Pittsburgh Observatory, the other to the Cincinnati Observatory, were filed in the folder on shooting stars

TO: The Director of the
Pennsylvania Observatory
at Pittsburgh

April 9

Dear Mr. Director:

I have the honor of drawing your attention to the following fact of great interest to the world of astronomy—in the northern skies on the evening of April 2–3, I discovered a shooting star moving at high speed from the northeast to the southwest. It appeared in the lens of my telescope at eleven thirty-seven and twenty-two seconds, then vanished at eleven thirty-seven and forty-nine seconds. Since then, despite the most careful surveillance, I've been unable to see it again. Accordingly, I'm writing to ask that you duly note and record the information in this letter, so that should the said meteor reappear, I'll be credited with making this invaluable discovery.

Please accept my highest regards, Mr. Director, and I remain most humbly at your service.

Dean Forsyth,
Elizabeth Street
Whaston

April 9*

Dear Mr. Director:

On the evening of April 2, from eleven thirty-seven and twenty-two seconds to eleven thirty-seven and forty-nine seconds, I had the good fortune to discover a new shooting star moving across the northern skies from the northeast to the southwest. Since then I've been unable to reconfirm the trajectory of this meteor. But if it reappears on our horizon, as I'm sure it will, it seems only fair that I be acclaimed as the discoverer of this major addition to the annals of contemporary astronomy.

Please accept my sincerest personal regards, Mr. Director, and all assurances of my continuing esteem.

Dr. Stanley Hudelson
27 Morris Street*
Whaston

5. Three weeks of impatience during which Dean Forsyth and Omicron on the one hand, and Dr. Hudelson on the other, don't find their shooting star again despite the most relentless skywatching

Addressed to the directors of the Pittsburgh and Cincinnati observatories, the foregoing two letters, double-stamped, triple-sealed, and complete with cover notes, called only for the simplest response. This response would most likely take the form of a straightforward acknowledgment that the said letters had been duly received and filed. The interested parties asked for nothing more. They wanted to lay the proper groundwork in case other astronomers, whether amateur or professional, also sighted the meteor. Dean Forsyth, for one, hoped to find it again any second now, and Dr. Hudelson also had high hopes. The possibility that their asteroid was lost in outer space, that it had escaped the earth's gravitational pull and would never be seen again by mortal eyes—this was something they flatly refused to accept. In accordance with known physical laws, their shooting star would show up again on Whaston's horizon; they would spot it going by, bring it back into focus, determine its coordinates, add it to the sky maps, and baptize it with the exalted name of its discoverer.

But on the day of its reappearance, it would emerge that two different conquerors had claimed the exact same territory—and what would happen then? If Francis Gordon and Jenny Hudelson could have known the perils of this situation, they would have exclaimed: "Dear God, help us get married before that wretched shooting star comes back!"

And Mrs. Hudelson, Loo, Mrs. Mitz, and all their acquaintances would have repeated the same heartfelt prayer.

But none of them knew any of this, and even though they'd noticed how perturbed the two rivals were, they had no suspicion of what was behind it all. Undoubtedly it had something to do with astronomy . . . but what?

So aside from Dr. Hudelson, the residents of the house on Morris Street weren't a bit troubled by what was going on in the far reaches of space. But though they didn't have any worries, they did have plenty of work—there were announcements to send to the friends of both families, there were rounds of visits, congratulations, and thank-yous to be made . . . wedding arrangements to get underway, invitations to go out for the church ceremony, ditto for the banquet, which was bound to involve around a hundred guests . . . satisfactory seating arrangements to devise . . . and wedding presents to select . . .

In short the Hudelson family weren't twiddling their thumbs, and if we're to believe little Loo, they faced a real time crunch. She reasoned it out this way: "When the first daughter gets married, it's a big deal. It's something new, nobody's had any practice at it, they're extra careful not to overlook something! Then when it's the second daughter's turn, it's old hat, everybody knows the drill, nobody worries about forgetting anything. So when I get married, there'll be nothing to it."

"Nope, nothing at all" Francis answered her. "And since you're almost fifteen, Loo, it probably won't be long now!"

"You just stick to marrying my sister!" the girl answered with an outbreak of giggles. "You haven't got time to worry about me!"

Meanwhile Mrs. Hudelson kept her promise and arranged to inspect the house on Lambeth Street. The doctor was too busy up on his observation deck to go with them.

"You do what you think is best, Flora, and I'll be fine with it," he replied when she invited him. "Besides, it's really up to Francis and Jenny. I myself don't have time—"

"Look here, dad," Loo said, "you're going to come down from your watchtower on the wedding day, aren't you?"

"Of course, Loo, of —"

"And you'll go to St. Andrew's with your daughter on your arm?"

"Of course, Loo, of —"

"And you'll wear your black dress coat, white vest, black trousers, and white tie?"

"Of course, Loo, of —"

"And while Father O'Garth says mass, you'll forget about your planets and participate?"

"Of course, Loo, of course, but that's off in the future! And right now the skies are clear, which doesn't happen very often in April. So you just run on without me."

And that's how Mrs. Hudelson, Jenny, Loo, and Francis Gordon left the doctor to fuss with his binoculars and telescope. And the sunny weather guaranteed that Dean Forsyth would be up to the same thing in the watchtower of his home on Elizabeth Street. And who knows—maybe the meteor they'd seen once before, the meteor that had since vanished into outer space, would shoot in front of their telescope lenses a second time.

The inspection team left that afternoon. They went down Morris Street, crossed Constitution Square, and got a friendly wave from Judge Proth on the way; they headed up Exeter Street, just as Seth Stanfort had done two weeks earlier while waiting for Arcadia Walker;* they reached the Wilcox subdivision and turned down Lambeth Street.

We should note that Loo recommended—no, insisted—that Francis bring along a good pair of pocket binoculars. Since he claimed they would have a terrific view from the windows of their new home, Loo planned to explore every inch of the available horizon.

They reached 17 Lambeth Street. After going in the front door, they began their inspection with the ground floor.

It really was a very attractive dwelling, smartly designed in a comfortable modern style. It had been well kept up. No repairs needed.

All they had to do was furnish it, and their furniture was already on order at Whaston's finest upholsterer. To the rear, a study and dining room opened onto the back yard—not huge, just a few acres, but offering the shade of two fine beech trees, a green lawn, and flowerbeds where the first buds of spring were already starting to open up. Kitchen and workrooms were in the basement, in the English fashion.

The second floor was just as attractive as the first. A central hallway ran between spacious rooms. Jenny could only congratulate her fiancé on his discovery of this lovely dwelling, an exceptionally good-looking species of suburban home. Mrs. Hudelson agreed with her daughter that they definitely couldn't have found anything better in all Whaston.

As for Miss Loo, she cheerfully left her mother, sister, and Francis to confer about wallpaper and furnishings. Like a bird fluttering around inside its cage, the girl darted into every corner of the house. She was delighted too, finding the place absolutely perfect. She repeated this assessment every time she ran into Mrs. Hudelson, Jenny, and Francis on one floor or the other.

And at a point when everybody was gathered in the parlor, she announced: "I've got my room picked out!"

"Oh have you?" Francis inquired.

"Don't worry, I left the best one for you," the girl added. "You'll be able to see the river. As for me, I'll be able to smell the garden!"

"And what would you need a room for?" Mrs. Hudelson put in.

"I need a place to stay, mom, when you and dad are traveling."

"But honey, you know your father hates traveling!"

"Except into outer space," the girl shot back, her hand whooshing through the air and off into some imaginary yonder.

"But since he never actually goes away, Loo . . . ?"

"It's fine, let her be," Jenny cut in. "Yes, she can have a room in our house, and she can drop by any time she wants! And she's welcome to stay here, mom, if it happens that you and dad *do* have business out of town."

Which was too far-fetched a possibility for Mrs. Hudelson even to contemplate.

"Wow," Loo said, "what a view, what a gorgeous view, you've got to have up there!" And by "up there" the girl meant the top part of the house where a railing ran around the base of the roof. From that location you could see every part of the horizon out to the nearby hills.

In fact Mrs. Hudelson, Jenny, and Francis were wise to go along with Loo. Since the Wilcox subdivision is pretty elevated and their house was located at its highest point, a vast panorama was visible. You could see up and down the Potomac, and even beyond to the village of Steel that Miss Arcadia Walker had left behind to meet up with Seth Stanfort. The whole town was on view below, with its clocks and churches, the high roofs of its public buildings, and its treetops* forming a vault of greenery overhead. To see all this, nosy little Miss Loo had to sweep her pocket binoculars side to side in all directions. She chattered away: "There's Constitution Square . . . there's Morris Street, and I can see our own place with our watchtower and the flag fluttering in the breeze. There's somebody out on the deck . . ."

"Your dad," Francis said.

"He's the only one it could be," Mrs. Hudelson stated.

"Right, it's him," the girl agreed. "I can make out his features. He's holding a telescope. And you'll see, it'll never occur to him to aim it this way. No, it's pointed up at the sky. We aren't that high up, dad! Over here, over here!"

Loo called and called, as if Dr. Hudelson could ever have heard her. Besides, even if he'd been closer, wouldn't he have been too wrapped up in his work to answer?

At this point Francis joined in: "If you can see your house, Loo, probably you can see my uncle's as well."

"Right," the girl replied. "Let me give it a try . . . I'll see if I can get a good look at the watchtower . . . it's got to be over here . . . uh huh . . . hold on . . . let me get it in focus . . . good . . . good . . . there it is . . . yep . . . there it is!"

39

Loo wasn't mistaken. It was Forsyth's house all right.

"I've got it . . . I've got it," she repeated triumphantly, as if she'd made some major scientific breakthrough that would put her name on the front page. Then, after looking at it a minute: "There's somebody up in the tower."

"My uncle no doubt," Francis replied.

"He isn't by himself."

"Omicron would be with him."

"No need to ask what they're up to," Mrs. Hudelson commented.

"Same thing as dad," Jenny responded. A gloomy shadow seemed to pass over the young lady's brow. She was in constant fear that the rivalry between Forsyth and Dr. Hudelson would lead to chilly relations* between the two families. But once the marriage had taken place, the young couple would be a major influence and could head off any potential conflicts between the two rivals. Francis would do his part. He would take his uncle in hand, while she would see to her father, during those scientific skirmishes that were bound to come up.

Their inspection over with, Loo once again said how pleased she was. Mrs. Hudelson, her two daughters, and Francis Gordon went back home to Morris Street. The next day they would see the landlord and sign the lease, then forge ahead with the decorating and furnishing. Before long the newlyweds would be able to move in.

And thanks to all the crucial things they had to do, from choosing linens to making the rounds of friends and acquaintances, the time was sure to fly during those fifty days between April 10 and May 31,* the date set for the wedding.

"We'll be ready, you'll see!" our impatient Miss Loo kept saying. And if they weren't, it wouldn't be any fault of hers, because she would be sticking her nose in everywhere.

Meanwhile Dean Forsyth and Dr. Hudelson were likewise wasting no time, but with other objectives in mind. They were risking physical and mental exhaustion during those clear days and calm nights when they searched the skies for their shooting star, which persisted in not reappearing above the horizon. And speaking of horizons, wasn't Whaston's too restricted? Didn't they need a far better view of the heavens? If they shifted operations to some high mountaintop, couldn't they track the meteor over a much wider stretch of sky? And they wouldn't have to go very far to do this, no need to leave North America for the heart of Mexico, no reason to set up shop on the proud South American summit of Mt. Chimborazo.* After all, right in Virginia's neighboring states of Georgia and Alabama, didn't the Alleghenies* offer mountain peaks lofty enough to improve things for our two astronomers? That high in the sky, nothing would be in the way, and at five or six thousand feet* above sea level, what a magnificent expanse of firmament their telescopes would be able to take in!

And though they never put their heads together on this subject, Forsyth and Dr. Hudelson were both wondering if they not only needed a less restricted horizon, but also a place that didn't have such cloudy skies.

Which, to tell the truth, is all they'd been getting for their pains. Though they'd had the benefit of mild weather and no fog, from sunrise to sunset, from dusk to dawn, there wasn't a sign of that meteor over Whaston.

"Is it really up there?" Forsyth asked after a good long spell at the eyepiece of his telescope.

"It's up there," Omicron replied with unflappable confidence.

"Then why can't we see it?"

"Because it's out of sight."

"But if it's out of *our* sight, is it out of everybody else's?"

And employer and employee kept on bickering while their bloodshot eyes returned to their wearying vigils.

Meanwhile similar comments were emerging in monologue form from the lips of Dr. Hudelson, no less aggravated by his lack of success.

The observatories in Pittsburgh and Cincinnati had answered their respective letters. Each answer duly noted the receipt of information regarding the appearance of a shooting star on the date of April 2 in the northern sector of Whaston's horizon. Each answer added that its institution's own observations hadn't managed to confirm the existence of this shooting star, but each promised to keep looking; and if the meteor was sighted again, Pittsburgh would inform Dean Forsyth, and Cincinnati Dr. Stanley Hudelson, immediately.

Understand now that the two observatories had replied independently, neither realizing that two different amateur astronomers were involved, each of whom would be claiming he was the first to make this discovery.

But on one point there were no doubts whatever—the watchers in those towers on Elizabeth Street and Morris Street could easily have taken a vacation from their exhausting vigils. The above-cited observatories were much better equipped for the task, owning telescopes many times more powerful and precise. If the meteor wasn't just some runaway rock, if it had a well-defined track, and if it finally reappeared under circumstances like those in which it had already been sighted, the telescopes and binoculars in Pittsburgh and Cincinnati were sure to spot it going by. Messrs. Forsyth and Hudelson would have been far better off leaving things to the directors of those two renowned institutions.

Not a chance. They were more addicted to skywatching than ever. That's because they sensed they were both chasing the same hare. Each man kept his doings to himself, each was gripped by all sorts of delusions, and neither had a moment's peace from worrying that the other would beat him to the punch. They were eating their hearts out, and for the sake of good relations between their families, you could only hope they never laid eyes on that miserable meteor again.

In fact there were now ample grounds for worry, and the worries could only get worse. Forsyth and Dr. Hudelson no longer set foot in each other's homes. In the recent past two days wouldn't have gone by without their exchanging visits or inviting each other over for dinner. These days there were no such visits, no more invitations—which was something to be thankful for, because it saved them both from having to say no.

For the two lovers it was a tough state of affairs. They still saw each other every day, and the door of the Morris Street home remained open to Francis. Something had changed, though, and it wasn't Jenny. Mrs. Hudelson still showed him the same trust and friendliness, but her husband seemed distinctly uncomfortable in his presence. And when they mentioned Dean Forsyth's name in front of Dr. Hudelson, the doctor's face would turn pale and then bright red from all the animosity he felt; and in similar circumstances Forsyth's expression would show the same regrettable signs.

Mrs. Hudelson tried hard to learn the reason for this new hostility between the two old friends. But her attempts got nowhere, and her husband only replied: "I'm not going to talk about it, the way Forsyth's been behaving!"

Behaving how? It was impossible to coax an explanation from him. Even Loo herself, the spoiled brat who got away with everything, couldn't worm the truth out of him. She even proposed to hunt up Forsyth in his watchtower. But Francis talked her out of it, and undoubtedly she would have gotten the same sort of answer from Uncle Dean as her father had given . . .

"I refuse to talk about it! I can't believe Hudelson's acting this way toward me!" And let the record show that when old Mrs. Mitz heard this and hazarded a follow-up question, Forsyth answered curtly: "None of your beeswax!"

Finally, however, Omicron blurted out the truth, which Mrs. Mitz promptly relayed to Francis. The boss had discovered a fabulous shooting star, and there was reason to think Dr. Hudelson had made the exact same discovery at the same hour on the same day.

So that was the reason for this idiotically vehement feud. Just as they were about to create even closer bonds of friendship, a meteor had come between these two old pals! A shooting star, an asteroid, an aerolite, just a stone—all right, it was a pretty big stone, but in any case it was a stumbling block over which Jenny and Francis's wedding procession was in serious danger of tripping.

And Loo couldn't help cussing like a boy: "To hell with that meteor! And ditto with the whole solar system!"

Time went by. April gave way to May. The mutually agreed-upon wedding date was twenty-five days off. But God only knew what might go wrong in the interim. What drastic developments might occur? What complications might toss a monkey wrench into the two families' plans? So far this disgraceful feud had been kept behind closed doors, but what if some unexpected circumstance brought it out into the open, what if the two rivals were publicly pitted against each other?

Yet the wedding preparations did go forward. Everything would be ready by the twenty-fifth of the month, even Miss Loo's gorgeous gown.

It's important to note that the first week of May featured atrocious weather: wind, rain, and a sky swept with endless piles of huge clouds. You couldn't see either the sun, which by then was soaring fairly high above the horizon, or the moon, which was nearly full and should have been lighting up the whole firmament.

So any serious skywatching was out of the question.

Interestingly, Mrs. Hudelson, Jenny, and Francis never dreamed of complaining. And even Loo, who usually hated it when it was wet and windy, was ecstatic over the continuing bad weather.

"If only it lasts till the wedding!" she kept saying. "Over the next three weeks, I don't want to see the sun, the moon, or one single star!"

And that's how it went, to the endless annoyance of the two astronomers in their towers and the heartfelt satisfaction of their families.

But this state of things couldn't last forever, and the weather improved during the night of May 8–9. A north wind drove away all the clouds cluttering the air, and once again the heavens were perfectly clear.

Up on their respective observation decks, Dean Forsyth and Dr. Hudelson went back to scouring the sky over Whaston from its far edges to its zenith. Would the meteor make another pass in front of their telescopes? Would they be lucky enough to sight it again, and which of the two would be the first to spot it?

One thing was certain: their attitudes hadn't changed an iota, and if their moods were equally vile, it was because their skywatching was so fruitless that they weren't sure they'd ever see that meteor again.

But a last-minute news item appeared in the papers on May 9 that tackled this issue.

The item read: "Friday night, at 10:47 p.m., a shooting star of amazing size moved across the northern part of the sky at high speed, heading from northeast to southwest."

This time neither Forsyth nor Hudelson had seen the meteor. But it didn't make any difference. They were positive this shooting star was the same one they'd described to the two observatories.

"At last!" the one exclaimed.

"Finally!" exclaimed the other.

So you can understand how delighted they were the next day—and also how irritated—when the newspapers gave fuller accounts as follows: "According to staff at the Pittsburgh Observatory, they first heard of this shooting star on April 9 from a Mr. Dean Forsyth of Whaston; and according to staff at the Cincinnati Observatory, they were told of it on the same day by one Dr. Stanley Hudelson, also of Whaston."

6. Which contains a variety of colorful tidbits on meteors in general and on the particular shooting star whose discovery was a bone of contention between Messrs. Forsyth and Hudelson

If ever there was a geographic region to make a continent proud, as proud as a father would be of one of his children, it was North America. If ever there was a nation to make North America proud, it was the United States. If ever there was a state, out of the fifty-one represented on its star-spangled flag, to make the U.S.A. proud, it was Virginia, with its capital in Richmond. If ever there was a city on the Potomac to make Virginia proud, it was Whaston. And if ever one of its citizens could have made all Whaston puff out its chest, it was on the occasion of this sensational discovery that was sure to rank high in the achievements of twentieth-century astronomy.*

Aside from the countless daily, twice-weekly, weekly, twice-monthly, and monthly news publications flourishing in the United States, you can readily imagine that it was the local Whaston papers that issued the most glowing reports on Dean Forsyth and Dr. Hudelson, at least early in the game. Didn't these two illustrious townspeople reflect glory on the whole city? What citizen wouldn't want to share in this? Wouldn't the name Whaston be inextricably linked to this discovery? Wouldn't it be recorded in the municipal archives, along with the names of these two astronomers to whom the whole scientific world owed so much?

So don't gasp in surprise, dear reader, and take my word for it when I tell you that the very same day, swarms of loudly enthusiastic Whastonians headed over to the two houses on Morris Street and Elizabeth Street. Needless to say, none of them knew about the rivalry between Forsyth and Hudelson. These delirious townspeople simply lumped the two men together. They couldn't have cared less about their private differences. Their two names would be connected for years to come, and in future millennia, wouldn't historians maybe claim that this discovery had really been made by just one man, somebody with the hyphenated moniker of Forsyth-Hudelson?

But one thing was for sure: in response to the cheering throngs, Dean Forsyth and Dr. Stanley Hudelson were obliged to make separate appearances on their respective observation decks. They bowed to acknowledge the roaring crowds.

Yet a close observer would have noticed that their faces didn't wear expressions of unalloyed delight. A shadow was passing over their triumphs like a cloud across the sun. Each man kept casting sideways glances at his competitor's watchtower. Each knew that his rival was also receiving the public's acclaim. Their telescopes had already told them so—and if those spyglasses could have been loaded cannons, who knows, they just might have opened fire on each other! Their eyes held such sheer, concentrated jealousy, they didn't simply look daggers, they looked bullets.

Even so, Dean Forsyth was applauded just as heartily as Dr. Hudelson, and vice-versa, by the same townsfolk parading in front of both homes.

And while these ovations were causing uproars in their two neighborhoods, what was going on with Francis Gordon, the old housekeeper Mrs. Mitz, Mrs. Hudelson, Jenny, and Loo? Did they have any inkling of the dismal consequences soon to come from those press releases by the Pittsburgh and Cincinnati Observatories? The secret was out now. Working separately, Forsyth and Dr. Hudelson had discovered a shooting star at the exact same moment, so it was obvious they were dealing with the identical meteor. Furthermore, if the two men laid separate claims to the honor, if not the rewards, of this discovery, couldn't it lead to an embarrassing scandal for both families?

It isn't hard to imagine—and understand—the feelings of Mrs. Hudelson and Jenny while those crowds were carrying on in front of their home. The two of them watched it all through their window curtains. Since the doctor had already put in an appearance on the observation deck, they were spared having to go out on the balcony of their room. With sinking hearts they imagined the consequences of the reports in the newspapers. If, out of their silly jealousy, Forsyth and Dr. Hudelson kept quarreling over the meteor, the public wouldn't just stand back and stay impartial. Both men would have their supporters, and during all the turmoil around town, during all the disorder that was likely to ensue, think what could happen to the two families and to the engaged couple—a modern-day Romeo and Juliet, caught up in a feud between the scientific Montagues and Capulets of this U.S. city!

Loo was livid; she wanted to throw her window open; she wanted to scream at the entire town; she was sorry she didn't have a hose handy to spray the whole crowd and drown their cheering with a blast of cold water. Loo's mother and sister would have had a rough time reining in her righteous wrath.

It was the same over on Elizabeth Street. The revelers were about to aggravate an already strained situation, and Francis Gordon would gladly have doomed the whole lot of them to the eternal bonfire. At first he intended to go up beside his uncle. But he didn't, afraid that he wouldn't be able to hide his irritation. So he let Forsyth and Omicron strut around on the deck by themselves.

And just as Mrs. Hudelson needed to restrain Loo's impulsiveness, Francis likewise had to curb the temper of old Mrs. Mitz. She wanted to sweep the streets clean of those crowds, and the domestic implement she wielded with such expertise could have done major damage. Still and all, it seems a tad harsh to greet well-wishers with whacks from a broom, and Francis felt obliged to intervene in his uncle's best interests.

"But Mr. Francis," the old housekeeper exclaimed, "listen to that racket! They're goin' honest-to-goodness crazy!"

"Sure seems like it," Francis agreed.

"And all because of some oversized pebble wandering around in the clouds!"

"You're right, Mrs. Mitz."

"And if it wants to fall out of the sky and smack half a dozen of 'em on the head, it's fine with me! What are those shooting stars good for anyhow, I ask you?"

"For starting feuds," Francis concluded, while the cheers reached a fever pitch outside.

And if this discovery really had so much glory associated with it, why weren't the two old friends willing to share it? Their two names could be attached to that meteor till the end of time. Otherwise there were no material advantages in it, no monetary benefits. It was strictly for the honor of the thing. But when it's a point of personal pride, when vanity gets stirred into the mix, there's no way you can talk sense to two fellows who were so stubborn they must have been descended from old Aliboron.*

But honestly now, just what was so glorious about sighting this meteor? Wasn't its discovery simply a matter of luck, wasn't it sheer accident that it had crossed Whaston's horizon at the exact moment when Dean Forsyth and Dr. Stanley Hudelson just happened to be squinting into the eyepieces of their instruments?

And anyhow, day and night don't these shooting stars, asteroids, and aerolites pass overhead by the hundreds, by the thousands even? And haven't other observers besides our two amateurs spotted the light trails of these flying objects as they streak through space? Is it even possible to count how many of these balls of fire are scooting along their erratic trajectories in the dark depths of the firmament? Experts say that six hundred million meteors enter the earth's atmosphere in one night, 1.2 billion during the daytime. And according to Newton, ten to fifteen million of these heavenly bodies are potentially visible* to the naked eye! "So if these two discoverers have made a discovery the astronomers haven't, big deal."

This last sentence was the wrap-up of an article in the *Whaston Punch*, which was the only newspaper to take a humorous view of things and which never missed a chance to display its usual irreverence.

The competition took things more seriously, turning the occasion into a parade of enough scientific knowledge—cribbed from the American equivalents of Larousse's encyclopedia*—to inspire envy in professionals at the most renowned observatories.

Kepler believed [said the *Whaston Daily Standard*] that shooting stars were of terrestrial origin; but it seems more likely that these phenomena really do come from outer space, since they always show signs of violent combustion. In Plutarch's day they were already viewed as pieces of rock that had hit the earth's surface after they'd been caught in its gravitational pull. Studying them carefully and comparing them to other rocks, one finds they have the same composition and contain nearly a third of all the elements; but the characteristics of these fundamental substances are different. Their particles can be as small as metal filings or as big as exceptionally hard peas or nuts, and inside cracks they show signs of crystallization. Some are entirely composed of iron—an iron in its primitive state—but more often they're mixed with nickel left unchanged by oxidation.

It was all very sound stuff that the *Whaston Daily Standard* was dishing out to its readers. Meantime the *Whaston News Journal* did a historical survey of the learned men down through the ages who'd studied these meteorites,* and it said:

Diogenes of Apollonia records that a piece of burning rock as big as a millstone hit the earth near Aegospotamos and terrified the citizens of Thrace. If a shooting star like that were to strike the steeple of St. Andrew's, the whole structure would be demolished. And while we're at it, we may as well give a complete rundown of these rocks that have come from the depths of space, gotten caught in the earth's gravitational pull, and been found lying on the ground: before the time of Christ, that flashing stone the Galatians revered as a sign from the nature goddess Cybele and which they sent to Rome; likewise another one that was discovered near Emesa in Syria and turned into a religious artifact by a cult of sun worshippers; that sacred slab found during the reign of Numa; the Black Stone that was treated with such tender loving care in Mecca;* the thunderous stone that was shaped into the famed sword of Antar. Since the time of Christ observers have described many of these space rocks, along with the circumstances of their fall: a stone weighing 260 pounds that fell near Ensisheim in Alsace;* a stone with a metallic black color that fell on Mt. Vaison in Provence and was the size and shape of a human skull; a stone weighing 72 pounds that fell near Seres in Macedonia,* gave off a stink of sulfur, and looked like it was made of iron slag;* a stone that fell in Lucé near Chartres in 1768 and was so hot, it was impossible to touch. And it's important also to mention the shooting star that landed near the village of Laigle in Normandy in 1803, which Humboldt described as follows: "At 1 p.m. under clear skies, observers saw a large shooting star moving from southeast to northwest. A few minutes later they heard a loud booming sound that lasted five or six minutes and came from a small, nearly motionless black cloud; this was followed by three or four other explosions so thunderous, they sounded like they were produced by a combination of gunfire and many drums beating. With each explosion the black cloud lost a part of the vapor forming it. No light was visible inside it. Going from the southeast to the northwest, over two thousand meteorites weighing up to 17 pounds fell in an oval-shaped pattern nearly seven miles long.* These stones smoked and glowed but weren't actually on fire, and they proved to be more brittle the first few days after their fall than later on." And finally here's the phenomenon recalled by the Permanent Secretary of the Royal Academy in Belgium: "In 1854 near Hurworth, Darlington, Durham, and Dundee, in a starry yet cloudy sky, a ball of fire appeared, twice as big as the moon and completely visible to our eyes.* Its dazzling light shot out from a blood-red mass. It trailed a long, bright, gold tail behind it, thick, compact, and standing out vividly against the dark blue sky. From its onset this tail swept in a steep, arching path. The shooting star's trajectory was from the northeast to the southwest, and it was so long, it stretched from one horizon to the other. It was spinning violently, or rather turning on its axis, while changing from bright red to dark red, and it vanished without any sign that it had either exploded or fallen."

The details given in this article from the *Whaston News Journal* were supplemented by additional ones from a competitor, the *Whaston Morning News*:

If the Hurworth meteor didn't explode, this certainly wasn't the case with the shooting star on May 14, 1864, which was visible to a skywatcher in Castillon on the Gironde estuary in France. Though it was only in sight for five seconds, its speed was so great that in this brief stretch of time, it swept through a full sixty-degree arc. Its bluish green color turned an amazingly brilliant white. And even though sounds can take two minutes to travel a vertical distance of 25 miles,* in this case there was a lapse of three to four minutes between the moment you could see the explosion and the moment you could hear it. So the force of this explosion had to be greater than the loudest explosions that could be produced on the earth's surface. As for the size of this shooting star, calculating from its altitude you could put it at no less than 1,500 feet across, and it must have been traveling at close to 12½ miles per second,* or two-thirds of the speed at which the earth orbits the sun.

After the above words in the *Whaston Morning News* came more words in the *Whaston Evening News*, these focusing on the many shooting stars that are almost totally composed of iron. It reminded its large readership of a meteorite found in the steppes of Siberia that weighed at least 1,500 pounds. But how puny this rock seems next to one discovered in Brazil that weighed no less than 13,000 pounds!* And let's not forget two other meteorites of the same type, one found in Olimpia near San Miguel de Tucumán that weighed over 30,000 pounds, the other weighing over 41,000 pounds* and found in the vicinity of Durango, Mexico.* Finally, in eastern Asia near the head-waters of the Yellow River, there's a hunk of solid iron some forty feet high that the Mongols have nicknamed "A Piece of the Axis," which is what the locals figure it really is, rather than something from space.

It's no exaggeration, in all honesty, to say that some members of the Whaston populace couldn't help feeling a tad jittery after reading the above article. For the Forsyth-Hudelson meteor to be visible under the conditions described, and from a distance that had to be substantial, it follows that this shooting star was probably much larger than the Tucumán or Durango meteors, or even the so-called "Piece of the Axis." Who knows, it may have equalled or surpassed that shooting star seen over Castillon, which was estimated to be fifteen hundred feet across—and imagine the weight of all that iron! Now then, since this latest meteor had already made one appearance on Whaston's horizon, wasn't it reasonable to assume it would come back? And if for some reason it ran out of steam at a point in its trajectory right over Whaston, it would land on the place with inconceivable violence! All in all, it was a good time to teach the ignorant and remind the learned about that nasty formula for falling objects—multiply their height and weight by the square of their velocity.

Consequently a certain nervousness held sway around town. This menacing, malevolent meteor was the main topic of conversation in the public forums, at home, and out in society. As for the women of the city, all they could think about were demolished churches and pulverized homes, and if some men shrugged their shoulders and viewed the whole thing as a fairytale danger, they were hardly in the majority. Around the clock, in both Constitution Square and the ritziest parts of town, multitudes of people were outside watching the skies. No matter what the weather was like, absolutely nothing interrupted their vigils. The opticians had never sold so many field glasses, pocket binoculars, and assorted ocular devices. The heavens had never been more thoroughly picked over than they were by the anxious eyes of the Whaston citizenry. Once the astronomers in Pittsburgh and Cincinnati* had sighted this shooting star, their press releases would confirm that its direction had to take it right over the town, and whether or not the meteor was visible, it could be a threat to Whaston any hour now—or minute or second.

But wasn't it reasonable to point out that this threat must have been just as great for the cities, towns, villages, and hamlets in other regions located under the meteor's trajectory? Sure, obviously. Over a period of time not yet determined, the shooting star would be obliged to circle the globe, so every patch of earth beneath its orbit was in danger. Nevertheless, to mix metaphors, if ever there was a town that was quaking in its boots, no other city, not even in the Old World, had a leg up on Whaston. And if this fear had been hazy to start with, then taken on concrete form, increased, and now clutched the whole town in its grip, it was because the shooting star had first been sighted over Whaston. Consequently this locality had to be the most prominent point on the meteor's trajectory. So the prevailing feeling could be summed up as follows: the citizenry felt like folks in a town under attack, their enemy was all set to open fire, and any second they expected a bomb to arrive and blow their homes to smithereens. And in this case it was quite a bomb!

Not surprisingly, one local newspaper found plenty of fodder for a series of humorous articles. These were quite popular even though they made fun of their own readers. Yes, the *Whaston Punch* aimed to get folks even more riled up by exaggerating and satirizing this threat, a threat for which the newspaper held Messrs. Forsyth and Hudelson personally responsible:

Who asked these two amateurs to get mixed up in this? What right do they have poking around in the solar system with their spyglasses and binoculars? Can't they leave the skies in peace and quit pestering the stars? Aren't there enough real experts around without these two snooping about in space? Heavenly bodies hate peeping toms, and their secrets are none of our business—so guess what? You got it. Now our town's in danger and nobody's safe anymore! You can guard against fire, hailstorms, and cyclones, but we defy you to take precautions against a meteor falling, a meteor maybe ten times the size of downtown Whaston! And if it explodes while it's falling—which often happens with that breed of bomb—it could trash the whole town with its debris, or, if the particles are on fire, maybe even burn us to the ground. Any way you slice it, this means inevitable destruction for our fair city! Why, we ask, didn't Messrs. Forsyth and Hudelson stay in the comfort of their living rooms instead of lying in wait for passing meteors? Their presumption and malfeasance have brought this vengeance on our heads! If Whaston is destroyed, if it's pulverized or burnt to a crisp by this shooting star, it will be their fault, they're the culprits. So we put it to any impartial reader (which automatically includes all *Punch* subscribers): what use are these skywatchers, stargaz-ers, and meteorologists, and what good has their work ever done for people on this planet? In the sublime words of a brilliant Frenchman, the famous gourmet Brillat-Savarin, "The discovery of a new star won't create as much happiness as the discovery of a new recipe!"

7. In which we see Mrs. Hudelson get annoyed with the doctor's attitude, while at Dean Forsyth's we hear old Mrs. Mitz give her boss a royal scolding

What did Dean Forsyth and Dr. Hudelson make of these witticisms in the *Whaston Punch*? Not a thing, and they probably wouldn't even read that irreverent editorial. After all, isn't ignorance bliss? But those more or less humorous quips were far from amusing to certain others who *did* see them. If the two men were just naturally oblivious, the same wasn't true of their families and friends, and their reactions weren't exactly ho-hum. Old Mrs. Mitz was apoplectic. How dare they accuse her master of luring this meteor that endangered the public safety! In her opinion Forsyth ought to sue the author of that article, and Judge Proth was certain to award stiff damages, not to mention the prison time those slanderous charges deserved. Francis Gordon had to step in and calm the old housekeeper down.

As for little Loo, she looked at the bright side and in between fits of giggling kept saying: "The paper's absolutely right! Why did Mr. Forsyth and daddy have to go and discover that stupid stone in the first place? If they hadn't, it would have snuck on by like thousands of others, and it wouldn't have caused an ounce of trouble!"

And the awful trouble at the forefront of the girl's mind was the rivalry all set to erupt between Francis's uncle and Jenny's father. She was worried about the consequences of this rivalry on the eve of a union that was supposed to bring the two families closer together.

We should point out that the least of her worries, her lowest priority, was the slim likelihood of the shooting star actually falling on

Whaston. Their town was in no more danger than any other located under the meteor's trajectory as it orbited the globe. In any case it was only a possibility, not a certainty, that it would fall to the earth, so why couldn't it stay up there forever like the moon or any other satellite subject to a planet's gravity? No, the best thing was for the townspeople to laugh off those whimsical predictions in the *Whaston Punch*—and that's just what they did, since, unlike the Forsyth and Hudelson families, they had no real grounds for being upset.

The inevitable came to pass. So long as Messrs. Forsyth and Hudelson had only been suspicious of each other, so long as it wasn't absolutely certain they were both on the same trail, no catastrophes would occur. If their friendship cooled a little, so be it. If they avoided each other even, so be that too. But after the appearance of those statements from both observatories, it was now a matter of public record that *two* skywatchers from Whaston were associated with the discovery of this meteor. What would happen next? Would both men claim they saw it first—not only in the newspapers but maybe in some appropriate court of law? Wouldn't there be uproarious debates on the subject? And if the *Whaston Punch* published new editorials full of reckless satirical banter, wouldn't it spur the two rivals to even greater heights of vanity, wouldn't it just add fuel to the flames—especially since America has such a bottomless supply of gasoline?* And soon the cartoonists and gossip columnists would get into the act, and things could only become more and more strained between the two watchtowers on Morris Street. and Elizabeth Street.

So it shouldn't surprise anybody that Forsyth and Dr. Hudelson avoided even the tiniest reference to that wedding day whose date was approaching too slowly, you can be sure, for the likes of Francis and Jenny. The two astronomers treated it like a nonevent. The instant it popped up in conversation, each man would suddenly remember something that needed doing up in his tower. Which was where they both spent their days, more consumed, more obsessed than ever. Most likely they weren't even aware of the loudmouthed nonsense regrettably being published by that satirical newspaper. How could word from outside have gotten up to their two watchtowers? Francis and Mrs. Hudelson went to great lengths to keep the real world out, fearing it would only make things worse, and the two rivals had other concerns besides reading small-town newspapers.

In essence the astronomers in Ohio and Pennsylvania still hadn't seen the meteor for themselves, so this was the reason Dean Forsyth and Stanley Hudelson were trying to find it again—without success. Was it too far off, out of the range of their instruments? This was a likely enough possibility, all things considered. But day and night they stuck to their guns, taking advantage of every opening in the cloud cover. If they kept on in this way, they would finish up two very sick people! But each man was willing to do anything he could to beat out the other.

As for determining the characteristics of this new asteroid—the exact position of its trajectory, its composition, its shape, its distance from the earth, the duration of its orbit—these details were clearly beyond Messrs. Forsyth and Hudelson. Ascertaining these attributes was the domain of specialists, and anyhow that mischievous meteor hadn't put in a second appearance over Whaston, or at least the two skywatchers hadn't gotten a glimpse of it with their substandard spyglasses. So both of them stayed in vicious moods. Nobody dared to go near them. Twenty times a day Forsyth would take out his frustrations on Omicron, who would snarl right back. As for the doctor, he was reduced to beating up on himself, punishment richly deserved.

Under these circumstances nobody in his right mind would have dreamed of talking to them about nuptial agreements or wedding plans.

Meanwhile a week had gone by since the publication of those press releases from the Pittsburgh and Cincinnati Observatories. The date was May 18. There were thirteen days to go till the wedding, though Loo claimed it would never happen because the date had been officially struck off the calendar. According to her, May 31 hadn't been scheduled for that year. This was her idea of a joke to brighten the gloom settling over the two households.

But it's important to repeat that Francis's uncle and Jenny's father ignored the upcoming marriage as if it had never been planned in the first place. At the least mention of this subject, each man would instantly stop talking and leave the room. The possibility of pinning them down came under discussion during one of Francis's daily visits to the house on Morris Street. But Mrs. Hudelson felt the best way to handle her husband was to do nothing at all. He couldn't be bothered with nuptial arrangements any more than he could be bothered with other household activities. Instead, when the wedding day arrived Mrs. Hudelson planned simply to tell him: "Here are your hat, coat, and gloves. It's time to head over to St. Andrew's for the ceremony. Give me your arm and let's go."

And he undoubtedly *would* go, without even asking why—so long as the meteor wasn't passing at that moment in front of his telescope lens.

But if Mrs. Hudelson's wishes prevailed in the Morris Street household, over on Elizabeth Street Francis Gordon's did not. Though the doctor wasn't compelled to explain his attitude toward Forsyth, his rival came under stiff pressure on this matter from his old housekeeper. Mrs. Mitz wasn't buying any excuses. She was outraged by her employer's behavior. She felt that the situation was becoming more and more serious, that there was a danger of the mildest incident creating a rift between the two families. And what would happen then? The wedding would be delayed, maybe called off, and the two young lovers would be in despair, her dear Francis heartbroken because Forsyth forced him to give up Jenny's hand. And if there was a public scandal, cutting off any possibility of a reconciliation, what would the poor boy do?

So on the afternoon of May 19, catching Dean Forsyth alone in the dining room, Mrs. Mitz stopped him just as he was about to go upstairs to his watchtower.

As you know, Forsyth dreaded making excuses to his old housekeeper. He was well aware that these excuses generally didn't pan out. So he felt his best move was to beat a retreat; any time your defeat is assured, discretion is the better part of valor.

On this occasion, seeing that the lower half of Mrs. Mitz's face wore an expression reminiscent of a bomb with a burning fuse, Forsyth headed for the other end of the room, intending to run for cover. But before he could turn the doorknob, his old housekeeper had caught up with him, her chin lifted, her eyes looking daggers at her boss, who averted his. And in a quivering voice that she made no attempt to modulate, she said: "I want a word with you, Mr. Forsyth!"

"With me, Mrs. Mitz? Uh, I don't have time right now . . ."

"Then you'll have to make time."

"I think Omicron's calling me . . ."

"He ain't, and if he does, he can just wait."

"But if my shooting star—"

"It can wait too."

"By heaven!" Forsyth exclaimed, starting to lose control.

"Anyhow," Mrs. Mitz continued, "the sky's dark, it's starting to rain, and you can't see a thing up there!"

It was true, only too true, and that was what infuriated both Forsyth and Dr. Hudelson. For the past two days, ultra-heavy clouds had been blocking the sky. During the day there wasn't a single ray of sunshine, during the night not a speck of starlight. The low-lying mists stretched like a shroud from one side of the horizon to the other, occasionally punctured by the arrowhead point of St. Andrew's steeple. Under these circumstances you couldn't do a scrap of skywatching, you couldn't make out a single asteroid passing by, and you definitely wouldn't be able to see that hotly disputed shooting star. The reader can likewise assume that weather conditions weren't any more helpful to astronomers in the states of Ohio and Pennsylvania, or to other observatories in the New World and the Old. In fact nothing new about the April 2 meteor had appeared in any paper. The sighting was already six weeks old, and it simply wasn't novel enough to hold the attention of the scientific world. In itself such a cosmic development isn't terribly rare, to tell the truth, and only a Dean Forsyth or a Stanley Hudelson would have watched for this shooting star with such maniacal impatience.

After her employer saw that she had him absolutely cornered, old Mrs. Mitz folded her arms and continued as follows: "Mr. Forsyth, by any chance have you forgotten you have a nephew named Francis Gordon?"

"Ah yes, young Francis," Forsyth answered, wagging his chin benevolently. "Of course I haven't forgotten him. And how's the dear boy doing?"

"Very well, believe me."

"It seems to me I haven't seen him in quite a while . . ."

"Not since breakfast two hours ago."

"We had breakfast together? Really?"

"Mr. Forsyth, can't you see what's in front of your nose?" Mrs. Mitz demanded, forcing him to face her.

"Of course, Mrs. Mitz, of course. What do you want from me? I'm a little busy at the moment . . ."

"So busy you seem to have forgotten a pretty important thing."

"What have I forgotten?"

"Your nephew's gettin' married."

"Married? Him?"

"Don't tell me you're gonna ask to whom!"

"Of course not, Mrs. Mitz, of course not. But what's the point of all these questions?"

"To get you to talk about the way you've been behaving toward the Hudelson family! You remember the Hudelson family, don't you, Mr. Forsyth? It's made up of Dr. Hudelson who lives over on Morris Street along with Mrs. Hudelson and her two daughters, Miss Loo and Miss Jenny. And the one your nephew's supposed to marry just happens to be Miss Jenny!"

And while the name Hudelson fell more and more emphatically

from old Mrs. Mitz's lips, Dean Forsyth clapped his hand to his chest, his side, and his head, as if this name were a bullet and he'd been shot at point-blank range. He gasped, he choked, his eyes were bloodshot, and when he didn't respond, Mrs. Mitz kept after him: "Well, did you hear what I said?"

"I . . . I . . ."

His jaws were so tightly clenched, he could barely mumble a sentence.

"Well?" the old housekeeper demanded, raising her voice.

He finally said: "So Francis is still considering this marriage?"

"As he lives and breathes," Mrs. Mitz snapped. "As we are too! And as I'd like to think you are!"

"What! My nephew's still set on marrying Dr. Hudelson's daughter?"

"Miss Jenny, if you please, Mr. Forsyth, and a sweeter girl would be hard to find."

"Even if I agreed," Forsyth continued, "that she might be a sweet girl . . . she's the daughter of a man whose name I can't even speak without choking on it . . ."

"Oh, that's too much!" Mrs. Mitz burst out, tearing off her apron so vehemently, it seemed like she was going to quit on the spot.

"Now calm down, Mrs. Mitz," her boss responded, a little alarmed at her threatening attitude.

The old housekeeper clutched her apron in her hand, strings dangling. "So, Mr. Forsyth, that's the sort of drivel you've got in your head?"

"But Mrs. Mitz, you don't know what Hudelson has done."

"What did he do?"

"He robbed me."

"Robbed you?"

"Yes, robbed me blind!"

"Did he pick your pocket? Steal your watch, your wallet, your handkerchief?"

"No, my meteor!"

"Oh, your meteor!" the old housekeeper snapped, sneering at Forsyth in her most caustic and unpleasant manner. "Your famous shooting star . . . and you've never seen it again, I bet!"

"Mrs. Mitz, you watch what you're saying!" Forsyth warned. That time she'd nailed the astronomer on his soft spot.

But there was no stopping Mrs. Mitz, now boiling with rage. "Your meteor!" she repeated. "Your own little thingamajig running around in the sky! And what makes you think it's yours any more than it's Dr. Hudelson's? Doesn't it belong to everybody, to me even? Did you plunk down your money and buy it? Did somebody leave it to you in his will? Was it maybe God's special gift to you?"

"Shut up, Mrs. Mitz! Shut up!" Forsyth hollered back, thoroughly losing it.

"I won't! You can't shut me up, Mr. Forsyth! Go call for help from silly old Omicron, see if I care!"

"Silly old Omicron?"

"That's what I said! And he can't shush me any more than the President himself could shush the angel Gabriel when God sends him to announce Judgment Day!"

This fearsome declaration left Forsyth speechless, his throat so tight that not a syllable could get through, his vocal cords too tangled up to emit a single sound. Answering her was beyond him. He was so paralyzed with anger, he couldn't even have shown his housekeeper the door with those time-honored words "Get out! You're fired!"

In any case Mrs. Mitz would certainly have ignored him, and he would have been the one to suffer if she'd hadn't. It takes more than some pesky meteor to split up a master and servant after forty-five years of employment! All the same, even if Forsyth had ended up giving in on the issue of the shooting star, Mrs. Mitz wouldn't have backed down on the issue of Francis marrying Jenny!

But in Mr. Dean Forsyth's own best interests, it was time this little scuffle ended, and being well aware that he was the anointed loser, he tried to beat a retreat without this move seeming too much like he was running away.

This time around it was the sun that came to his rescue. Suddenly the clouds parted. A shaft of light shot through the window facing the garden. For at least three days Old Sol had stayed in hiding and hadn't been visible to the citizens of Whaston, and therefore to the eyes of the two notables feverishly waiting for him to come back.

At that very moment, no doubt, Dr. Hudelson would be climbing up to his tower, if he wasn't there already, and this thought popped instantly into Forsyth's head. He could picture his rival taking advantage of this lucky opening in the clouds, stooping over on his observation deck, peering into the lens of his telescope, scouring the far reaches of space. And who knows, maybe their meteor was zipping through the sky, on display in all its glory?

Forsyth couldn't hold still. This time he didn't wait for Omicron to yell down to him. The sunshine had the same effect on him that gas has on a balloon. He shot upward. Once inflated he could only move in a vertical direction, so he turned to the door, dropped his metaphorical ballast, and shot furiously toward the old housekeeper.

But Mrs. Mitz stayed in his way and didn't seem inclined to let him through. Would he have to grab her by the arms, struggle with her, and call to Omicron for help? No, he had another option: if he went out of the room into the garden, there was a second door leading to the tower that wasn't guarded by any Cerberus, male or female.*

This move turned out to be unnecessary. Clearly the confrontation had been a physical strain for the old housekeeper. Though she was used to speaking her mind to her boss, she'd never before pitched into him like this. Normally her complaints had focused on Forsyth's absentmindedness, his slovenly personal habits, showing up late for meals, going out in cold weather without bundling up, coming inside with a runny nose and aching joints. But this time a more serious issue was involved. It was something that stirred old Mrs. Mitz to her very core, and she was determined to go to bat for her beloved Francis and his Jenny.

And in light of the vehement way Forsyth had talked about Dr. Hudelson, whom he'd branded a common thief, wasn't this situation bound to get more desperate by the day? The two rivals seldom went out, true. They no longer visited each other, also true. But ultimately there might be an accidental meeting in the street or the home of some mutual friend, and then what would happen? Undoubtedly a catastrophe, followed by the two families breaking off relations for good. Now then, this was a development that had to be averted at all costs, and that's what the old housekeeper had been trying to do. But as an important part of this plan, she meant to serve her boss notice that she wasn't budging one inch on this matter.

Consequently Mrs. Mitz left her spot in front of the door and dropped into a chair. The coast was clear. Fearful that a new batch of clouds would cover the sun again, maybe even for the rest of the day, Forsyth took a step toward the doorway.

Mrs. Mitz didn't move. But just as her employer opened the door to slip into the hallway leading to the foot of the watchtower, she said: "Mr. Forsyth, you just remember one thing. Francis Gordon and Jenny Hudelson *will* get married, and they'll get married right on schedule. The wedding day is the thirty-first of this month. Everything will be ready for you—your white shirt, tie, and vest; your black coat and trousers; your tan gloves, polished boots, and top hat! What's more . . . I'll be there watching you!"

Forsyth didn't say a word, but dashed up the tower stairs three steps at a time.

As for old Mrs. Mitz, she'd gotten back on her feet to deliver this Summons to Appear. Afterward, shaking her head, she sank into her chair again, and a couple of good-sized tears glistened in her eyes.

8. In which the situation gets worse and worse as Whaston's newspapers start to take sides, some with Forsyth, some with Dr. Hudelson

But the weather showed a sincere inclination to improve. In this second month of spring, the aneroid barometers took well-deserved vacations after their wintertime trials and tribulations. Worn out from all their jumping around between highs and lows, their needles were glad to take a breather and stay put. Which meant astronomers could bank on a series of fair days and fine nights, just right for the precisely detailed observations they needed to make.

It follows that these benign atmospheric conditions were equally helpful to the denizens of Whaston's two watchtowers. In fact, during the night of May 20–21, the shooting star crossed the town's horizon from the northeast to the southwest, and the two rivals both spotted it at the same instant.

"There it is, Omicron! There it is!" Dean Forsyth shouted at 10:37 p.m.

"That's it!" Omicron confirmed, taking his boss's place at the eyepiece of the telescope. Then he added: "I only hope old Hudelson isn't up in his tower right now!"

"Or if he is," Forsyth stated, "that he won't be able to see the meteor . . ."

"Your meteor," Omicron said.

"My meteor!" Forsyth repeated.

Oh well, they were both wrong. "Old Hudelson" was on his observation deck, spyglass aimed northeast, and he picked up the shooting star the moment it emerged from the clouds on that side, and just like the other two, he didn't lose sight of it till the instant it vanished into the haze in the southwest.

What's more, they weren't the only ones who spotted it in that part of the firmament. The Pittsburgh and Cincinnati Observatories, plus plenty of other skywatchers in both the New World and the Old, could also vouch for the meteor in question. Besides, it was probable that its movements could be regularly observed, if the clouds would kindly refrain from hiding it for the next several weeks. The speed, distance, and timetable of its orbit around the earth could be worked out with mathematical precision, and presumably it was at least as fast as the records set by Stiegler and other globetrotters back then.*

Naturally the newspapers were committed to keeping their readers up to date on everything pertaining to this shooting star. Since astronomers were keenly interested in it, the public followed suit. The Whaston rags tried to supply accurate information even more industriously than their competition elsewhere, which was perfectly understandable since the two initial discoverers lived in their city. But in any case the meteor was visible under such conditions that the observatories couldn't help but analyze it. It wasn't one of those aerolites that skim the horizon and then vanish for good, one of those asteroids that are visible only for a brief moment before they're lost in space, or one of those interplanetary pebbles that fall to the earth the instant they appear. No, this meteor kept coming back, it was circling the globe like a second satellite, it deserved all the attention it could get; and since it got plenty—culminating in this devoted narrative—it deserved to be ranked among the most interesting phenomena ever recorded in the annals of astronomy.

So, driven by vanity, Forsyth and Dr. Hudelson staked their conflicting claims, to heck with the consequences—and if you find this inexcusable, too bad. But you'll understand soon enough.

Meanwhile it was now possible for the professionals, i.e., scientists, to meticulously analyze the meteor, and they did so. The various observatories aimed their finest telescopes at it, and into their lenses squinted the best-qualified eyes.

First off, based on press releases they'd received, the newspapers informed the public about the trajectory of this shooting star.

Its trajectory unfolded from the northeast to the southwest, in the process passing directly over Whaston—and if it fell at that point, it would land right on the town.

"But it isn't likely to fall!" insisted the *Whaston Morning News*, legitimately concerned with bucking up its subscribers. "It's moving at a steady, uniform, predictable speed, and there's no reason to think it might collide with something that could knock it out of its orbit."

This was clear enough; so for all the cities under the meteor's trajectory, Whaston included, there were no real grounds for worry on that score.

"To be sure," the *Whaston Evening News* chimed in, "there are space rocks that have fallen to the earth in the past and will do so in the future. But they're mostly small, they're just meandering through the cosmos, and they only fall when they get caught in our gravitational pull."

This explanation was flawless, and it didn't seem applicable to the meteor under discussion, which looked regular in its movements and no more likely to fall than the moon. At certain times, though, meteor showers can stream across the sky, and to take just one example, during the night of November 12–13, 1833, in less than nine hours it "rained" an estimated two hundred thousand aerolites and shooting stars over one location alone.

"Given the frequency of these meteor showers,* isn't it reasonable to wonder if, down through the centuries, our planet hasn't put on weight from those thousands, millions, and billions of stones falling on it? And if the earth's volume, mass, and gravitational pull have increased as a result, won't that change its orbit around the sun and its rotation on its axis? And who knows, isn't it possible the moon's orbit might even shift, bringing it nearer the earth?"

The *Whaston Daily Standard* was the publication making these observations, and immediately the *Whaston Punch* added its usual two
cents: "Oh come off it! Isn't it enough that some new shooting star
is threatening to flatten us? Now the moon is in danger of dropping
on our heads? This is all the doing of Mr. Forsyth and Dr. Hudelson,
and we hereby denounce them as enemies of the people!"

You couldn't help thinking that this fiendish newspaper was carrying out some private vendetta against those two individuals. Maybe
they'd let their subscriptions lapse.

The question of the meteor's distance also received careful attention. It was some 125 miles above the earth's surface,* hardly what had
been attributed to the magnificent shooting star sighted on March 14,
1863,* over Holland, Belgium, Germany, England, and France, whose
speed reached 40 miles per second, in other words, 2,400 miles per
minute, or over 140,000 miles per hour, a speed much greater than
that of the earth's orbit around the sun.* The new meteor wasn't that
fast by a long shot, since it was doing only a little better than 1,000
miles per hour.* But its altitude was sufficient to keep it from smack-
ing into the mountaintops of the New World and the Old, since the
tallest peaks in the Tibetan Himalayas, the Dhaulagiri and the Chomo
Lhari,* aren't higher than 33,000 feet* above sea level.

So, given that the shooting star was moving faster than 1,000 miles
per hour,* pretty close to the speed of the earth's equator as our globe
rotates on its axis, and likewise given that it was about 125 miles above
the earth's surface,* here's what it all comes down to: the meteor took
exactly twenty-four hours to orbit our planet, in contrast with the
moon, which takes twenty-eight days. It follows from this that if the
skies had stayed clear, the meteor would have been continually visible to countries located under its trajectory from the northeast to the
southwest.

But even for telescopes with the proper range, wasn't it reasonable
to ask how the meteor could be visible 125 miles up?* Wouldn't it have
to be pretty big?

To this perfectly natural question the *Whaston Daily Standard* gave
the following reply:

Based on its apparent altitude and dimensions, this shooting star
would have to be about 1,500 to 2,000 feet across.* Observations
to date allow us to say that much. But it still hasn't been possible to determine its composition reliably. It's visible, at least
to users of reasonably powerful binoculars, simply because it
shines so brightly, which is probably due to atmospheric friction—though the air is much thinner at that altitude, since at
barely eleven miles up,* it's already 90% less dense than on the
earth's surface. But this meteor isn't simply a clump of gaseous
matter, is it? To the contrary, doesn't it consist of a solid nucleus
followed by a luminous tail? But as for how big it is, and what
its nucleus is composed of, those are things we don't know and
may never know.

Now then, is this meteor likely to fall to the earth? No, apparently not. Probably it has been orbiting our planet since time
immemorial, and if the professional astronomers have missed it
till now, shame on them. It's our two fellow citizens, Mr. Dean
Forsyth and Dr. Stanley Hudelson, who deserve all the glory
coming from this magnificent discovery.

Regarding the question of whether or not this shooting star
will explode, as meteors of this sort often do, Herschel provides
an answer with this in-depth explanation: "The heat that meteorites contain when they hit the earth, the molten characteristics they display, their tendency to explode when they enter
pockets of heavier air—all this, in line with the laws of physics, can be adequately explained by the air condensing as a result
of the meteor's tremendous velocity, and by its heat interacting
with the rarefied air." As for an explosion proper, that's caused
by the pressure exerted on the meteor's solid core. This is what
happened to the 1863 shooting star. At the altitude where it was

sighted, the air's density was reduced by 90%, yet that meteor was still under a pressure of 675 atmospheres, which only solid iron can handle without shattering.

These were the explanations offered to the public. In short, the shooting star was behaving conventionally, and so far it didn't seem one bit different from other shooting stars—whether it broke free of the earth's gravitational pull, whether it continued to orbit the globe, whether it exploded and scattered its pieces across the ground, or whether it would fall to the earth as so many others have in the past and will in the future. All in all, there was nothing here out of the ordinary. For the scientific world it was business as usual, nor was there much in it to hold the interest of the general public.

Only the townspeople of Whaston—it's important to emphasize this—were deeply intrigued by everything concerning the meteor. This came from the fact that it had been discovered by two respected fellow citizens, and it seemed destined to be theirs, to become their own personal property. However, like the rest of the mortal world, the townsfolk might have shrugged off this cosmic event (or "comic event," as the *Whaston Punch* referred to it), if the newspapers hadn't played up the rivalry between Forsyth and Dr. Hudelson, a rivalry that was assuming more serious proportions by the day.

In actuality there wasn't any real reason to get worked up over this shooting star, but circumstances were about to change the public mood in a big way. Then you'll see the extremes to which human passions can go when they run amuck.

Meanwhile the wedding day had been approaching to where it was now just a week away. Mrs. Hudelson, Jenny, and Loo in one camp, Francis Gordon and good old Mrs. Mitz in the other, were getting more and more nervous. They lived in constant dread that some unexpected scandal would erupt, that two thunderclouds with positive and negative charges would collide and lightning would strike! They knew that Forsyth's temper wasn't improving, that Dr. Hudelson lost his at the tiniest provocation. Yet the sky was generally clear, the air was clean, and Whaston's horizons were wide open. At a set time every twenty-four hours, the two rivals could watch their meteor going by overhead, glitteringly adorned in its halolike coma.* They devoured the sight of it, they caressed it with their eyes, they assigned their names to it, the Forsyth Meteor, the Hudelson Meteor. It was their child, their flesh and blood. It belonged to them like a baby to its mother. Its appearance never failed to excite them. After making many observations, they developed theories concerning its speed and shape, then they communicated their brainstorms to the respective observatories of Cincinnati and Pittsburgh, each reiterating that he'd been the first to make this discovery.

Soon the *Whaston Daily Standard* even published a letter to the editor that was distinctly hostile to Dr. Hudelson, a letter attributed to Dean Forsyth. It said that certain people must have really sharp eyes, if all they could do was look through somebody else's telescope and see things that had already been seen.

In the *Whaston Evening News* the next day, this was answered by a letter noting that the lenses of certain telescopes obviously needed a good cleaning, since the things their users thought were meteorites were simply specks of dirt.

And meanwhile the *Whaston Punch* had published a cartoon with remarkably good likenesses of the two rivals, who were equipped with gigantic wings and racing in hot pursuit of their shooting star, which sported the head of a zebra sticking out its tongue at them.

Thanks to these articles with their inflammatory content, the situation between the two antagonists was worsening by the day, yet it still hadn't gotten in the way of the proposed wedding. Though they ignored it, at least they didn't impede it. If, to avoid a face-off, they failed even to participate—a truly disgraceful possibility—the ceremony would take place all the same. Francis Gordon and Jenny Hudelson would still

> be joined heart to heart
>
> till death do them part

like in the old Breton song. Afterward, if the two pigheaded ones saw fit to wage an all-out war, at least by that point Father O'Garth would have safely wrapped up the matrimonial proceedings at St. Andrew's.

Nothing changed during the uneventful days of May 22–23. But if things didn't get worse, they didn't get any better either. At mealtime in the Hudelson household, nobody made the tiniest reference to the meteor, and Miss Loo was furious at not being able to deal with the topic as it deserved. Her mother had pressed on her that it was better to keep quiet on this subject so as not to aggravate the situation. But from the way she sliced her meat, it was clear the girl wished the shooting star could be chopped into teensy pieces that could be swallowed up without a trace. As for Jenny, she couldn't hide her sadness, which the doctor gave no sign of noticing. And no doubt his obtuseness was due to his being so caught up in the cosmos.

Naturally Francis Gordon no longer appeared at mealtimes, and he was allowed his daily visits only when Dr. Hudelson was back up in his tower.

What's more, when the young man joined his uncle at table, meals weren't any more cheerful in the Elizabeth Street household. Forsyth said little, and when he spoke to old Mrs. Mitz, her monosyllabic answers were as chilly as the weather had just been.

Once on May 24, as Forsyth was leaving the table after finishing breakfast, he said to his nephew: "Are you going over to Hudelson's today?"

"That's right, uncle," Francis answered firmly.

"And why shouldn't he?" the old housekeeper wanted to know.

"I wasn't speaking to you, Mrs. Mitz!" Forsyth snarled. "I asked Francis—"

"And I gave you my answer, uncle. Yes, I go over there every day."

"So should *you*, Mr. Forsyth," Mrs. Mitz couldn't help remarking, folding her arms and looking her boss in the eye.

"After what the doctor did to me!" Forsyth exclaimed.

"And just what did he do, uncle?"

"He dared to sight—"

"The same thing you sighted yourself, the same thing anybody's free to sight, the same thing others will sight any minute now! Because all we're talking about is a simple shooting star—no different from a thousand others anybody can see over Whaston!"

"And it isn't any more unusual than the cornerstone of this house —it's just a silly piece of rock!"

That comment came from Mrs. Mitz, who was having a tough time keeping her temper. And, now out of control, the exasperated Forsyth fired back: "All right then, Francis—I order you to stay away from Hudelson's house!"

Startled by his uncle's presumption, the young man restrained himself with difficulty. "Sorry to have to disobey you, uncle," Francis stated, "but I'm going anyway."

"You bet he's going!" old Mrs. Mitz hollered in turn. "He'll see Mrs. Hudelson, he'll see Miss Jenny, his fiancée—"

"My fiancée, uncle, the lady I'm about to marry!"

"Marry?"

"That's right, and nobody's going to stop me!"

"We'll see about that!"

And with these words, the first he'd ever spoken in opposition to the marriage, Forsyth left the room, went upstairs to his watchtower, and viciously slammed the door.

Yet, despite his uncle, Francis Gordon was bound and determined to keep up his usual visits to the Hudelson family. But what if the doctor, like Forsyth, didn't want him there, what if he opposed the marriage too? There was good reason to fear the worst. Blinded by their mutual jealousy, the two antagonists were consumed by the nastiest hatred of all—the hatred two men feel when they tie for first place!

That day Francis had a hard time hiding his dark mood when he faced Mrs. Hudelson and her two daughters. He had no intention of mentioning the fracas he'd just had with his uncle. It would only make the ladies more anxious. Hadn't he decided to ignore his uncle's orders? If he had to manage without Forsyth's consent, then manage he would. After all, he was of age, and everything would be fine if the doctor didn't withhold his consent too . . . because, though Francis was legally free to disregard his uncle, Jenny wasn't in the same position with her father.

It was at this juncture that Loo got the idea of making a direct appeal to Dean Forsyth. This fifteen-year-old budding mediator was convinced, you see, that she could succeed where others had failed. Remember now, she was a young American female, a species that doesn't know the meaning of fear. They enjoy complete freedom, they come and go as they please, and they change their minds at the drop of a hat. So the next day and without a word to her sister or her mother, the girl pranced down the street, used to going out by herself,* while Mrs. Hudelson assumed she was heading off to church.

But Miss Loo wasn't going to church, which by and large would have been a more productive destination, and she soon stood at Forsyth's front door.

Francis was away, so it was Mrs. Mitz who let her in.

As soon as she learned the purpose of this visit, the old housekeeper told the girl some hard truths: "It's sweet of you, dearie, but believe me, it won't do a lick of good to appeal to him. My boss is crazy, certifiably insane, and my one last fear is that your dad will go crazy too, because then we'll be doomed for sure."

"You're saying I shouldn't talk to Mr. Forsyth?" Loo persisted.

"Yep, you're wasting your time, because he wouldn't even see you—or if he did, who knows if he wouldn't cut loose with some nasty words that could finish things for good!"

"But Mrs. Mitz, I know I can coax him! I'll smile and say, 'Oh, Mr. Forsyth, it doesn't have to be this way, does it? You wouldn't want this poor meteor to upset anybody, would you? You want your neph-ew to be happy, don't you? And my sister, and all of —'"

"It won't work, dearie," the old housekeeper responded. "I know what he's like, he won't budge an inch. He's too far gone, he's off his rocker, like I said. Listen, even I can't do a thing with him, so you'd only be wasting your breath. Forget about speaking with Mr. For-syth—it'll only end up in some explosion that'll make things even worse, and then the whole wedding'll be out the window."

"But what can we do? We've got to try something!" the girl pleaded.

"Be patient, dearie, we only have a few more days to go! Take my advice, the best thing is for you to head back home, but say a little prayer at St. Andrew's on the way, and ask the Good Lord to straight-en things out. I'm sure He'll give you a listen."

And with that the old housekeeper kissed the girl on both cheeks, then showed her to the door.

Loo took Mrs. Mitz's advice, but only after stopping first at her dressmaker's and verifying that her gown would be ready in time . . . it would and it was gorgeous. Then Loo headed over to church and begged the Almighty "to straighten things out" by sending two new and even more spectacular shooting stars, one for each of the rivals to discover on his own, so they could forget this old one that had been such a pain in the neck.

In less than a week—six days, to be exact—it would be May 31, the date when the wedding of Francis Gordon and Jenny Hudelson was scheduled to take place.

"Assuming nothing goes wrong," old Mrs. Mitz kept saying.

And if the situation didn't actually improve, at least there were no signs of anything happening to make it worse. Besides, what reasonable person would dream of preventing or delaying the marriage of two young lovers over such an issue as a shooting star? And even if Forsyth and Dr. Hudelson refused to face each other during the ceremony—well, their families would make do without them. After all, once they'd given their consent their presence wasn't essential. The main thing was that they didn't withhold their consent—or at least that the doctor didn't, because, though Francis was merely his uncle's nephew, Jenny was her father's daughter and couldn't marry against his wishes.

This was the reason for Mrs. Mitz's stipulation "Assuming nothing goes wrong." But Loo, whistling in the wind, repeated twenty times a day: "I can't believe that would happen!"

Francis was of the same mind, though he was less confident than his future sister-in-law: "Dr. Hudelson and my uncle are completely at loggerheads, but I can't see their feud getting any worse. Thanks to both of them, that blasted shooting star is now a matter of public record, so it won't have any further effect on this! It crosses the sky on a regular basis, and I expect it'll keep on till the end of time. The doctor and my uncle have both staked their claims, which have been noted and filed, and that's that. Time heals all wounds, so their rivalry will end up healed as well—once Jenny and I've gotten married and we've brought our two families even closer together. So all I ask is to be six days older!"

Ah, if mankind only had the magic power to skip from May 26 to May 31! After all, what's one week out of the three thousand that make up your average human lifespan? But this kind of time travel is still beyond us, and Francis Gordon could only resign himself to living out the 144 hours till his wedding day.

In any event what he'd said about the meteor was true. The good weather kept up and the skies over Whaston had never been better behaved. There was only a little morning and evening fog that evaporated at sunrise and sunset. Not a single cloud sullied the clear sky. The meteor put in regular appearances, rising and setting in the same parts of the firmament just like the stars themselves, though without picking up those extra four minutes that ultimately total the 366 days of the sidereal year.* Yes, it moved with the faultless precision of a chronometer. So in Whaston, as in every other locale where it was visible, battalions of binoculars lay in wait for it, then chased after it as it zipped along. Its luminous tail shone brilliantly on the moonless nights, so thousands of lenses could watch its every move.

Of course Messrs. Forsyth and Hudelson feasted their eyes on it, reaching for it as if to hug it to their panting bosoms. Honestly, it would have been better for everybody if it had stayed hidden behind some heavy cloudbank! The sight of it could only fan the flames of their antagonism. So Mrs. Mitz would stand in her window before going to bed and shake her fist at the shooting star. It was an empty threat, and the meteor continued blithely on its way through the star-spangled skies.

We can't help mentioning that the shooting star was a big hit with the public, and in every town it passed over, it was greeted by cheering crowds, especially in Whaston. Thousands of eyes watched for it to show up, then stayed glued to it till the moment it vanished below the horizon again. It almost seemed to be the private property of that delightful Virginia city, simply because two of its leading citizens had been the first to single it out from the swarms of asteroids up there.

And we should also mention that the townsfolk had split into two camps: those supporting Dean Forsyth and those Dr. Hudelson. Some newspapers sided vehemently with the former, others gave vociferous backing to the latter. Now then, according to press releases from the Pittsburgh and Cincinnati Observatories, both of these Whaston skywatchers had sighted the meteor on the same day—or rather the same night, hour, minute, and second—so it seemed prudent to duck the question of who should get the final credit. But neither the *Whaston Morning News*, the *Whaston Evening News*, nor the *Whaston Daily Standard* was willing to let go of the issue. From the heights of the two warring watchtowers the conflict had descended to the desks of the news editors, and dire complications were easy to foresee. Already there were announcements of public meetings to discuss the matter, no doubt with plenty of intemperate language, given the unbuttoned personalities found in the land of the free. And suppose the participants locked horns! What would they do next? Couldn't things get physical? Wouldn't they be whipping out bowie knives and revolvers?*

So Mrs. Hudelson and her daughter Jenny looked on fearfully as the town grew more frenzied by the day. Loo had no luck comforting her mother, nor Francis his fiancée. They were all too aware that both rivals were growing more and more agitated, were getting riled up to a point past forgiving. They remembered all the things, real or imagined, that Dr. Hudelson had said. And if the doctor came down from his tower to rant in front of his supporters during meetings of the Hudelson camp, and if his rival did the same with members of the Forsyth contingent, wouldn't the two maniacs cause a huge riot?

Wouldn't a horrifying battle break out, spilling blood in the streets of this once-peaceful town?

At this juncture there was a figurative clap of thunder, and it reverberated around the world.

Had the shooting star just exploded, and was the sound of it echoing and reechoing across the skies?

No, rest easy on that score. It was nothing less than a late-breaking news item that raced with electric speed along the telegraph and telephone lines of all the democracies and monarchies in the Old World and the New. And if ever a piece of scientific information was capable of provoking amazement, it was this news item whose absolute accuracy even the most skeptical were forced to accept.

And the piece of information we're referring to didn't hail from the watchtowers of Dean Forsyth or Dr. Hudelson, nor even from the Pittsburgh or Cincinnati Observatories. No, it was the observatory in Boston that had made this unexpected discovery, during the night of May 26–27, and it's hardly surprising that it sparked a major uproar.

At first many people refused to believe it. Some assumed it was an error that would soon be acknowledged, others figured it was a hoax cooked up by pranksters.

Yet the experts at the Boston Observatory seemed to be serious men who were above playing practical jokes. But even supposing that the solemn astronomers at this major national institution had been capable of "thumbing their noses at the universe," as a Washington newspaper quipped, the observatory director would have done his duty and put an immediate stop to it—unless the whole crew of them had gone loco for twenty-four straight hours.

But that didn't seem to be the case, and there were solid grounds for accepting their information as the real thing.

Here, then, is the press release those scientists sent to the leading U.S. cities, where it was immediately published in a thousand newspapers. As you can see, no telegraph lines have ever transmitted a more incredible yet truthful message:

The shooting star reported to the Pittsburgh and Cincinnati Observatories by two distinguished citizens of Whaston, Virginia, and which seems to be orbiting the earth with flawless regularity, has just undergone scrutiny from the standpoint of its physical composition.

Following due examination and study, these are the results of that scrutiny: the rays given off by this shooting star have been subjected to spectral analysis, and the pattern of their light waves provides conclusive evidence of the meteor's composition.

Its nucleus, which is surrounded by the halolike coma that's the source of the rays we've studied, isn't a gas but a solid. It isn't pure iron as most meteorites are, nor is it formed of chrysolite, that silicate of magnesium compounded of little balls of gravel.

This shooting star is made of gold—solid gold. And if we can't calculate its value down to the penny, it's simply because we can't measure the exact size of its nucleus at such a distance and under the present circumstances.

This was the news item that came to the world's attention. Its impact is easier imagined than described. Some thirty miles in the air,* a globe made of gold was circling the earth. A mass of precious metal that had to be worth billions of dollars. A ball of fire whose brilliance was either innate or caused by the heat from its speed through the atmosphere.

And it quickly became clear that the Boston chemists were dead right, and as soon as the international community also analyzed the meteor's rays, they confirmed that those rays could emanate only from a nucleus made of gold—and gold that wasn't too hot to remain in a solid state.*

As for the town of Whaston, it could take the credit for this discovery, thanks to those two citizens whose names would reverberate down through the ages, Dean Forsyth and Stanley Hudelson!

Unfortunately this piece of news wasn't about to end their rivalry, turn them back into old friends, or reduce the strain on their two families. No, each man was more determined than ever to claim the honor of making this astounding discovery.

Apparently the Good Lord hadn't been listening to little Loo's prayers. No new meteors were putting in personal appearances for Francis's uncle or Jenny's dad, and the two men battled more and more fiercely over this mass of gold whose trajectory took it directly above Whaston.

That same morning Judge Proth was standing at his window, while his housekeeper Kate bustled around the room. He was taking a peek outside, and trust me, he hadn't the slightest interest in seeing if the shooting star was passing over Whaston. This phenomenon had no fascination for him whatever. No, he was casually looking around Constitution Square, which was just outside the front door of his quiet home.

But if the meteor held no interest for Judge Proth, it held plenty for Kate, and two or three times already she'd paused in front of her employer and asked him the same question she was now repeating a fourth time:

"It's really made out of gold, sir?"

"So it would appear," the judge answered.

"Seems like you don't care one way or the other, sir."

"I don't, Kate."

"And yet if it's really gold, it's got to be worth millions."

"Not just millions, Kate, but billions. That's right, billions of dollars are going by overhead, but they're out of our reach, I'm afraid."

"That's a shame."

"How so, Kate?"

"Just think, sir—there wouldn't be any poor people left on earth."

"There would still be just as many, Kate."

"But, sir—"

"It takes a while to explain. In the first place, Kate, do you know how much a billion actually is?"

"Sort of, sir."

"It's a thousand millions."

"That much?"

"Yes, Kate. And even if you lived to be a hundred, from the day you were born till the day you died, you wouldn't have enough time to count up to a billion."

"You're kidding, sir!"

"It's the truth."

His housekeeper seemed aghast at the notion that a whole century wasn't long enough to count to a billion.* Then, picking up her broom and feather duster, she went back to work. But every minute or so she would pause and glance at the sky.

The weather was as magnificent as ever, perfect for skywatching.

The impulsive Kate couldn't help gawking at the sky overhead, that firmament on which all Whaston was keeping an eye. The meteor attracted them like a magnet. But Kate managed to bring her sights back down to earth, where she pointed out to her boss a couple of individuals standing at the bottom of Exeter Street.

"Sir," she said, "look at those two women waiting over there."

"I see them, Kate. What about them?"

"I recognize one of 'em. The taller of the two, the one who keeps stamping her foot."

"She certainly does seem impatient, Kate. But who is she? I know her from somewhere . . ."

"Oh sir, that's the lady you married two months ago—she and her future husband wouldn't get off their horses, remember?"

"Miss Arcadia Walker?" John Proth asked.

"Yes, and her new husband's name was Seth Stanfort."

"That's her all right," the judge stated.

"But what's she doing here?" Kate went on.

"I haven't the faintest idea," Proth answered.

"Could it be, sir, that she needs your services again?"

"I seriously doubt it," the judge stated. And after closing the window, he went back out to the garden to commune with his flowers.

The old housekeeper was right. It definitely was Mrs. Arcadia Stanfort, who that day, at that early hour, was back in Whaston with her chambermaid Bertha. And the two of them were striding impatiently back and forth, looking up and down Exeter Street.

Just then the town clock struck ten. Mrs. Stanfort actually seemed to be counting the strokes.

"He still isn't here!" she exclaimed.

"Could Mr. Stanfort have forgotten your appointment?" Bertha asked.

"Forgotten?" the young woman repeated. "He didn't forget our appointment when the judge married us, and he won't have forgotten this one either!"

"Then be patient, ma'am."

"Be patient, be patient! That's easy for you to say, Bertha!"

"After all," the chambermaid continued, "maybe Mr. Stanfort is having second thoughts."

"Second thoughts?"

"Yes, about following through on your plans."

"We've made up our minds and we're going ahead with it," Mrs. Stanfort answered firmly. "It's too late for second thoughts. This situation simply can't go on, it'll only get worse! My paperwork's all in order, isn't it?"

"Yes, ma'am."

"And Mr. Stanfort's is too, right?"

"All you need is the judge's signature," Bertha answered.

"And this one will do the trick just as well as the first," Arcadia added. Then she took a step or two toward Exeter Street, followed by her maid. "Mr. Stanfort's still not in sight?" she asked even more impatiently.

"No, ma'am, but maybe Mr. Stanfort isn't taking the road from Wilcox."

"But if he's coming from Richmond . . ."

"It's been two whole weeks since you split up, ma'am, and I haven't seen Mr. Stanfort since. Who knows what road he'll take to Whaston."

After this comment of Bertha's, Mrs. Stanfort turned back toward the square. "No, not a soul, nobody!" she repeated. "He's making me wait, after all our arrangements! Today *is* May 27, correct?"

"Yes, ma'am."

"And it's almost ten thirty?"

"Just five minutes to go."

"All right, Mr. Stanfort better not think I'll run out of patience, because I'll wait all day if I have to! And I'm not leaving Whaston till Mrs. Seth Stanfort has been turned back into Miss Arcadia Walker!"

No doubt the curiosity seekers in the hotels around Constitution Square would have noticed the young woman's restlessness, just as two months earlier they'd noticed the impatience of that horseman who'd been waiting to escort her to the magistrate. In fact Mrs. Stanfort's unusual agitation might have left them even more puzzled than before—and then wouldn't their imaginations have been off and running! But that day every man, woman, and child had something else on his mind—and just then Mrs. Stanfort was the single exception in all Whaston. Barely twenty-four hours had gone by since the big news had flashed around the world. And once again it was the friendly city of Whaston that was the most feverishly interested. Its citizens had thoughts only for that marvelous meteor passing regularly over their town. The gossips hanging around Constitution Square, and the doormen in the hotels, weren't one bit curious about Mrs. Arcadia Stanfort. But while waiting for the shooting star to show up, they were just as impatient as she was waiting for her husband. Despite what some people claim, we can't be sure that the moon really exerts an influence over the human mind and that moon madness is an actual fact. But we can be forgiven for noting that there were a gigantic number of people around the world who suffered from "meteor madness," who skipped meals at the thought of a hunk of stone worth billions going by overhead. Oh, if only they could somehow get ahold of it and cash it in . . .

Though arriving from different locations, Mr. and Mrs. Stanfort had gone off together to Richmond after being married by the justice of the peace. There, a few weeks earlier, they'd set up their new living quarters, complete with all the up-to-date amenities their fortunes could buy. Located in the wealthiest, most desirable section of Virginia's capital, their dwelling overlooked the James River, whose left bank the city occupies. The newlyweds stayed there just a week, during which time they paid visits to several members of Mrs. Arcadia Stanfort's family, who were among the town's leading citizens.

Maybe if cold weather had started setting in, the distinguished couple would have hunkered down in their new dwelling for the duration of the winter. But the first buds of April were already covering the branches, and what could be more delightful than a honeymoon while spring was being sprung. Before their marriage, as you know, both Mr. Stanfort and Miss Walker loved to travel, and this craving definitely persisted after they became man and wife. You could even say that their union had taken place on the road, or at any rate in a Whaston street. Equipped with marriage licenses duly made out by court clerks in Boston and Trenton, these two young people had thought it was an innovative idea to get married under the eccentric circumstances we've seen.

So a week after returning to Richmond and at a typical American tempo, these two U.S. speed demons had crossed, if not visited, the fields and mountains of nearby North and South Carolina.

What went wrong during that high-speed trip via railroad, steamboat, and stagecoach? Had the newlyweds disagreed about which routes to take? Didn't they see eye to eye on things? Had clouds darkened the skies of their honeymoon? Were there wrong notes in their wedding march?

All we know is that three weeks after leaving town, Mr. and Mrs. Stanfort returned to their Richmond home by different routes. Then, a week after that, the husband went out one door, the wife another. And if they had any further contact, it was strictly by letter and other long-distance methods. And they didn't use the telephone—where two voices have to talk, listen, and interact over an electric wire—but the more impersonal telegraph, when they made an appointment for 10 a.m. on May 27 in the town of Whaston.

Now then, it was already ten thirty, and only Mrs. Arcadia Stanfort had shown up for their appointment. And she asked again: "Can you see him, Bertha?"

"No, ma'am."

"Could he have changed his mind?"

"Maybe so."

"Well, I haven't changed mine!" Mrs. Stanfort replied firmly. "And I'm not planning to!"

Just then shouts erupted at the end of the square. Passersby rushed over to look. Several hundred people poured in from the nearby streets, and soon there was a substantial crowd. In the meantime, hearing this outburst of voices, John Proth left his garden and popped out on his front step, his loyal Kate beside him.

"There! Up there!"

Those shouts came from busybodies hanging around the square and out the windows of the hotels overlooking it.

And the words "There! Up there!" were such an appropriate answer to the question in Mrs. Stanfort's mind, she couldn't help exclaiming, "Finally!"

"Afraid not, ma'am," her chambermaid had to tell her. "He still isn't in sight!"

And even if he was, why would the crowd be so worked up about it? Why would they care?

Besides, everybody was looking at the sky, fingers pointing at the northeastern part of the horizon.

Was the notorious meteor putting in its daily appearance over Whaston? Had the townsfolk come out to wave as it went by?

No, it wasn't time for the telescopes in our two watchtowers to start tailing the meteor after it popped above the horizon. It wouldn't be visible before nightfall. As you may recall, it orbited the earth once a day. Dean Forsyth and Dr. Hudelson had first sighted it after sundown, and that's the only time it could be seen, if the clouds elected not to hide it from mortal eyes.

So what was the crowd going on about?

"It's a balloon, ma'am," Bertha said. "Look, there it is—passing over the steeple of St. Andrew's."

"A balloon!" John Proth echoed in answer to Kate, who was hoping it was their pet meteor.

A hot air balloon rose lazily into the stratosphere. The famous Walter Wragge was flying it with his assistant's help.* This balloon flight had the objective of studying the shooting star under the most favorable conditions, and it was intended to last into the evening. Since the wind was blowing from the southwest, the hot air balloon could ride ahead of it, some three to three and one-half miles up.* So maybe Walter Wragge would be able to make out the gold nucleus in the middle of its halolike coma. And who knows—the world might finally find out how big it was!

Naturally, once this balloon ride had been announced, Dean Forsyth thoroughly alarmed old Mrs. Mitz by insisting, according to Francis, on "going along too." Ditto the doctor, likewise to the trepidation of Mrs. Hudelson. But the famous balloonist had room for only one other person in the car of his balloon. At which point the two rivals launched a heated exchange of letters arguing their respective cases. Ultimately Walter Wragge passed over both men in favor of his assistant, an infinitely more rational choice.

About two thousand feet up, the stronger currents at that altitude caught the balloon and swiftly carried it off to the north, where it lay in wait for the shooting star. It vanished to a last round of cheers from the crowd.*

As worried and impatient as she was, Mrs. Stanfort watched it so intently that she didn't see her husband walk up, his step calm and measured.

"Here I am, ma'am," Seth Stanfort said, bowing.

"Really, sir," Mrs. Arcadia Stanfort began, while Bertha stood discreetly to the rear.

And they traded the following questions and answers in tones that grew chillier and chillier.

"So, Mr. Stanfort, you're finally here, are you?"

"I didn't want to miss our appointment, Mrs. Stanfort."

"I've been here a full hour."

"I'm sorry I kept you waiting, but I needed to come by train. It had engine trouble and pulled in late."

"For a moment I thought you'd gone off in that balloon."

"What? Then things would really be up in the air!"

Mrs. Stanfort started to grin but caught herself, and her husband became just as serious.

"This is no time for jokes," the young woman went on, "and since we both had our say at our last meeting—"

"There's no point in going over it again," Seth confirmed, "because we both know exactly where we stand."

"We do, and furthermore I think our last conversation can be summarized in a single sentence."

"Which is?"

"It's time for us to go our separate ways."

"Agreed."

"And end our relationship for good."

"My sentiments exactly."

"But rest assured, Mr. Stanfort, I fully recognize all your good qualities."

"And believe me, I'll always appreciate yours."

"We thought we liked the same things, and when it comes to traveling, that's true enough . . ."

"And yet, Mrs. Stanfort, we could never agree on our destination."

"No, and when I wanted to go south, you wanted to go north."

"And when my plans called for heading east, yours called for heading west."

"So, Mr. Stanfort, I'll say again what I said before: we're wrong for each other."

"I think so too, ma'am, just as I said during our last conversation."

"You see, sir, I've always lived by myself. I've never had to worry about what anybody else wanted."

"I'm like that too, ma'am, and what's more, many American girls are taught the same values. I don't say they're right or wrong, but they don't prepare people very effectively for the obligations of marriage."

"True," Arcadia replied, "yet I'll admit my personality can be a little severe—but I definitely would have had warmer feelings for you, if, say, I'd had a chance to admire you for some great piece of heroism . . ."*

"And that chance hasn't come up, I'm afraid," Stanfort acknowledged. "You're very adventurous and you like going into danger, but I haven't had an opportunity to risk my life for you. Which I wouldn't hesitate to do if the need arose. I'm sure you realize that."

"I do, Mr. Stanfort."

We must comment that this dialogue had gradually changed from bitter to bittersweet.

But instead of calling each other Seth and Arcadia, they'd reverted to Mr. Stanfort and Mrs. Stanfort, which soon gave way to those curt sir's and ma'am's that most couples have long since discarded, even after just two months of marriage. So it was high time this conversation drew to a close, and not surprisingly it was the young woman who brought things to a head.

"You recall, sir," she said, "why we agreed to meet again in Whaston?"

"I've no more forgotten than you have, ma'am."

"Have you brought all your paperwork?"

"It's in order, ma'am, as I'm sure yours is."

"Once we're divorced, sir, both of us can go back to that single life more suitable to our personalities. But it's possible, even likely, that we'll meet up as we travel around the globe."

"And it'll be a pleasure to see you again, ma'am, and to greet you with all the courtesy you deserve."

"I'll expect no less from you, sir."

"It's inevitable, ma'am, because I can't possibly forget that I once had the honor of being married for two whole months to Miss Arcadia Walker."

"And for those same two months, sir, I've had the privilege of being wed to Mr. Seth Stanfort."

Really now, both of them could have dispensed with these nostalgic admissions, which weren't about to change a thing: they'd wanted to reach an agreement and they had. They were bound and determined to get a divorce, an option that was becoming as common as those old stage marriages between leading men and leading ladies. As a matter of fact, divorce proceedings in the United States are a high-speed operation. In this amazing American Union where unions have become so short-lived, you can split up in no time. It's even easier to get untied than tied.* In such states as North Dakota, South Dakota, and Oklahoma, all you have to do is set up a bogus residence, and you don't even have to appear in person to get a divorce. Hired consultants can take care of everything for you, from gathering witnesses to hiring signatories. They can smooth anything over, and their services are well known in big cities across the land.

But Mr. Seth Stanfort and Miss Arcadia Walker didn't need to go to such lengths, though they would have if they'd had to. No, it was right there in Richmond, in the heart of Virginia, in the actual place where they resided, that they went ahead with the legal proceedings and tended to all the formalities. And if they decided to go back to Whaston to undo the same bonds of matrimony they'd tied just two months earlier, it was simply because they wanted to get divorced at the same place they'd gotten married, and in a locality where nobody knew them. Given the slapdash manner in which they'd taken this step, normally considered to be the most important in a person's life, they had good reason to wonder if the magistrate would even remember them when they went back to him.

And so the conversation between Mr. and Mrs. Stanfort finished along these lines:

"Now, sir, all we have to do is go ahead with it."

"I think so, ma'am."

"We need to go over to Judge Proth's home, sir."

"I'm with you, ma'am."

And instead of going single file, they walked side by side, just three steps apart, over to the justice of the peace.

Standing in the doorway, old Kate saw the couple approaching, ran to her boss, and said: "Judge! Judge! They're coming!"

"Who?"

"Mr. and Mrs. Stanfort."

"The Stanforts? What do they want?"

"We'll soon find out!" Kate answered.

In fact their visitors were only a hundred paces from the judge's house, and when his housekeeper saw them come into the courtyard, she said: "You want to speak with Judge Proth?"

"We do," Mrs. Stanfort answered.

"A legal matter?"

"A legal matter," Mr. Stanfort answered.

Based on that response it obviously wasn't a social call, so Kate didn't escort Mr. and Mrs. Stanfort into the living room but into Judge Proth's study.

Both of them sat down without saying a word and waited for the magistrate to arrive, which he did a few moments later.

As friendly and easygoing as ever, Judge Proth expressed his delight at seeing Mr. and Mrs. Stanfort again, then asked how he could be of service on this occasion.

"Two months ago, judge," Mrs. Stanfort answered, "we appeared before you so that you could marry us."

"And it was a pleasure," Proth stated, "to make your acquaintance."

"Today, judge," Mr. Stanfort added, "we're appearing before you so that you can divorce us."

Though he certainly hadn't anticipated this proposal, Judge Proth was a man of the world who saw that this was no time to attempt a reconciliation, so he said calmly: "Well, at least I'll have the pleasure of renewing our acquaintance."

The two petitioners bowed.

"Is your paperwork in order?" the magistrate asked.

"Here's mine," Mrs. Stanfort said.

"And mine," Mr. Stanfort said.

Judge Proth took the documents, examined them, made sure they were well and truly executed, then replied simply: "I'm able to issue a divorce decree."

And there was no need to call in witnesses, since all the formalities had been tended to. In his most elegant script, Proth drew up the decree that would dissolve the marriage between these two young people.

This done, he got up and held out his pen to Mrs. Stanfort: "All I need are your signatures," he said.

And without any comment, hesitation, or unsteadiness of fingers, Mrs. Stanfort signed her maiden name of Arcadia Walker.

And Mr. Seth Stanfort added his own signature, just as coolly.

Then, after nodding to each other and bowing to the magistrate, Mr. Stanfort and Miss Walker left the study, walked out into the street, and separated, one heading out Wilcox way, the other in the opposite direction.

And when they were out of sight, Judge Proth, who'd followed them to the front door, said to his old housekeeper: "Kate, do you know what I ought to add to that sign outside?"

"No sir, what?"

"*Marriages on Horseback, Divorces on Foot.*"

And Judge Proth returned philosophically to the pathways in his garden, which needed a little raking.*

11. In which the number crunchers have a field day arriving at dollar amounts with great appeal to human greed

"One thing's for sure," snapped impatient Miss Loo as she got up at seven o'clock that morning, "if we can just hang on for the next four days, at eleven-thirty on May thirty-first Francis Gordon and Jenny Hudelson will walk out of St. Andrew's as husband and wife!"

The girl was right, but it all depended on nothing going seriously wrong beforehand.

But the situation between Dr. Hudelson and Dean Forsyth showed no signs of improving. That exchange of letters over the flight planned by the balloonist Walter Wragge definitely didn't help. If the two rivals bumped into each other on the street, it was sure to result in a heated dialogue, and God only knew what would happen next . . .

Luckily both of them stayed put in their respective towers. Probably they were simply skywatching rather than deliberately avoiding each other. But their families still had to allow for unexpected developments, which always seem to make things worse instead of better. Yet if they could only hang on for the next four days—that was Miss Loo's thinking, and her mother, sister, and future brother-in-law also had their fingers crossed.

However it didn't seem that the shooting star would be the cause of any new complications. Aloof and unconcerned, it followed its standard route from the northeast to the southwest without showing the slightest inclination to deviate from that path, at least so far. It tooled along at full throttle while millions of human eyes watched it go. No king or queen of the wealthiest country, no diva at the biggest opera house, no dancer in the ritziest ballet, had ever been the source of more feverish attention. As you know, whenever there's a simple solar eclipse, the price of sunglasses* jumps tremendously. Imagine, then, how expensive telescopes, field glasses, and pocket binoculars became in every country where the meteor was visible! And wasn't it just possible that one of those tireless skywatchers would put the finishing touches on this discovery, either by accurately determining the new asteroid's composition, or by ascertaining the exact size of its gold nucleus?

And weren't Dean Forsyth and Dr. Hudelson on the same stubborn quest? While they waited to see whom the asteroid would be named after, if either of our rivals had managed to crack the meteor's mysteries, it would be a huge feather in his cap! Weren't these remaining secrets of the shooting star the topic of the day, the question on everybody's lips? And if the greatest fear of the ancient Gauls was that the sky might fall on their heads, modern humanity had the opposite desire: they wanted that shooting star to stop in its tracks, give in to the force of gravity, and lavish our planet with the billions its nucleus was worth.

"Boss," Omicron kept repeating during his long nighttime vigils on the observation deck of their watchtower, "isn't it possible to figure out the weight of our shooting star?"

He'd gotten into the habit of saying "our," though this possessive modifier offended the ears of Mr. Dean Forsyth.

"It's very possible," his employer answered.

"And how about figuring out its value?"

"That's possible too."

"Oh, if only we could be the ones . . ."

"It makes little difference, Omicron, whether it's us or somebody else, just so long as it isn't that filthy scoundrel Hudelson!"

"Not him! Please not him!" asserted Omicron, who pretty much shared all his boss's sentiments.

No doubt the doctor himself was of the same mind and had no intention of letting his rival get the best of him.

Meanwhile the general public only wanted to know what the meteor was worth in dollars, francs, or pounds sterling, and they didn't care who figured it out, so long as they finally got a satisfactory answer.

Even so, this was more a point of curiosity than of greed, since those airborne millions would most likely remain out of reach till the end of time.

But really now, wasn't it asking too much of human nature for everybody simply to shrug off those riches roaming through the skies barely twenty miles* overhead?

So students of the human psyche weren't one bit surprised that interest mushroomed outrageously at the news this meteor was made of gold. And there were countless attempts to put a price tag on it, but since nobody knew how big its nucleus was, these efforts didn't have any factual basis. The most advanced instruments were still unable to penetrate its haughty rays and determine its shape and size. But nobody could dispute that it was entirely composed of this most precious of metals, since this characteristic could be verified at any time by subjecting its rays to spectral analysis. And whatever its value was, it had to be beyond anybody's wildest dreams.

In fact that same day the *Whaston Daily Standard* published the following item: "If we accept that the nucleus of the Forsyth-Hudelson meteor"—this newspaper gave it a hyphenated label—"is shaped like a ball that only measures about thirty feet across,* its weight, if it were made of iron, would be over forty-one hundred tons. But as pure gold, it would weigh over eleven thousand tons,* and it would be worth more than six billion dollars."*

Even with such modest dimensions, the shooting star would still be worth a fabulous sum!

"Boss, can this really be possible?" Omicron asked, flabbergasted by the above news item.

"It's not only possible, it's a certainty," Dean Forsyth answered. "And all you have to do in order to determine its volume is to use this formula:

$$V = \frac{\pi D^3}{6} \quad \dots \text{"}$$

Omicron could only bow his head before this formula, which was completely unintelligible to him, and he couldn't help repeating in a voice that quivered with profound feeling: "Six billion dollars . . . six billion dollars . . . !"

"That's right," Forsyth confirmed, "but it's so disgusting that this newspaper insists on linking my name with you-know-who's."

And no doubt you-know-who was thinking similar thoughts.

As for Miss Loo, when she read this item in the *Whaston Daily Standard*, the scornful expression on her pink lips put even those six billion bucks in their place.

Even in America, as you know, it's in the nature of news reporters to want to top each other. If the first writer says two, the next one says three, simply because you can't keep rehashing the same old story. So not surprisingly, that same night the *Whaston Evening News* did a follow-up, siding with Hudelson (while the *Whaston Morning News* would side with Forsyth), even though the *Daily Standard* had made them joint discoverers. The *Evening News*'s response read as follows:

We don't know why the *Daily Standard* is so timid in estimating the meteor's size. Are its dimensions so piddling that its nucleus measures only thirty feet across? Why turn an asteroid into a pebble when it could just as easily be a boulder? Didn't the top experts in the field assign a diameter of over 1,350 feet to that shooting star seen on March 14, 1863, and over 1,600 feet* to the one seen on May 14, 1864? All right, let's take things a bit far-ther than the *Daily Standard* but stay well within the realm of probability: we'll assign a diameter of 300 feet* to the Hudelson meteor. Now then, based on this new figure, its revised weight if made of iron would be over 4,100,000 tons, and if pure gold would be over 11,000,000 tons,* which means it would be worth over six trillion two hundred and fifty billion dollars.*

"Leaving off the cents," quipped the *Whaston Punch* when it quoted these monstrous, mind-boggling numbers.

But whether they went along with the estimates of the *Daily Stan-dard* or those of the *Evening News*, Whastonians were now convinced that every twenty-four hours billions and billions were passing over their town, and over others under the meteor's trajectory.

And after good old Kate read the above item, she took off her read-ing glasses and said to Judge Proth: "All these big numbers don't mean a doggoned thing to me, judge. What I want to know is how much this treasure's worth to each person, if it fell to the earth and was divvied up among the whole human race."*

"Fair enough, Kate. And it boils down to a simple problem in long division, so we'll start by assuming there are about one and a half bil-lion people in the world—"

"That many?"

"Yes, so you and I are only the tiniest fraction of that whole."

"But how much would we get?"

"Hold on, Kate," Proth answered. "There are so many zeros in both the divisor and the dividend, I have to be careful I don't get mixed up and give you a wrong answer." He worked the problem through on a corner of the newspaper, then said: "It comes to about forty-two hundred dollars per person."*

"Forty-two hundred dollars!" the old housekeeper shrieked, clasp-ing her hands. "Everybody would be rich!"

"No, I'm afraid they'd still be poor!" Judge Proth replied. "Because the price of gold would go down—it wouldn't be worth any more than the grains of sand on a beach! And even if we assume that it keeps its value, imagine how many people would go right out and squander their forty-two hundred dollars on drinking and partying. Soon they'd be just as broke as they were before!"*

And with that the philosophical judge turned his back on the world's follies and went out to sprinkle his flowers.

You may have noticed that Judge Proth spent more time in his garden than in his chambers. That simply speaks well of Whaston's citizens, a peace-loving lot with little interest in litigation. But every so often John Proth would have to hear a serious case that called for as much common sense as knowledge of the law. And sure enough, within forty-eight hours a matter of this kind was going to draw the public in droves to his courtroom.

Meanwhile the fair weather held up. The needles on people's aneroid barometers seemed to have gotten permanently stuck at thirty and one-half inches.* Day and night the skies stayed clear. There was only a little morning and evening mist, which promptly vanished at sunup or sundown. So skywatchers had a pleasant and productive time all around.

But their cups would have run over if they'd been able to find out the exact size of the asteroid's nucleus. However, it was very difficult to pinpoint its contours in the midst of its brilliant tail. Even the best telescopes hadn't managed this.

It's true that around 2:45 a.m. on the night of May 27–28, Dean Forsyth thought he'd verified that the nucleus was globular in shape. The light around it had dimmed for an instant, and a brilliant golden ball became visible.

"Omicron!"

"Boss?"

"Look, look!"

Omicron peered into the eyepiece of their telescope.

"Can you see it?" Forsyth said.

"Yes . . . it looks like . . ."

"That's right!"

"We've got it . . . finally . . . rats, it's already out of sight!" Omicron exclaimed.

"It doesn't make any difference! I saw it! I've finally had a piece of good luck! I'll notify the Pittsburgh Observatory first thing tomorrow morning! And this time that rascal Hudelson won't have a leg to stand on!"

No doubt about it, Forsyth had seen that the meteor's core was shaped like a ball, and for a few extra seconds Omicron had too. But wouldn't Hudelson have detected this fact as well? That same night, the doctor had tracked the shooting star from the instant it appeared above the northeastern horizon to the second it vanished below the southwestern one. He would likewise have seen its nucleus and would similarly be planning to notify *his* contacts at the Cincinnati Observatory. And the two rivals would be right back at each other's throats.

Luckily this danger didn't materialize, because others had already made the same discovery under absolutely authoritative circumstances. What's more—as you'll read in an announcement from one of America's most renowned institutions, the Naval Observatory in Washington D.C.—scientists hadn't just seen the meteor's nucleus on that noteworthy night, they'd determined its size and shape with the greatest accuracy.

So the next day Dean Forsyth, Dr. Stanley Hudelson, and readers worldwide came across the following item in their morning papers: "Last night at 2:45 a.m., astronomers at the U.S. Naval Observatory in Washington D.C.* examined the new shooting star under exceptionally favorable conditions and were able to measure its nucleus. The meteor is globular in shape and has a diameter of exactly 164 feet."*

So if the shooting star wasn't three hundred feet across as the *Whaston Evening News* had speculated, it was more than the modest 30 feet suggested by the *Whaston Daily Standard*. The truth lay right in between those two estimates, and it was still impressive enough to gratify the greediest people—if the meteor wasn't destined to orbit the earth till the second coming.

In a nutshell, the number crunchers knuckled down and soon learned the facts: with V the globe's volume, π being 3.1416, and D the diameter, they used the formula:

$$V = \frac{\pi D^3}{6}$$

Taking this formula, gangs of math whizzes went feverishly to work and came up with the following result: since the diameter of the meteor's core was 164 feet, the gold composing it had a weight of 1,389,393 tons,* and its market value was over 781 billion dollars.*

Even if its nucleus wasn't three hundred feet across and worth six trillion two hundred billion dollars, per the *Whaston Evening News*, you can see that the meteor would still fetch an enormous sum of money. And if it were divvied up among the billion and a half people living on earth, each person would still get about $530.*

When Forsyth heard about the market value of his shooting star, he shrieked: "And I'm the one who discovered it, not that villainous doctor! It's mine, all mine, and if it ever falls to the earth, I'll be worth 781 billion!"

Meanwhile Dr. Hudelson for his part was shaking his fist in Forsyth's direction and saying over and over: "I own it, it belongs to me and my heirs! It's out in space, but it's still my property! If it ever drops out of the sky, it'll be mine and I'll be a billionaire 781 times over!"

No doubt about it, compared to Messrs. Forsyth and Hudelson, such American financial wizards as Vanderbilt, Astor, Rockefeller, Pierpont Morgan, Mackay, and Gould—to say nothing of Rothschild overseas—would all be small-time operators.

That was the thinking of our two rivals, and if they weren't afflicted with softening of the brain, it's simply because they were both so hardheaded.

Francis Gordon and Mrs. Hudelson could easily see where things were going with the two men. But what could they do about it? How could they keep the two competitors from sliding farther and farther down this slippery slope? It was impossible to talk calmly with them, definitely not about that wretched shooting star, nor even about the wedding ceremony now due to take place in just three more days. The two rivals seemed to have forgotten this fact, or rather they were only thinking about their feud, which the local newspapers kept fueling in such a shameful manner. It was as if the Capulets and Montagues had come back to life in Whaston, Virginia, whose townspeople were just as polarized as the Italians in old Verona. Articles in the once-placid newspapers got nastier and nastier, and every day the insults flew thicker and faster. There was a real danger these normally civil men might be goaded into challenging each other to a duel;* the effect of this meteor on human emotions was so intense, so virulent, there was a distinct possibility it could lead to bloodshed.

Therefore the two families were especially afraid that Forsyth and Dr. Hudelson would haggle over their asteroid firearms in hand, that they would settle the business in an American-style shootout. And that damned *Whaston Punch* kept making matters worse, constantly stirring things up with its cartoons and one-liners. Honestly, if this newspaper wasn't actually pouring oil on the fire—or gasoline rather, since we're in the U.S.A.—its daily jokes were at least adding a pinch of salt, which only made the flames crackle more merrily.

"Oh, if I could just fix this situation!" Miss Loo exclaimed that day.

"And what would you do, baby sister?" Francis Gordon asked.

"Do? Easy. I'd send that stinking ball of gold so far out into space, the best telescopes would never see it again!"

In other words, if the shooting star were to vanish, maybe a little sanity could return to the deeply troubled minds of Dean Forsyth and

Dr. Hudelson. And who knows, once the meteor was out of sight and gone for good, maybe their rivalry would vanish as well.

But this possibility didn't seem terribly likely. The wedding was just three days away, and afterward the shooting star would still be there—and there it would probably stay for all eternity, since its steady, unvarying orbit was regulated by the laws of gravity.

Then an idea started to take form in the public consciousness, an idea that seemed extremely simple but also, alas, hopelessly impractical. It wasn't just forming in Whaston but in every city, town, village, and hamlet that lay under the meteor's trajectory around our planet.

Here, in all its simplicity, is the idea that was running through people's minds: "What if, by some method, we could cause the fall of this shooting star that's worth all those billions? If it isn't going to fall by itself, what if, just for an instant, we could interrupt its orbit around the earth . . . ?"

Yes . . . then its fall would be a certainty. But who could come up with this "method"? Wasn't it beyond all human power? Could anybody create an obstacle for the shooting star to smack into, an obstacle strong enough to stand up against a speed of one thousand miles per hour?*

So the inventors piled helter-skelter into their inventing. And the newspapers reported their nuttiest proposals: how about building an extra powerful cannon, like the one concocted years ago that tried to hit the moon, or that later one whose recoil was so tremendous, they hoped it would knock the earth off its axis? Fine, but as everybody knows, those two contraptions were completely fictitious, the pipe-dreams of some woolgathering French novelist.*

"Oh, if only this shooting star were made of iron, like most meteors out in space!" the *Whaston Daily Standard* commented one day. "Then you'd have no problem pulling it out of the sky—you'd just have to build an ultra powerful electromagnet!"

Yes, but it was made of gold, not iron, and magnets have no effect on that precious metal. Besides, if it *were* made of iron, it would amount to 519,000 tons of the stuff,* and there'd be no point in trying to lay hold of it. Don't we have enough of that substance already, since the earth itself is simply an enormous hunk of iron carbide?

So they taxed their imaginations, cudgeled their wits, and wracked their brains to the bursting point. Human greed can go to such extremes! People simply couldn't live with the thought that all those billions were just out of reach. From the instant that meteor arrived out of the blue—maybe after escaping from the gravitational pull of some other planet—and then went into orbit around our globe, it belonged exclusively to the earth. And nobody would have dreamed of letting it go off and orbit our planet's bigger or smaller neighbors in the solar system.

At which point the *Whaston Punch* dealt with this solemn issue by turning the whole business into a miser's monologue:

"This meteor is ours, all ours, and nobody's going to take it away from us! Other planets may want a piece of the action, so we've got to stay on the alert! We've got to keep an eye on big old Jupiter, who might kidnap our meteor with its gravitational field! We've got to guard against that old flirt Venus, who might seduce it away just to have another gold trinket! And don't forget who else is lurking nearby—Mercury, patron of pickpockets! So watch out, everybody, watch out!"

Ever since the meteor's market value became known to the world, this was the general drift of people's thinking. Meanwhile, like clockwork, the shooting star kept appearing above the northeastern horizon and vanishing below the southwestern one over all the countries lying under its orbit. And in one of those localities, a certain Virginia town, there were two men, two former friends, who kept devouring that golden-rayed meteor with their eyes, while they waited for a chance to devour each other.

During those fine, clear nights back then, there were maybe only two human beings in all Whaston who weren't keeping their eyes on the shooting star, for the simple reason that Francis Gordon and Jenny Hudelson only had eyes for each other. As for little Loo, she sent it angry looks every waking minute.

And if Mrs. Hudelson and old Mrs. Mitz gave themselves daily pep talks in their respective households about that aerolite maybe leaving for good, wandering off into outer space, and dwindling into a dead issue, their hopes were soon dashed. That big billion-dollar ball kept coming back, coming back to arouse the greed of a human race consumed by money lust, coming back to cause misfortune for these two decent families who were continually aware that they teetered on the brink of catastrophe.

Anyhow the wedding day kept getting closer and closer. May 28 was ready to turn into May 29 on that year's calendar. There were only forty-eight hours to go till the church bells at St. Andrew's would peal out and summon the two lovers to the marriage ceremony.

But that same afternoon, the Whaston telegraph office, like many others in both the New World and the Old, received the following announcement from the Boston Observatory:

"After closer scrutiny we have verified that the speed of the meteor's trajectory is gradually diminishing. We conclude from this fact that it will eventually fall to the earth."*

"It will fall . . . it will fall . . . it will fall to the earth!"

If ever a future tense was overused, and with such worldwide emotion, this was the occasion. From that moment on, the pronoun "it" referred only to the meteor. As for the verb, the burning question was when the time would come to shift to the present and past tenses.

True, when the Boston Observatory revealed that the meteor's nucleus was made of gold, it did result in a record-setting outbreak of mass hysteria. But this was nothing compared to the global frenzies that erupted at the announcement that the giant meteor was going to fall out of the skies. When this news was telegraphed to Europe, Asia, America, Africa, Australia, New Zealand, and Oceania, nobody dreamed of doubting it. The Boston astronomers were internationally renowned and were incapable of committing any error that might reflect negatively on their justly famous observatory.

So the *New York Herald* was perfectly right to state, in a special edition that had a huge print run: "We've heard from the Boston Observatory, and we know where we stand—it's a dead certainty that the shooting star will eventually fall to the earth."*

Apparently the laws governing the earth's gravity weren't operating to their full capacity in this instance. In the world of astronomy, all the experts quickly confirmed that the shooting star was noticeably losing speed, and maybe interested parties would have spotted this fact sooner if they'd been watching for it. But as the saying goes, "they had something else on their minds." From early on they only wanted to know how big the meteor's nucleus was and how much it was worth, though they hardly imagined they could ever actually bank those billions. The shooting star had been following a perfectly regular, well-defined trajectory, and who would have guessed it was due to drop out of the skies and fall to the earth! Nobody in a thousand years!

Nor had Dean Forsyth and Dr. Hudelson foreseen this development. Each was passionately claiming to have sighted the meteor first, though this feat had nothing to do with its market value, with those billions nobody was going to get one sou, one pence, or one cent of. No, as we can't say too often, they were fighting over whom, Forsyth or Hudelson, this great astronomical phenomenon should be named after. In other words they were in it only for the honor and glory.

Anyhow our two rivals could now see for themselves that the meteor was definitely slowing down. It took longer to appear in the northeast, longer to disappear in the southwest, and longer to travel between those two points in the Whaston skies. Possibly Messrs. Forsyth and Hudelson regretted that they weren't the first to discover this fact, but this time the honors unquestionably went to the Boston Observatory.

At this juncture two issues popped up, even in the minds of those men, women, or children who weren't normally very inquiring. All around the world two gigantic question marks hung in the air:

When would the meteor fall?

Where would it fall?

The second question answered itself, assuming the shooting star kept to its old trajectory from northeast to southwest. If it did, it could only fall on one of the localities situated under this trajectory. That was plain enough.

Answering the first question took longer. But the experts weren't discouraged and managed to get a firm handle on it by continually monitoring the meteor's loss of speed.

All right, that being the case, wouldn't a third question pop up to join the other two? And wouldn't it be a good deal trickier since there were so many interested parties involved, and on a playing field where the most basic human instincts are bound to collide?

Once the shooting star fell to the earth, to whom would it belong? Who would bank those billions from the gold inside that shining halo? No doubt its coma would vanish, and anyhow rays of light aren't substantial enough to have a cash value. But the nucleus would remain, and it wouldn't be hard to turn it into genuine coin of the realm.

Right, so to whom would it belong?

"To me!" Dean Forsyth exclaimed when this question crossed his mind. "I saw it first! I was the first one to spot it in the skies over Whaston!"

"It's mine!" Dr. Hudelson cried out at the same instant. "I'm the man who made this discovery!"

That very night of May 29–30, both of them watched it go by with an intensity that was more furious than ever, and they would have done anything to snatch it out of the sky. And it was still barely twenty miles up, trapped overhead by gravitational forces that would soon induce it to come down to earth. And on that clear night it shone with such brilliance, the stars and planets paled by comparison—even Jupiter and Venus, even Vega or Altaira in their respective constellations of Lyra and Aquila, even the brightest star of them all, Sirius in Canis Major.

Oh well, the townsfolk wouldn't be marveling at that incomparable sight for much longer, since the meteor was soon due to come crashing to the ground. No problem, people could hardly wait till it did! They were consumed with selfish cravings, everybody in our whole greedy world—except for a few philosophical souls who could rise above such human weaknesses, or a few wiser heads such as Whaston's justice of the peace, his honor John Proth.

On that afternoon of May 30, the judge's courtroom was packed. Of all the curiosity seekers who wanted to squeeze inside, three-quarters couldn't. Out in front of Proth's home, swarms of busybodies were green with envy as they thought of those who'd had the good luck—or the quick reflexes—to be crammed into the hall. No doubt about it, if the judge hadn't taken precautions to protect his garden, his flowers would have undergone a public trampling. But nobody could get in that way, because old Kate was mounting guard.

Mr. Dean Forsyth and Dr. Stanley Hudelson were present in that courtroom. Both would be called before the justice of the peace, where one at a time each man would claim to be the discoverer—and therefore the owner—of the shooting star. The two rivals would face each other at long last.

So to the boundless despair of Mrs. Hudelson, her daughters, Francis Gordon, and old Mrs. Mitz, it wasn't just about honor and glory anymore—if the judge declared himself competent to decide the case, he would also have to rule on the dollars and cents. As you can imagine, when a magistrate has to pronounce judgment between members of his own jurisdiction, it's a fairly touchy situation. But true to his calling, John Proth would do his level best to reconcile these two parties; yet in order for him to succeed, it's no exaggeration to say that he would need to be the shrewdest mediator in North America.

Beforehand, much to his satisfaction, Proth quickly settled a number of other cases on his docket, and several disputants who'd arrived shaking their fists left arm in arm. Could he engineer the same result with the two enemies now waiting to address him? He was less than optimistic.

"Next case," he said.

"Forsyth versus Hudelson and vice-versa," his clerk called out. Which is how the case was listed on his calendar.

"The parties may approach the bench," the judge added, sitting straighter in his chair.

And each man emerged from his accompanying band of supporters. They approached side by side, then looked each other up and down, eyes glaring, fists clenched, two cannons loaded to the muzzle and ready to fire away at the tiniest provocation.

"What seems to be the trouble, gentlemen?" Judge Proth asked, his tone of voice indicating he knew perfectly well what it was.

Forsyth went first, saying: "I'm here to claim what's rightfully mine!"

"So am I!" Dr. Hudelson instantly butted in.

Then they launched into a full-volume duet. And believe me, their voices didn't blend melodiously or follow any known rules of harmony.

Judge Proth quickly intervened, rapping his desktop with an ivory letter opener, like an orchestra conductor trying to halt some out-of-tune cacophony by tapping his baton on his music stand.

"One at a time, gentlemen," he said, "and in alphabetical order. Since Mr. Forsyth's name starts with F and Dr. Hudelson's with H, Mr. Forsyth has the floor."

And God only knew what bitterness sprang up in Hudelson's bosom simply because his name started with the eighth letter of the alphabet instead of the sixth.

So while the doctor was corking himself with his last ounce of strength, Forsyth stated his case. During the night of April 2–3 at eleven thirty-seven and twenty-two seconds, he, Dean Forsyth, had been skywatching in his tower on Elizabeth Street when he sighted a shooting star just as it appeared above the northeasterly horizon. He tracked it the entire time it was visible, then early the next morning he wired the Pittsburgh Observatory to inform them of the new meteor and to establish himself as its discoverer.

When it was Dr. Hudelson's turn, it was more of the same. He gave an identical description of spotting the meteor from his watchtower on Morris Street and then firing off a telegram the next morning to the Cincinnati Observatory.

And both men spoke with so much clarity and conviction, the whole courtroom trembled with silent excitement, then held its breath as it waited for the magistrate to rule on these clear-cut claims.

"It's quite simple," said the judge, an old hand with the scales of justice and able to tell at one glance if the pans were perfectly balanced.

Yet those words "quite simple" caused a good deal of surprise in his audience. They didn't seem to apply to this situation at all. It couldn't be *that* simple.

But since this brief comment fell from the lips of Judge Proth, it was automatically significant. Everybody had heard about the fairness of his interpretations and the soundness of his verdicts. So the whole courtroom was on pins and needles waiting for him to elaborate.

They didn't wait long, and here he is word for word, giving the conjunction "inasmuch" a healthy workout in fine legal style:

"Inasmuch as the first party, Mr. Dean Forsyth, alleges that on the night of April 2–3, he discovered a shooting star crossing the skies over Whaston at thirty-seven minutes and twenty-two seconds past eleven o'clock, and inasmuch as the second party, Dr. Stanley Hudelson, alleges that he sighted the same shooting star at the identical hour, minute, and second—"

"Yes, yes!" yelled the doctor's supporters, wildly waving their hands.

"No, no!" retorted Forsyth's, stamping their feet on the floor.

Judge Proth quietly sat out this hullabaloo, and when it was over he continued as follows:

"—but inasmuch as the entire matter turns on a question of hour, minute, and second, a question that lies exclusively in the domain of astronomy and is beyond our strictly judicial competence . . . the court accordingly declares itself incompetent to hear this case."

Surely the judge couldn't have replied any other way. And since it appeared that neither disputant could supply irrefutable proof of the exact instant he saw the meteor, it definitely seemed that they couldn't go ahead with their claims, that they had no grounds for fighting any further, and certainly not on the field of honor.

But neither their supporters nor the men themselves could leave it at that. If, instead of reconciling the two parties, Judge Proth hoped he could just wash his hands of the business by declaring his court incompetent, his hopes were quickly dashed.

Because, following the wholesale muttering that greeted his decision, a voice rang out, and it was Forsyth's.

"I want to say something!" he said.

"So do I!" the doctor added.

"Though I've never needed to reconsider my rulings, even under the gravest circumstances," the magistrate replied with his perennial cheeriness, "and though this matter, I repeat, is beyond the competence of a justice of the peace, I'll allow statements from Mr. Forsyth and Dr. Hudelson, provided they agree to speak one at a time."

Maybe it was asking too much of these rivals to give in even on this simple point. They answered in unison with the same torrent of words, the same vehemence of vocabulary, neither one willing to wait a second for the other.

The best thing, the judge felt in his heart, would be to dismiss them and simply wrap up the proceedings, which struck him as reflecting badly on the two distinguished gentlemen and even on Whaston's upper crust as a whole. But Proth noticed that their wrangling was heading in a new direction, that it was less about matters of astronomy and more about property rights.

In essence the shooting star was due to fall to the earth, and once it did, to whom would it belong? Dean Forsyth . . . or Dr. Hudelson?

"It'll belong to Forsyth!" shouted fans of the watchtower on Elizabeth Street.

"No, to Dr. Hudelson!" shouted the Morris Street claque.

A gracious philosophical smile on his kindly face, Judge Proth hushed the courtroom with an easygoing gesture, and his expression indicated that he felt perfectly comfortable making a statement of his own.

The hall was silent again, and believe me, it couldn't have been quieter on that day around 900 BC when Solomon decided the famous dispute between the two mothers.*

"Gentlemen," Proth said, "the first matter you submitted to the court called for determining which of you had made a particular scientific discovery. There it was a point of honor, and the honor couldn't be divided up between you.* That was that. But now the meteor's ownership has come under dispute, and there I don't have the essentials to hand down a well-founded verdict, yet I *do* think I can give you a sound piece of advice."

"What?" Mr. Forsyth yelled.

"What?" Dr. Hudelson hollered.

"This," Judge Proth said. "In the event that the shooting star should fall to the earth —"

"Which it will!" said Dean Forsyth's supporters in chorus.

"Which it will!" repeated Dr. Stanley Hudelson's to a man.

"So be it," the magistrate answered, with a deferential politeness not exactly characteristic of judges, even in America. Then with a benevolent air, he addressed his two constituents. "And yet in this case," he continued, "we're concerned with a shooting star valued at 781 billion dollars. So my advice is: divide it up between you."

"Never! Never!"

This word, the ultimate negative, rang out on all sides. Messrs. Forsyth and Hudelson would never agree to divvying up that money. True, it still would have been worth nearly four hundred billion to each man; but in that whole land of Vanderbilt, Astor, Gould, and Morgan, there wasn't enough money to heal their wounded vanity. To make even the tiniest concession was, for either of them, as good as admitting that the other man had been the meteor's true discoverer.

With his knowledge of human dealings, Judge Proth wasn't awfully surprised that the courtroom unanimously rejected his advice, sound as it was. He wasn't a bit put out, and when the hubbub swelled tremendously and he saw that he was having zero effect on it, this time he got up from his seat: court was adjourned.

But then order was restored, as if the whole assembly suddenly sensed that somebody was about to say something important.

Which is what happened, and from somewhere in that packed hall these words rang out: "Judge, are you deferring this case to some other date when you'll give your final ruling?"

Apparently this was a new question mark in the public mind.

The judge sat down again and gave this simple answer: "The court had hoped to resolve the ownership question by encouraging the two parties to divide the proceeds. They rejected this solution."

"And we'll keep on rejecting it!" shrieked Dean Forsyth and Dr. Stanley Hudelson in perfect unison, as if their words were coming out of the horn of an old phonograph player.*

After a moment's silence, Proth said: "The court defers judgment on the question of the meteor's ownership . . . till after it has fallen to the earth."

"But why wait till it falls?" Forsyth demanded, not willing to accept any delays.

"Yes, why wait?" the doctor echoed, also wanting an instant ruling on the dispute.

Judge Proth stood up again and declared in a wry tone of voice: "Because on the day it falls, there's a real likelihood that a *third* interested party will emerge, who'll also claim a share of the meteor money."

"Who? What party?" The question shot from every corner of the courtroom, and the audience started getting more and more out of hand.

"The country where the meteor ultimately falls—it will have excellent grounds for a claim simply because it owns the land."

The good judge might also have mentioned that there was some likelihood the shooting star would fall into the sea, belong to nobody, and lie in Davy Jones' locker till the end of time.

The audience digested these last remarks by Judge Proth, who'd finally left the courtroom. It was certainly possible that a third party could emerge to claim an extra share of that unearthly treasure once it became earthly, but would this possibility quiet the passions of the two factions? Maybe after a little time and reflection, because they definitely needed to allow for this contingency. But in their current emotional state, they weren't giving it a thought. They could focus only on the case of Forsyth versus Hudelson, which, in a nutshell, had been left unresolved. Good grief, the court was deferring judgment till the meteor actually fell out of the sky! And when would that happen? Next month? Next year? The next century? God only knew. No, what the two disputants wanted was an instant verdict, and they felt the judge had used a cheap trick simply to calm the public down.

So when everybody was back outside in the square, they split up into two groups, augmented by all the busybodies who couldn't squeeze into the courtroom. And there was a hellacious uproar—shouts, insults, threats, probably even flurries of fisticuffs. Clearly Forsyth's supporters were itching to lynch Dr. Hudelson, and Hudelson's supporters wouldn't have balked at lynching Forsyth back, in the approved manner of American conflict resolution.

Luckily the authorities had taken precautions against this regrettable but all-too-possible enormity.* A large number of policemen were patrolling Constitution Square. Just as the two groups lunged at each other, the law forcefully intervened and separated the warriors in the nick of time.

But they weren't able to keep Forsyth and Dr. Hudelson from meeting face to face. And the former said to the latter: "You, sir, are nothing but scum of the earth, and I can guarantee that my nephew is never going to marry your daughter!"

"And you, sir," the doctor replied, "are an out-and-out criminal, and my daughter is never going to marry your nephew!"

There you have it, the dreaded event had come to pass—a total and irreparable rift between the two families.*

And meanwhile Judge Proth was strolling around his flowerbeds and saying to old Kate: "I only hope that damned meteor doesn't fall on my garden and hurt my geraniums!"

13. In which we see a third claimant emerge and assert rights of ownership, just as Judge Proth predicted

We won't even attempt to describe the deep dismay felt by the Hudelson family. It was only matched by Francis Gordon's desperation. He was a decent young fellow and wouldn't have hesitated for a second to break off relations with his uncle, dispense with his consent, and face the inevitable consequences of his displeasure. But the steps he could take against Forsyth he couldn't against Dr. Hudelson. Once the doctor refused to give his daughter's hand to Francis, the young lawyer would have to give up any hope of marrying the girl. Mrs. Hudelson tried to get her husband's agreement, tried to make him reverse his decision, but it was no use—no amount of pleading or scolding could get that bullheaded man to back down. And even Loo, little Loo herself, was mercilessly rebuffed. She begged, she coaxed, she even wept, but none of it did the slightest good.

"No, no!" Dr. Hudelson repeated. "I'll never agree to an alliance between my family and the family of that man—he not only stole my meteor, he treated me like scum right out in public!"

Whereupon he himself had retaliated by labeling Forsyth "an out-and-out criminal." So to coin a phrase, it takes two to tangle.

As for old Mrs. Mitz, she confined herself to addressing her boss along these lines: "Mr. Forsyth, you're a heartless brute!"

Anyhow Forsyth had eyes, and as night fell over Whaston, they took turns peering into the eyepiece of his telescope, watching for the meteor's arrival, checking to see if it was still slowing down.

But the globe of gold went by as usual from one horizon to the other, and thousands of skywatchers had no trouble viewing its magnificent brilliance.

When night was over, the sun appeared again; but the bells in St. Andrew's steeple, which were supposed to ring out for the wedding of Francis Gordon and Jenny Hudelson, kept mum that day.

However, the shooting star was indeed losing speed little by little, in accordance with a law of mechanics whose effects were currently being worked out by astronomers at the various observatories. One result of this loss of speed was that the meteor was getting lower in the sky, and it would fall to the ground once its speed was too slow to withstand the earth's gravitational pull. At the time of its discovery it was some twenty-five miles overhead, but this distance had undergone a twenty-five percent reduction and was now reckoned at only about eighteen miles.* So between its entrance and exit, it was onstage for a longer period of time, which meant you should have been able to study it under highly auspicious conditions. Unfortunately the east wind was in charge at that point, and it filled the sky with dense mists imported from the Atlantic. This heavy cloudbank made the meteor tricky to see. Besides, thanks to its reduced speed, it was moving along its orbit from the northeast to the southwest not just at night but at various times during the day, so it became harder and harder to keep an eye on it. Even so, it gave no signs of changing its trajectory and faithfully stayed on its original path.

Besides, there was no longer any need to track its movements with telescopes or binoculars. Calculating from the data already gathered and carefully verified, experts would be able to supply the specifics the public were hungering for. Interested parties—and you'll soon find out the extent of their interest—immediately became more concerned with those two old questions:

When would the meteor fall?

Where would it fall?

Concerning the first question, the Boston Observatory sent a release to the newspapers that suggested it could fall during the period July 15–25.

Concerning the second question, the data were still insufficient to provide an acceptable answer for those interested parties mentioned above.

Anyhow the big event wouldn't take place for another six weeks at the earliest and eight at the latest. There was a whole month and a half to go till that memorable day when the planet earth would finally be smacked by this golden cannonball the Creator of All Things had fired at it from outer space.

And as the irreverent *Whaston Punch* pointed out in its brazen pages: "Let's be grateful we're the ones the grand gunner is aiming at! After all, He could just as easily have drawn a bead on Jupiter, Saturn, Neptune, or any other member of our solar system! But no, he saved this cosmic goodie for that ancient daughter of the stars, the earth goddess Cybele, mate of the god of fertility Attis*—in other words, Mother Earth herself will get this queenly gift worth 800 billion smackers."

The thought of banking all those billions got the world's greedy unanimously fired up, and just as Judge Proth had predicted, interested parties were soon filing claims countering those of the meteor's two discoverers—and by interested parties we mean the various nations located beneath the meteor's trajectory, onto one of whom the shooting star would be obliged to fall.

These were the lucky localities that lay under the meteor's path: the United States, Nicaragua, Costa Rica, the Galapagos Islands, the Antarctic regions, the East Indies, Afghanistan, the Kirgiz Republic, the Ukraine, Norway, Lapland, Greenland, Labrador, and Quebec.

As you can see from this starting lineup, only Europe, Asia, and North America would be decently represented in this competition: North America by Greenland, Labrador, Quebec, the United States, Nicaragua and Costa Rica; Asia by the East Indies, Afghanistan, and the Kirgiz Republic; Europe by Norway and northwestern Russia. Out of the whole vast Pacific, only a single island group could watch the shooting star pass directly overhead: the humble Galapagos at longitude ninety-two degrees west and latitude one degree, forty minutes south. Much farther south, down in the Antarctic, the meteor would blaze a bright trail over this huge icy expanse that's still largely unexplored,* ditto up north over those Arctic regions around the pole.

As this rundown shows, parties with a vested interest included Americans in the United States, Nicaragua, and Costa Rica; Britishers in India and Quebec; Asians in Afghanistan; Russians in the Kirgiz Republic and east Lapland; Danes in Greenland; and Norwegians in the Lofoten Islands.

So the total had now increased to seven groups of claimants, and from the start all the newcomers seemed determined to assert their rights aggressively. Which shouldn't surprise anybody, since the lucky countries were none other than America, England, Russia, Denmark, Norway, and Afghanistan. Up against these powerful governments would the claims of Dean Forsyth and Dr. Hudelson stand a dog's chance? Assuming that either or both were recognized as the meteor's discoverer, did it automatically follow that they were entitled to a share in this golden goodie? It wasn't as if this shooting star was a chest of buried treasure, part of which went to the person who found it and the greater part to the owner of the land in which it lay buried. After all, what difference did it make that Forsyth and Hudelson were the first to sight the meteor over Whaston? Wouldn't others have sighted it sooner or later? And whether anybody saw it or not, the thing was still going to fall to the earth. Neither Forsyth, the doctor, nor any other skywatchers would have the tiniest rights in the matter.

This clear-cut proposition appeared in a legal analysis published by the various newspapers. And you can imagine how furious the two rivals were at this wholesale rejection of their claims to those cosmic billions. And who knows, if the two were equally victimized, mightn't it bring them back together, unifying their respective homes, families, and watchtowers?

In any case, though it hadn't been possible to persuade Messrs. Forsyth and Hudelson into going halves on the shooting star, maybe the nations located under its trajectory would prove more reasonable. As a matter of fact, any deal or arrangement that divvied up the golden ball among them—whether they got equal shares or shares proportional to their geographic presence—would have guaranteed each of them an enormous sum, enough to let them balance their budgets or even, gasp, pay their bills ahead of time.

So in a matter of days they'd set up an international commission, and its purpose was to protect the interests of all the nations whose geographic locations left them in a position to receive the precious meteor.

In this commission the United States was represented by Mr. Newell Harvey of Boston, England by Mr. Whiting of Montreal, Russia by Mr. Saratov of Riga, Norway by Mr. Lieblin of Oslo, Denmark by Mr. de Schack of Copenhagen, Afghanistan by Mr. Oullah, a member of the ruling family, Nicaragua by Mr. Truxillo of León, and Costa Rica by Mr. Valdejo of San José.

Not surprisingly, the vast polar continent of Antarctica didn't have a representative in this international commission: the place was uninhabited and would stay that way.* But if the shooting star just happened to land there, Antarctica was sure to become densely populated in no time: multiple expeditions would set out to capture that globe of gold, and they wouldn't hesitate to scour the countryside from McClary Glacier to Louis-Philippe Peninsula. Which would definitely lead to that geographic event so devoutly desired by explorers, the discovery of the South Pole!*

Folks also wondered about the Galapagos archipelago with its population of giant tortoises: these reptiles aside, how would the various islands in this group—Albemarle, Chatham, Norfolk, etc.—be represented in this commission?* It was a natural enough concern, since the

United States had paid three million dollars* for these islands in 1884. But they only occupied a surface area of 5,675 square miles* over four degrees of equatorial latitude. The chances of the shooting star landing thereabouts were slim to none. But if the meteor *did* happen to fall on one of those islands, the citizens of Ecuador, their former owners, would be devastated! Actually the U.S.A. had a much better chance with its southeastern states of Virginia, South Carolina, Georgia, and Florida; ditto England with its long Canadian prairies bordering the Saint Lawrence River, with the island of Sri Lanka below India, and with Labrador and Quebec; likewise Russia with the Kirgiz Republic; likewise Denmark with the huge region of Greenland; and likewise the vast, barren tracts of Afghanistan, which extend over eight degrees of latitude.*

Obviously Norway didn't stand as good a chance as the other countries, since the meteor's trajectory passed over only the Lofoten Islands and a thin strip of seashore on the western mainland; but the Norwegians still wanted their rights upheld, so their representative took his place among the other members of the international commission.

The commission was scheduled to meet on June 17 in New York City. To arrive in time, its English, Danish, Norwegian, Nicaraguan, and Costa Rican members booked passage on the fastest steamers. The delegate who really had to work fast was the representative sent by the ruling family of Afghanistan. By a stroke of luck he was able to board a French cruise ship to Suez.* From there a liner took him to Marseilles; then, after cutting through France, he crossed the Atlantic on a German steamer and reached New York in the nick of time.

From June 17 on, the international commission worked around the clock. They hadn't a second to lose. This business was unprecedented in the annals of astronomy, and its climax could be approaching more swiftly than people had originally thought. No doubt about it, the meteor was gradually slowing down, plus it was simultaneously drawing nearer to the earth. Day after day the professional journals kept coming up with new figures for its speed and distance, and it was just possible their calculations would indicate, within a degree or two, which country it was going to fall on.

Not surprisingly, as soon as the Americans, Brits, Norwegians, Danes, and even the Afghans began exploring the consequences of this development, there was lively discussion on all sides. Apparently the various countries had the wisdom not to emulate Messrs. Forsyth and Hudelson and were open to sharing the enormous treasure, so their respective delegates came to the table with that clear intention.

But this was easier said than done, and the sticking point was the question of who got how much. In a nutshell, a country's chances were greater or lesser depending on how much acreage it had under the meteor's trajectory. Consequently the delegates debated with compass in hand, and we can be forgiven for wondering if this instrument of measure wasn't about to turn into a murder weapon.

Moreover, as session followed session, fewer and fewer participants were seeing eye to eye. The U.S.A.'s Mr. Harvey was especially pigheaded in guarding his country's interests, always taking great pains to include the Galapagos Islands in the American Union. "You can't deny it!" he would endlessly repeat. "They're the only dry land in the whole Pacific where that shooting star could fall!"

Speaking for the government of Great Britain, Mr. Whiting brought a lordly disdain to the proceedings and refused to make the tiniest concession. Ah, what an actor he was! He was the haughty representative of a nation* that wouldn't dream of soiling its hands by chasing after mere trillions; but despite this lofty indifference, he didn't give an inch, since the United Kingdom based its claims on the fact that the meteor's trajectory passed over two of its possessions, parts of India in the Old World, plus a large slice of Canada and Labrador in the New.

But the Britisher had to yield the floor to Mr. Saratov, who proceeded to club his competitors with Russia's huge holdings in the Kirgiz Republic.

Sure enough, Mr. Oullah jumped in for Afghanistan, answering that his country was just as big as Kirgiz. And you wouldn't believe the vehemence of this man's oratory, how he interrupted, shouted, and raged! No doubt it was because this mideastern country desperately needed the money, but maybe it was also because he was working on commission and a bigger deal meant a fatter paycheck.

One member of the assembly, however, made more modest demands. It was Mr. Lieblin, representing Norway. In essence his country expected little from its tiny piece of Lapland or its Lofoten Islands and knew it didn't stand much of a chance. So he concentrated on arguing that every country under the meteor's path deserved an equal share in the proceeds. But England, Russia, and the United States instantly made it clear that they would never go along with this proposition, and things didn't look promising for the old Land of the Vikings.

What's more, Mr. Lieblin ran into fierce competition from Mr. de Schack. The delegate from Denmark offered to the commission's eyes the whole vast expanse of Greenland, right under the meteor's orbit from the northeast to the southwest. He claimed to have evidence—which he didn't produce—that the meteor would fall in Greenlander country. So Mr. de Schack wasn't about to settle for less than his full share. His country was in a solid position to win the whole works, a grand total close to eight hundred billion dollars,* which meant those lucky Danes would never have to pay taxes again.*

Given all their conflicting interests, were the delegates really getting through to each other? Wouldn't the bigger nations lay down the law to the smaller ones? Couldn't the former plausibly claim the lion's share? Or to smooth things over, would they all agree to divide up the proceeds eight ways and give everybody an equal share, the handsome sum of one hundred billion dollars?

Don't hold your breath. Human greed is an eternal factor and in this instance it was on a rampage. The sessions grew stormier and stormier. The debates seemed to be getting increasingly personal. Mr. Newell Harvey of Boston and Mr. Valdejo of Costa Rica traded insults. Luckily they didn't have followers with them, or this particular meteor hunt would have ended in bloodshed.

Needless to say, the newspapers of the various countries—both those that were directly involved in the business and those that weren't—kept arguing the pros and cons in page after relentless page. But the issue, like the shooting star, was still up in the air, and you wondered if the business could be resolved before the meteor fell to the earth.

In fact it looked like the only thing that could conclusively settle the matter, the only thing that could end all the conflicts, would be for the meteor to fall in the open sea. But what were the chances of this actually happening? How did the landmasses of America, Europe, and Asia compare to the vast expanses of the Pacific, Indian, Arctic and Antarctic oceans? Wouldn't it be infinitely better all around if that ball of gold plunged into the sea and lay in Davy Jones' locker for eternity?

Still, it can't be denied that most people refused to accept this possibility. No way was this meteor going to slip through their fingers! What, that huge hunk of precious metal, that golden sphere with a radius of eighty-two feet, might end up somewhere beyond all reach?* After appearing in the skies, could those billions shift to a new orbit and vanish back into space? Never! A thousand times no! If anything like that happened, a billion and a half earthlings would have howled in protest!

Consequently the international commission never even considered this possibility. For its delegates, the shooting star was due—any day now—to become a terrestrial treasure. The only question left was who the meteor would belong to. What lucky country would pocket the thing?

But really now, as the French journal *l'Économiste* tried to point out, wouldn't it have been both easier and more equitable to let this windfall benefit the whole planet and not just one country, to simply portion it out to every nation in the New World and the Old according to the respective sizes of their populations?

As you would expect, America, England, Russia, Norway, Denmark, Afghanistan, Nicaragua, and Costa Rica gave this suggestion a collective raspberry. France had made this proposal with the willing support of Germany, Italy, and all the other left-over monarchies and democracies, mainly because the meteor didn't pass over any of them and they wouldn't have been able to lay a finger on it. For obvious reasons this proposal had no chance of being accepted, and it wasn't.

To make a long story short, after ten days of discussions that got nowhere, the international commission adjourned following a session that required the intervention of Boston's finest.

So the issue was automatically settled, and who knows, maybe it was for the best.

Since the participants couldn't agree on how to divide the meteor, neither equal shares nor proportional, it would belong to whatever country it ended up falling on.

If this outcome didn't please the eight interested parties, it was praised by all the countries with no stake in the matter—naturally. In short the whole business was simply a lottery with a single unbelievably high grand prize, a lottery where the players were the United States, England, Russia, Denmark, Norway, Afghanistan, Nicaragua, and Costa Rica. And winner takes all.

As for Forsyth's and Hudelson's rights in the matter, nobody paid them the slightest attention, and God knows they'd appealed to the international commission and tried to get a hearing. But the trip they'd made to Boston had turned out to be a total waste, because the commission kicked them out as if they were lowlife interlopers. Honestly now, what earthly rights did *they* have? Sure, they'd been the first to see the meteor after it got caught in the earth's gravity. But so what? Was it their power that caught it? Wouldn't it have happened anyway?

You can imagine how furious they were when they got back to Whaston, and they were even angrier at the commission than at each other.

"It belongs to us! It belongs to us!" they kept telling their supporters. "And we'll say so till our dying day!"

Actually all they had to do was bide their time and file a claim with the winning country. And who knows, that country might be in such a good mood, it would readily agree to hand over a paltry few billion to Messrs. Forsyth and Hudelson.

As for their families, neither man gave them a thought, though their loved ones suffered dreadfully from the rift the two rivals had created. Francis Gordon was in despair, Jenny was pining away, and Mrs. Hudelson couldn't do a thing to cheer her up. She had no further meetings with her lover, who stayed away from Morris Street. Per the doctor's strict orders, he had to give up seeing her.

As for Miss Loo and old Mrs. Mitz, they saved their bad language for the shooting star, which kept getting lower in the sky as it lost speed. And both of them passionately hoped that it would vanish into the deepest trench in the ocean. Then, with both the asteroid and the money out of the picture, maybe the two rivals could patch up their quarrels and dislikes.

For both the young girl and the old housekeeper, this was their dearest wish, and to tell the truth, wasn't it the most desirable thing for everybody? Hadn't the *Whaston Punch* published a sardonic editorial that conclusively demonstrated how the shooting star would make the whole world poorer instead of richer?

Fall, proud asteroid [the editorial writer had orated]! Fall, and you'll cause as much damage as a relentless hailstorm pouring out of the clouds and pounding the earth for months or even years! Fall, and world poverty and wholesale bankruptcy will fall with you! Isn't the annual production of gold already increasing at an alarming rate? From 1890 to 1898 didn't it climb from

120 million dollars to 300 million? Yet jewelry and other luxuries account for a yearly total of only 72 million, with no more than 36 million paid out in interest! If we tally the fortunes in Europe alone, we get frozen and liquid assets of no more than 235 billion dollars with liquid capital peaking at 100 billion, which breaks down to about 59 billion for England, 49.4 billion for France, 40.2 billion for Germany, 32 billion for Russia, 20.6 billion for Austria, 15.8 billion for Italy, 5 billion for Belgium, and 4.4 billion for the Netherlands! We can't give such an estimate for the New World, but assuming that its fortunes are half those of the Old, this would bring the total to only 320 billion! All right, compare this figure to the estimated value of the shooting star, i.e., 800 billion dollars. You can see what's coming: we'll have over three times as much gold as we have already, and it won't be worth a fraction* of what it is today. Which means financial conditions are in for a change! So fall, vile meteor, go ahead and fall, and mine owners in California, Australia, the Transvaal, and the Klondike will starve to death beside their gold deposits.*

All of this editorializing was quite realistic. If the meteor fell, it would cause a financial catastrophe, so the best thing was for it to break loose from the earth's gravity, shoot into space, and stake out some new orbit a couple of million leagues away!

Yet, once again, most people must have been mesmerized out of their wits by the sight of that shooting star, because instead of looking for ways to pull it down, they should have been figuring out how to make it go away.

That's how things stood, and they would soon be coming to a head. Actually the skies were mostly cloudy and in most places didn't allow for uninterrupted scrutiny of the meteor's movements, but telescopes could still follow it long enough to determine its speed and altitude. Both were slackening in accordance with the laws of mechanics, and the meteor would have to fall to the earth in a matter of weeks, maybe even days. While it traveled through the stratosphere, you could hear it hissing as if it were some sort of gigantic bomb. Which should have been ample cause for worldwide alarm, because if it dropped on some hamlet, village, or town, you can easily imagine the destruction this 1,389,000-ton object would cause! Taking its altitude into account, then multiplying its weight by the square of its speed, there was good reason to believe it would bury itself well below the earth's surface.

"That's right," certain newspapers predicted, "and if it *does* plow deep into the ground, it will break through the earth's crust, it will penetrate the central cavity where all the iron carbide making up our planet exists in a molten state, then it will vaporize and won't be worth a plugged nickel!"

During the morning of June 29, after the Boston Observatory finished their latest batch of calculations, telegraph lines worldwide carried the following news item: "Observations made today enable us to communicate the following information to interested parties on both continents. Until now it hasn't been possible to establish conclusively when and where the meteor would fall. Soon it will be possible to do so with total accuracy.

"Sometime between August 7 and August 15, the meteor will fall to the earth, and somewhere between latitude 70° and 74° north and between longitude 45° and 60° west, it will land in the country of Greenland."

As a result of this telegraphed message, markets everywhere took a nosedive, because the value of gold shares in both the New World and the Old was about to drop by seventy-five percent.

⇒ 14. In which we see droves of curiosity seekers grab at the chance to visit Greenland and watch the amazing meteor fall out of the sky

During the morning of July 5, everybody in the major port of Charleston, South Carolina, was on hand for the departure of the S.S. *Moʒik*. There were so many inquisitive Americans who wanted to dash off to Greenland, every available cabin on this 1,650-ton ship* had been booked for days. And the *Moʒik* wasn't the only vessel sailing for those parts—many other steamers of various nationalities were getting ready to head up the Atlantic to Davis Strait and Baffin Bay inside the Arctic Circle.

The huge crowds were in a state of terrific mental excitement. The Boston Observatory couldn't possibly have been in error, because any expert who made a mistake under such exceptional circumstances would never be forgiven and would deserve everything he got from the outraged public.

Don't worry, the Boston scientists were absolutely correct. The shooting star definitely wasn't going to land in American, British, Russian, Norwegian, or Afghan territory, nor in the inaccessible polar regions, and certainly not in the open sea where no human being could get to it.

No, it was about to fall on the soil of Greenland, in that huge country belonging to Denmark,* the lucky winner out of the eight European, Asian, and American nations.

True, it's an enormous piece of land, and nobody's clear if it's a continent or an oversized island.* So a major worry was that the meteor might come down someplace far inland, several hundred miles from the coastline, where it would be tremendously difficult to reach. No problem, though. People would overcome these difficulties, they would brave the Arctic temperatures and snowstorms, and even if it landed at the North Pole itself, then that's where they would unquestionably go—and with more fervor than Parry, Nansen,* or any polar explorer before them, because their motivation was a hunk of gold worth almost eight hundred billion dollars.

Besides, they had hopes that the landing site would soon be narrowed down, just like the date when the meteor was supposed to fall. Nobody doubted that this detail would be worked out before the first ships reached Greenland's coast.

If you, dear reader, had booked a cabin aboard the *Mozik* along with all the hundreds of other people—including a few thrill-seeking women—you would have noticed four passengers who were already quite familiar to you. Their presence, or at least the presence of three of these travelers, wouldn't have surprised you one bit.

Two were Mr. Dean Forsyth and Omicron, who'd left their Elizabeth Street watchtower behind, the third was Dr. Stanley Hudelson, who'd likewise vacated his tower on Morris Street.

In fact, the instant that the opportunistic shipping lines announced cruises to Greenland, the two rivals had immediately bought round-trip tickets. If need be, they would have chartered their own boats to Upernavik, capital city of this Danish possession.* As far as grabbing the gold first, making off with it, and taking it back to Whaston, this was obviously out of the question. But not surprisingly, both of them wanted to locate it the instant it hit the ground.

And who knows, maybe its owners of record, the Danish government, would give them a finder's fee out of all those billions that had dropped from the sky! Similarly, who knows if it might even become possible to settle the unanswered question of which one of these two Virginians should get the credit for discovering this shooting star, among the most amazing ever seen on the earth's horizon: after all, the meteor could simply be listed under the hyphenated name of Forsyth-Hudelson—that way, both men could take their places alongside Herschel, Arago, Leverrier, and other big names in the annals of astronomy.*

Needless to say, Forsyth and the doctor didn't have adjoining cabins aboard the *Mozik*. During this ocean voyage they kept as far apart as they had in Whaston. They refused to have any contact with each other, and supporters of theirs who'd come along adopted the same policy.

Mrs. Hudelson, it should be pointed out, wasn't exactly heartbroken at her husband's departure, nor had old Mrs. Mitz tried to talk her boss out of going. Maybe they hoped the two men would come back home good friends again. Couldn't circumstances arise that might appeal to their better natures? Which is what Miss Loo thought too, and the young lady had even asked to go along with her dad to Greenland. Maybe this wasn't such a bad idea, but Mrs. Hudelson put the kibosh on it. The trip would take about three weeks one way, so it could turn out to be extremely tiring. Besides, what about the difficult living conditions in Greenland? What if the meteor took a long time to fall? In that harsh climate the temperature drops quickly, and what if it turned cold while they were waiting? And if it came to that, what if Forsyth and Hudelson stubbornly decided to winter in that country above the Arctic Circle, as if they were Laplanders or Eskimos? No, it wouldn't have been wise to let Miss Loo go along, though she hated to give up the idea. Instead she stayed behind with her mom, who was already plenty upset with the doctor, and her sister Jenny, who needed constant bucking up.

Therefore, since little Loo wasn't traveling on the *Mozik*, Francis Gordon decided to go with his uncle. Even while Hudelson was away, Francis would have felt thoroughly uncomfortable flouting his strict orders and showing up at the house on Morris Street. So it was better for him to go along on the trip—just as Omicron was doing—to help out in case problems arose between the two enemies and to make the most of any development that might improve this dismal state of affairs. He felt sure that things would get better by themselves after the shooting star had fallen to the earth, whether it became Denmark's property or vanished into the depths of the Arctic Ocean. Because, despite everything they'd said, the astronomers in Boston could have been wrong in asserting that the asteroid would fall on Greenland proper. At that latitude it sits between two large bodies of water barely thirty degrees apart. So any deviation due to atmospheric conditions would be enough to send the adored meteor into the sea and beyond the grasp of greedy humanity.

This, let's remember, was Miss Loo's dearest wish, and Francis Gordon was in complete agreement.

But among the steamship's passengers was an individual who wouldn't have been overjoyed at this outcome. This was none other than Mr. Ewald de Schack, the international commission's delegate from Denmark. This small country under King Christian IX was on the verge of becoming nothing less than the wealthiest nation on earth. If the treasury building in Copenhagen wasn't big enough, they'd make it bigger; if it didn't have enough vaults, they'd add more. That's where the eight hundred billion properly belonged, not at the bottom of the sea.

And what a stroke of luck it would be for this little kingdom, where nobody would pay any sort of taxes ever again, where poverty would be abolished! Like lovely Danae at the hands of Jupiter in the old myth, Denmark would be showered with gold; but being shrewd and cautious, the Danes* were sure to spend this enormous mass of wealth with exceptional discretion, so there was reason to hope that the money markets wouldn't suffer any difficulties.

In short Mr. de Schack had become cock of the walk on board, and he was a man who knew his worth. He put on lordly airs with Dean Forsyth and Dr. Hudelson, and the two rivals seethed with resentment whenever they bumped into the representative from Denmark, who was denying them any share in their immortal discovery.

And maybe Francis Gordon wasn't half wrong in counting on this state of affairs to bring about a reconciliation between the doctor and his uncle.

The run from Charleston to the capital city of Greenland was some twenty-six hundred nautical miles.* It was scheduled to take about three weeks, including a layover in Boston for the *Moẑik* to refuel. Otherwise, like the rest of the ships bound for the same destination, she carried several months' worth of supplies; there were so many curiosity seekers heading that way, it would have been impossible to provide for their needs at Upernavik.

So the *Moẑik* headed north while hugging the east coast of the United States. She stayed in sight of shore nearly the whole time, and the next day she passed Cape Hatteras off North Carolina.

During the month of July, skies are generally clear over the North Atlantic. Thanks to the sheltering coast and winds from the west, the steamer mostly had smooth seas. But sometimes the wind reversed direction, and then the ship's rolling and pitching would produce their usual effects on the passengers' digestion.

But if lucky little Omicron was immune to seasickness, and Mr. de Schack had the cast-iron stomach of a multibillionaire, this wasn't the case with Forsyth and Dr. Hudelson. It was their first time at sea and they were paying heavy tribute to King Neptune. But they weren't sorry for an instant that they'd embarked on this adventure. Even though they wouldn't get a crumb of that shooting star, at least they would be on hand when it fell, they would look at it, they would touch it, and they would know in their hearts that it had become viewable on the earth's horizon because of them!

Needless to add, Francis Gordon had no trouble with seasickness. He didn't get the slightest touch of nausea or the heaves during this cruise. So for several weeks he took care of both his uncle and his potential father-in-law with the same sympathetic concern. And whenever the waves under the *Moẑik* smoothed out again, he would fetch the two invalids out of their cabins, take them to the promenade deck for some fresh air, and plump them into cane-backed chairs not too distant from each other, making sure that the distance shrank a bit each time.

"How are you feeling?" he would ask, spreading a blanket over his uncle's legs.

"Not too good," Forsyth would answer, "but I guess I'll make it."

"Sure you will, uncle."

Then he would pile cushions around the doctor. "How's it going, Dr. Hudelson?" he would repeat in a cheerful voice, as if the Morris Street prohibition had never taken place.

And the two rivals would relax there for a few hours, not glaring at each other but not looking away either. And sometimes Mr. de Schack would happen by, as steady on his feet as an old salt, oh-so-sure of himself, head held high like a man whose life and dreams are made up of nothing but gold. Then Messrs. Forsyth and Hudelson would sit up in their chairs, lightning would flash from their eyes, and if they'd had the proper voltage, they would have blasted the Danish delegate to kingdom come.

"Meteor robber!" Mr. Forsyth would mutter.

"Asteroid pirate!" Dr. Hudelson would intone.

But Mr. de Schack would pay them no mind. He wouldn't even deign to acknowledge their presence on board. He would come and go with snooty nonchalance, with the lofty confidence of a man who's about to make his country more money than it would need to buy back Schleswig-Holstein from Germany,* more money than it would take to pay off the national debts of every country on the planet, which, after all, only added up to a measly thirty-two billion dollars.*

By and large, though, they had good weather for the trip. Ships out of ports on the east coast were also heading up north, likewise making for Davis Strait. And no doubt plenty more were crossing the Atlantic with the same destination in mind.

The *Mozik* went by Sandy Hook without calling at New York City, aimed her prow to the northeast, and hugged the New England coastline up to Boston; then, during the morning of July 13, she docked at the Massachusetts capital. She needed only a day to refuel, which was essential because she wouldn't be able to take on coal in Greenland.

The trip hadn't been too rough, yet most of the passengers got seasick. Consequently some of them decided to abandon ship at Boston, and a half dozen or so now left the *Mozik* for good. Needless to say, Forsyth and Dr. Hudelson weren't among them. Give up going to Greenland? For these two it was unthinkable. Never mind the rolling and pitching; when that meteor bit the dust, they would be there to see it or perish in the attempt.

The departure of those less hardy, less committed souls freed up several cabins on the *Mozik*. But there was no shortage of travelers standing by to board her in Boston.

Among these newcomers you could make out a gentleman of distinguished appearance: he stood to the front of a line that was clamoring for one of those vacant cabins, and he wouldn't take no for an answer. This gentleman, who didn't hide the great satisfaction he felt at muscling his way on board, was none other than Mr. Seth Stanfort, ex-husband of Miss Arcadia Walker, whose marriage had been dissolved by Judge Proth in Whaston as we all know.

After their divorce, which was now two months old, Stanfort had gone back to Boston. With his usual wanderlust, he'd traveled to Canada and visited the metropolises of Quebec, Toronto, Montreal, and Ottawa. Was he trying to get over his ex-wife, trying to erase any memory of Mrs. Arcadia Stanfort? It didn't seem likely. At first the two spouses were happy, later they were unhappy. A divorce as eccentric as their marriage had split them up. Probably they would never lay eyes on each other again, and if they did, would they even recognize each other?

In brief Seth Stanfort had just arrived in Toronto, Canada's current capital,* when he heard of the telegrams about the shooting star. Even if it had been due to fall many thousands of miles away in darkest Africa or Asia, he would have moved heaven and earth to get there. It wasn't that this cosmic phenomenon had any intrinsic interest for him, but the thought of witnessing a sight that few others could, of seeing what millions couldn't, tremendously appealed to him. The gentleman was a daredevil who loved changes of scene, and he had the money to go any outlandish place he wanted.

But this time he didn't need to travel halfway around the world. This cosmic spectacle was scheduled to take place in Canada's backyard. No doubt there would be a large audience on hand for the last act of this meteoric melodrama. Seth Stanfort would only be one of many, but this intriguing event was potentially a once-in-a-lifetime experience, and he didn't mind following the crowd to Greenland.

So Stanfort took the next train to Quebec, then boarded another that crossed Canada and New England in the direction of Boston. But when he reached Boston there weren't any boats available. The last ship had left two days earlier, packed with passengers.

Stanfort had to cool his heels. Then he read in the shipping news that the *Mozik* out of Charleston had scheduled a layover in Boston and that it might be possible to board her. Clearly he had to work fast. According to the announcements from the Boston Observatory, the meteor was going to fall during the period of August 7–15. It was already July 11, there were over eighteen hundred nautical miles between the respective capitals of Massachusetts and Greenland, and steamers often had to battle countercurrents from the North Pole.

Two days after Stanfort's arrival, the *Mozik* entered Boston Harbor, and as we know, the gentleman was lucky enough to nab one of her freed-up cabins.

Hugging the coastline, the *Mozik* left Boston and passed off Portsmouth and then Portland, alert for any messages about the meteor that might be signaled by the semaphores on shore.* When the skies were clear, the passengers had no trouble seeing it go by overhead, but they couldn't reckon its decreasing speed closely enough to pinpoint just when and where it would come down. There wasn't a peep out of the semaphore stations. Maybe the one in Halifax would be more informative, once the steamer was off that major Nova Scotia port.

It had nothing to say for itself, and the travelers were heartily sorry they couldn't take a shortcut to the east by heading into Fundy Bay. If they'd been able to sneak between Nova Scotia and New Brunswick, they wouldn't have had to cope with the choppy seas that harassed them all the way to Cape Breton Island. Despite Francis's attempts to cheer them up, Messrs. Forsyth and Hudelson were equally miserable. And right off Omicron heard the following exchange, as the ship rolled sharply and moved the two men closer together on the promenade deck:

"It's your meteor that's the cause of all this!"

"*Your* meteor, if you don't mind!" answered the doctor, while Francis was trying to make him more comfortable.

Aha! They'd stopped squabbling over who'd seen it first! But they still had a decent distance to go before they would be pals again.

Luckily, seeing that his passengers were in such a bad way, the *Mozik*'s captain had the bright idea of avoiding those dreadful swells from the open sea. He detoured into the Gulf of St. Lawrence, which was sheltered by the whole island of Newfoundland, then sailed up through the Strait of Belle Isle in order to reconnect with the ocean, thereby guaranteeing the customers a much smoother ride. Then, crossing over Davis Strait, he made for the west coast of Greenland.

This took a while, but by the morning of July 21 they'd raised Cape Farewell at the tip of Greenland. The waves of the North Atlantic dash against this cape with tremendous ferocity, as career fishermen from Newfoundland and Iceland can testify.

Fortunately they didn't have to go up the east coast of Greenland, since the astronomers claimed that the shooting star would fall in the neighborhood of Davis Strait or Baffin Bay rather than on the side facing the open ocean. Besides, the east coast is practically unapproachable, there are no harbors for ships to put into, and the shoreline gets a terrific pounding from the Atlantic. On the other hand, once you're in Davis Strait there are plenty of opportunities to take cover inside fjords or behind islands, and except when the wind blows from the south, it's plain sailing.

Just above Cape Farewell is the little harbor of Lindenau,* where a speedy British cruise ship out of St. John's in Newfoundland had already dropped anchor. This ship brought some news of great interest to these travelers whose compulsive curiosity had led them into the seas above the Arctic Circle.

Thanks to their latest observations, the experts at the Boston Observatory were able to calculate with greater precision where in Greenland the meteor was about to fall. It would land within a radius of twelve to fifteen miles* of Upernavik. This was good news, and the semaphore station at Lindenau signaled it to the *Moʒik* as she went by. No need to worry about the golden ball falling into the watery deep. No reason to go into those harsh, forbidding wilderness areas in northern Greenland. They'd narrowed the landing site down to a patch of some twenty to thirty square miles. The passengers were overjoyed to see this difficult trip coming to an end, and they didn't give a thought to the ordeal of the return trip. So when easy-spending Seth Stanfort ordered champagne all around for his fellow travelers in the *Moʒik*'s lounge, Dean Forsyth and Dr. Hudelson were among the first to respond to the toasts he proposed in the meteor's honor.

True, there would have been even greater pleasure, not only on board but worldwide, if they'd had a better idea of when the great event would occur, at least the day if not the hour. But this detail still hadn't been worked out, and they had no choice but to sit tight and wait for the second week of August.

The cruise continued with the passengers in a better mood. The wind was now a stiff breeze out of the northeast, and on the far side of Greenland waves crashed against its coastline with appalling violence. So it was lucky for the *Moʒik* that she'd set her course up Davis Strait and into the higher latitudes of Baffin Bay.

From Cape Farewell up to Disko Island, this whole stretch of Greenland coastline mostly features high rugged cliffs of great age. This barrier offers protection from winds off the sea, and ships have a wide choice of havens—roadsteads, coves, and even genuine harbors. Furthermore, during winter this coastline is less clogged with the ice accumulating in the Arctic Ocean due to polar currents. On the other hand, the mountains inland are covered with year-round snow, and if the shooting star fell in the midst of them, it would be tough to get to.

It was under these conditions that the *Mozik*'s speedy propeller was churning the waves of the fjord that shelters Nuuk. Seafood being the main thing Greenlanders eat, the ship docked at this town for a few hours so her cook could make a bulk purchase of fresh fish. Afterward the *Mozik* passed the entrances to the respective harbors of Holsteinsborg and Christianshåb, so hidden by their walls of rock that you wondered if they were actually there. For the hordes of fishermen in Davis Strait, these villages are handy retreats, and they're always lively places during the winter season. What's more, plenty of ships visit these parts in pursuit of right whales, narwhales, walruses, and seals, sometimes sailing to the far end of Baffin Bay, which connects with the Arctic Ocean via Smith Sound.

By July 22 the steamer had made it to Disko Island, the biggest of the many that dangle from this whole Greenland coastline like a string of beads. Godhavn is its capital and is located on the south side of the island, whose cliffs are made of basalt. The houses in this Danish outpost are built from timber, not stone, and the rough-hewn beams in their walls are coated with a heavy layer of pitch to make them airtight. In his capacity as sole passenger not mesmerized by the meteor, Francis Gordon was intrigued by the sight of this blackened town, whose roofs and window frames added a dash of red here and there. He wondered what life was like during the harsh winters of that climate, and he would have been surprised to learn that it wasn't much different from life in Copenhagen. Though sparsely furnished, several of the homes here were comfortable and came with all the amenities including living rooms, dining rooms, and even libraries, because its upper classes, if we can call them that, are all from Denmark. The governing authority hereabouts is a superintendent who makes annual rounds as far as Upernavik, which is located farther to the north and is the true capital of Greenland.

Leaving Disko Island astern, the *Mozik* set about crossing Waigat Strait, which separates this island from the mainland,* and by 6 p.m. on July 25, she'd dropped anchor in Upernavik Harbor.

In which we'll see a passenger on the *Moẑik* meet up with a passenger on the *Oregon* while waiting for the marvelous meteor to meet up with the planet earth

The word "Greenland" suggests vistas of verdant fields, and no doubt this name was bestowed on the place with tongue in cheek, because it really should have been dubbed "Whiteland." In actuality the fellow who named it was a tenth-century mariner named Erik the Red, who probably didn't exemplify that color any more than this nation does green. But maybe this Norwegian had hoped to motivate his various countrymen to come over and colonize this huge High Arctic region. In any event it definitely didn't work;* the enticing name didn't hornswoggle anybody, and today the indigenous population of Greenland doesn't amount to much more than ten thousand.*

Honestly, if ever there was a country that wasn't fit to welcome a meteor worth eight hundred billion dollars, this was it—a thought that must have been racing through the minds of all those passengers whose compulsive curiosity had just brought them to Upernavik Harbor. Why couldn't the thing have chosen to fall a couple hundred leagues south on the wide prairies of Canada or the United States, where it would have been so easy to get to? Of all countries Greenland was the hardest to travel over, with its many mountain ranges, scads of precipices, glaciers galore, and regions that are virtually impossible to negotiate—what a setting for such a noteworthy event! And if that shooting star fell deep in the interior or on the east coast, how could anybody get within reach of it?* Who would dare emulate what Whymper did in 1867, Nordenskiöld in 1870, Jensen in 1878, or Nansen* in 1888? Who would have the rare courage, skill, and stamina needed to conquer all the obstacles, to venture into that mountainous labyrinth, to climb at altitudes of 6,500 to 10,000 feet,* to cope with blizzards, to face winter temperatures from forty to eighty degrees below zero?*

And yet there were precedents, really and truly! Haven't shooting stars elected to fall on Greenland in the past? Today doesn't the Stockholm Museum display three chunks of iron, most likely from meteorites, that weigh twenty-six and one-half tons each* and were found by Nordenskiöld in Ovifak on Disko Island?

Luckily, if the astronomers were correct, the shooting star was due to fall in a highly accessible region and during the summer months—that coming August, to be exact—when the temperature would be above freezing. It's likewise an established fact that as the Gulf Stream travels through Davis Strait, Baffin Bay, Smith Sound, Kennedy Channel, Robeson Channel, and into the glacial Lincoln Sea,* it warms up the west coast of Greenland, so the temperature sometimes climbs as high as sixty-four degrees Fahrenheit.* It's for this reason that the country's main outposts happen to be at Julianehåb, Jakobshavn, the north Greenland municipality of Nuuk, Godhavn, and the south Greenland municipality of Disko Island, which is the busiest port in these parts. Some of these localities actually manage to live up to that name of "Greenland" given to this corner of the New World. Their gardens have the soil to nurture a few vegetables, and grass grows here and there, though farther inland botanists can only gather mosses and seed plants. After the ice melts, pastures appear along this coast, allowing you to keep livestock. Of course you won't see many cows or bulls, but you'll find a hardy breed of wild goat that does well in this climate, and chickens thriving in their chilly barnyards, not to mention reindeer and a canine population that twenty years earlier had numbered at least eighteen hundred dogs.

After, at best, two or three months of summer, winter then returns with endless nights, harsh winds from the pole, and frightful blizzards that blot out the sky. Above the hard shell of the ground hovers a sort of gray dust, a mixture of microscopic plants and a kind of powdered ice called cryoconite, which Nordenskiöld was the first to study and which experts believe may come from meteorites that have entered the earth's atmosphere.

So it can be inferred from this that asteroids and aerolites—at least a thousand of which, we repeat, pass through our planet's atmosphere every twenty-four hours—favor* this corner of the world, which may explain why the Forsyth-Hudelson meteor was likely to fall in just this region.

But it wasn't due to land in Greenland's vast interior, so its fall wasn't automatically guaranteed to benefit interested parties in Denmark. During the voyage Mr. de Schack, the Danish delegate, frequently discussed this topic with Francis Gordon. In fact they often chatted with each other. Francis told him about the conflict between the two rivals, and Mr. de Schack showed a good deal of sympathy, holding out the possibility that he could intercede with his government and maybe persuade it to set aside a fraction of those astronomical billions for Mr. Forsyth and Dr. Hudelson.

"However," he added, "I'm not so sure we'll ever lay our hands on that treasure."

"But," Francis answered, "if the astronomers are right in their calculations—"

"Exactly," Mr. de Schack asserted, "and I'll admit they've narrowed it down to within a league or two. But we're dealing with a pretty narrow patch of land here, and there's a very good chance the shooting star will fall into the water where nobody can get at it."

"I don't care if it winds up at the bottom of the sea!" Francis snapped. "It'll be worth it if the doctor and my uncle can be friends again! They could finally quit fighting over which of them that damned meteor should be named after!"

"Hold it, Mr. Gordon!" Denmark's representative shot back. "We can't just shrug our shoulders! After all, that meteor's worth plenty, and we'd hate to see it go! But I'll admit we've got good reason to worry!"

In all honesty, the situation in Upernavik was well calculated to trouble Mr. de Schack. This outpost didn't just sit on the edge of the sea, the place was completely surrounded by it. Upernavik is one island in the middle of a large chain of islands scattered along the coast of Greenland. It measures barely twenty-five miles around,* and you'll admit that's a pretty skimpy target for an interstellar bullet. If the meteor's aim was even slightly off and it missed the mark, the waves of Baffin Bay would swallow it up. And those High Arctic waters are deep, three to six thousand feet down* according to the sounding lines. You just try fishing up an object weighing 1,389,000 tons from that sort of depth! To tell the truth, it would be better if it fell into the vast wilderness inland, where at least it wouldn't be absolutely impossible to retrieve. And it would be better still if it landed a few degrees farther down the coast—say at Jakobshavn, the port that the *Mozik* just passed on its way to Upernavik and that's located at latitude sixty-seven degrees, fifteen minutes north above the Arctic Circle.

In fact the vast Greenland interior unfolds right to the north, south, and east of this port. There a whole fleet could dock, there whalers on the prowl in Baffin Bay and Davis Strait can find a safe haven from stormy seas during the six-month winters. There, during the all-too-brief summers, greenery actually pokes through the melting snow. In short, Jakobshavn is the most important outpost on the superintendent's rounds to the north; it's more than a village, it's a town comparable to Godhavn on Disko Island. During the warm-weather months it's an excellent supply stop. And sure enough, the various cruise ships stocked up on their way to Upernavik, buying enough to feed several thousand curiosity seekers for a stay of absolutely no longer than a couple of weeks. Because the passengers would most likely remain on board till the actual day when the shooting star was sighted somewhere over the island.

Ultimately Upernavik berthed the *Moʒik* plus a dozen other steamships from America, Britain, France, Germany, Russia, Norway, and Denmark that had been chartered to sail up this Greenland coast. A few miles east of this outpost, the tall peaks of mountains in the interior stand out. In front of them, sheer cliffs rear up at the edge of the volcanic regions in Greenland.

At this latitude, it's worth noting, there are twenty-four days out of the year when the sun shines all around the clock. So everybody would be able to inspect the meteor in broad daylight, and if it did happen to fall in the neighborhood of the outpost, the bright sunlight would allow you to see it from far away.

The day after their arrival, a motley crowd wandered around the various timber cottages in Upernavik, whose government headquarters displayed the red and white colors* of Denmark's flag. The men and women of Greenland had never had so many people visit their far-off shores. The locals are Eskimos of the Kalalit, or Karalit, tribes, and their total population may amount to around twenty thousand.* Thanks to religious instruction from United Brethren missionaries, some six thousand have converted to Christianity.

An interesting ethnic type, these Greenlanders live mostly on the west coast; the men are small to medium-sized: stocky, muscular, with short legs, delicate hands and joints, yellowish complexion, face broad and flat, tiny nose, eyes brown and on the narrow side, thick, tousled black hair, with their gentle expressions almost resembling those of the seals living thereabouts, and like those animals they're protected from the cold by layers of fat. Males and older females dress almost identically: boots, trousers, parka. But the young women are all charm and smiles—they're into the latest styles, flaunt bobbed haircuts, and are decked out in multicolored ribbons. What's more, they no longer go in for tattooing, thanks to the influence of the missionaries, and both sexes adore singing and dancing. These locals have huge appetites. They'll enthusiastically consume over twenty pounds of food a day,* but their diet is restricted to venison, seal meat, fish, seaweed berries, and edible rockweed. As for what they drink, it's rarely alcoholic, because they touch liquor only once a year, during festivities honoring King Christian IX.

As you can imagine, the arrival of so many outsiders in Upernavik was quite a surprise for the several hundred natives living on this island. And when they realized just what was behind this influx, they felt even more surprised. These hapless people were about to learn of the power gold wields over humanity. But they weren't scheduled to be the beneficiaries of this windfall. If that wealth fell on their soil, it wasn't likely to go into their pockets, though pockets were plentiful in their outfits, unlike those of the Polynesians, say. But they weren't destined just to be disinterested onlookers in this "deal," which had drawn so many travelers to this particular island. Even some Eskimo families had left Godhavn, Jacobshavn, and other communities along Davis Strait to come up to Upernavik. And who knows, after the dust settled maybe Denmark would end up with so much money, she could give her New World colonies a slice of the same benefits and advantages her European subjects were due to enjoy.*

Anyhow it was high time for this event to actually occur, the climax of this whole business we've been narrating, and for several reasons.

First, if more steamships kept arriving in these parts, Upernavik's harbor wouldn't be big enough to hold them all, and what other havens could they possibly find among these coastal islands?

Next, it would be August in a few days, and ships didn't dare linger in these high latitudes. In September winter would return, bringing ice back down from the straits and channels to the north, and it doesn't take Baffin Bay very long to freeze over. Consequently it would soon be time to get going, exit these parts, and leave Cape Farewell behind—or risk being trapped in the pack ice for a savage Arctic winter that can last seven or eight months.

So if the shooting star didn't fall near Upernavik during the first two weeks of August, ships would have no choice but to leave the area, because it was out of the question for their passengers to winter under such harsh conditions.

Yet who knows if Dean Forsyth, Omicron, and Dr. Hudelson would have agreed to leave, or, instead, if they wouldn't have insisted on waiting for their shooting star? Honestly now, if one of our rivals stayed behind, wouldn't the other stay too?

But there were arguments against this, and when the occasion arose Mr. de Schack made them to the two men at the request of Francis Gordon, who felt he would be less persuasive than a representative of the Danish government and a member of the international commission. "If the meteor doesn't fall to the earth between August 7 and August 15 as the Boston astronomers have predicted," de Schack pointed out, "that means those astronomers were wrong. And if they were wrong about the time, couldn't they also be wrong about the place?"

This was an obvious possibility. No doubt the official mathematicians didn't have all the data they needed to obtain infallible results. Instead of landing in the neighborhood of Upernavik, what if the shooting star were to fall on some other spot under its trajectory around the earth . . . ?

And when Mr. de Schack considered this possibility, it sent chills down his spine.

During these endless hours of waiting, needless to say, our curiosity seekers took long strolls around the island. The rocky ground was mostly flat but swelled a little toward the island's center, so it made for easy walking. The prairies here and there offered more yellow than green and featured shrubs that would never turn into trees, a few stunted sequoias, white birches that still grew above the seventy-second parallel, plus some mosses, grasses, and brushwood.

As for the sky, it was mostly overcast and was often swept with low gray clouds driven by winds out of the east. The temperature didn't get above the mid-thirties.* So the passengers were glad to reboard their ships and enjoy those amenities the village failed to offer, including a style of cooking you won't find in Godhavn or any other outpost along this coast.

Unfortunately the cloud cover made it hard to see the shooting star. Was it still slowing down? Was it getting closer to the earth? Would it fall in the near future? There were so many tremendously important questions neither the experts nor the curiosity seekers could answer. But from fleeting glimmers that peeped through the clouds, the meteor definitely seemed to be up there,* still following its path from the northeast to the southwest. Under the wind you could sometimes hear hissing sounds, which indicated the shooting star was still orbiting through space. But the fact is that since the *Mozik* had dropped anchor three days earlier, her passengers were getting restless and were especially worried that the whole trip might turn out to have been a waste of time.

One of those for whom the hours didn't pass too slowly was Mr. Seth Stanfort. He was, as the saying goes, "comfortable in his own skin," and though he enjoyed good relations with Mr. de Schack and Francis Gordon, he wasn't impossibly bored when he had to make do without them. He'd come to Upernavik as a simple curiosity seeker, blithely dashing off to a place where there wasn't anything very unusual to see. If the meteor did actually fall here, he would be happy to look it over. If it didn't fall, nobody would take his leave more serenely than he, and he would head back to America, where he would go haring off after some new fad, footloose and fancy-free.

During the morning of July 31, four days after the *Mozik*'s arrival, one last vessel hove in sight off Upernavik. A steamship was gliding through the chain of islands and islets and coming into harbor.

What nationality was this ship? It came from the United States, a fact revealed by the fifty-one stars on the flag* flapping from the tip of its fore-and-aft sail.

No doubt this steamship would be dumping off a new batch of curiosity seekers to take part in this meteoric melodrama: though they were latecomers, they weren't too late to get in on the action, since that globe of gold—if it was continuing to revolve through the air—still couldn't be seen from the ground.

But since this steamship obviously hailed from an American port, wouldn't it be bringing some fresh news about the shooting star? Who knows if the astronomers hadn't worked up some more accurate calculations about the time, if not the place, the meteor would fall?

And in his ongoing distress, Francis Gordon kept telling himself: "Oh, if that blasted meteor would just go back where it came from, then Dr. Hudelson and my uncle could put it out of their minds for good, and after that . . ."

But if this was the young fellow's innermost desire, it wasn't shared by Messrs. Forsyth and Hudelson, nor for damned sure by Mr. de Schack or a single one of the curiosity seekers who'd paid good money to visit this island.

Around 11 a.m. the S.S. *Oregon* dropped anchor in the midst of the flotilla. She let down a lifeboat to take one of her passengers ashore, obviously somebody in a bigger hurry than the other travelers.

In point of fact this was one of the astronomers from the Boston Observatory, Mr. Wharf, who went right to headquarters, where the governing authority over the north district was presiding while on his rounds to Upernavik. The superintendent in turn sent for Mr. de Schack, and the delegate from Denmark made his way to the cottage over which the national flag fluttered.

Everybody was on tenterhooks, and they had a hunch this passenger from the *Oregon* was the bringer of crucial news. By any chance was the meteor planning to give our planet the slip, "go AWOL," and skip out for other parts of the galaxy, just like Francis hoped?

Not to worry. In actuality it was a piece of news, or data rather, that would appease everybody's curiosity and that the superintendent would forward to every ship.

Thanks to their latest observations of the meteor's movements, the astronomers had carried their calculations even farther—"out to the fourth or fifth decimal," as mathematicians say. The new figures didn't change anything that concerned the meteor's falling in the vicinity of Upernavik, but they did reduce the period of time previously put at August 7–15. There would no longer be a margin of ten days, just the three days of August 3–5, during which the shooting star would fall on this island, much to the delight of onlookers from the ships and of pocketbooks back in Denmark.

"At last! Finally! It isn't passing us by!" Forsyth and Dr. Hudelson exclaimed in turn.

And Denmark's delegate to the international commission was on the receiving end of more congratulations than even the aforementioned mathematicians could tote up. People greeted him as if he were the meteor's sole owner and proprietor, bowing even lower than they would to the richest American tycoons. Wasn't he the symbolic possessor of those eight hundred billion dollars, the very incarnation of Denmark itself?

That was on July 31. In another ninety-six to a hundred hours, the much-sought-after shooting star would be lying on the soil of Greenland.

"Unless it goes to the bottom!" Francis Gordon mumbled to himself, still hoping and praying.

But whether or not this business was destined to come to a head, whether or not the meteor and the planet earth were destined to link up till death do them part, we should note that a second meeting was also taking place, which no doubt would be followed by another parting of the ways.

Mr. Seth Stanfort had been strolling along dockside and watching the *Oregon*'s passengers disembark, when he stopped in his tracks at the sight of a female passenger whom one of the lifeboats had just dropped ashore.

Stanfort looked again, made sure his eyes weren't playing tricks, went up, and said in a voice that expressed both surprise and pleasure: "Miss Arcadia Walker, if I'm not mistaken?"

"Mr. Stanfort!" the lady answered.

"I never expected to see *you* on this out-of-the-way island, Miss Walker . . ."

"Nor I you, Mr. Stanfort."

"And how have you been, Miss Walker?"

"Never better, Mr. Stanfort, and you?"

"Just fine!"

Then they started in chitchatting like two old acquaintances who'd just met up again by the sheerest accident.

And right off Miss Walker pointed at the sky, asking: "It hasn't fallen yet, has it?"

"Not yet, don't worry. But from what I've just heard, it won't be long now."

"Then I'll be here for it," Arcadia said delightedly.

"So will I!" Stanfort replied.

There's no getting around it, they were two remarkable individuals, two people of the world, and to call a spade a spade, two old friends. And the same spirit of inquisitiveness had just reunited them on the shores of Upernavik. As we know, after their second visit to Whaston's justice of the peace, they went their separate ways without any reproaches or recriminations, a couple who simply didn't suit each other and who'd broken up without any hard feelings. Mr. Stanfort and Miss Walker had traveled north of their own volition. On the same whim they'd both come to this island off Greenland, so why should they pretend they didn't recognize each other or weren't acquainted? Is there anything sillier or more immature than two people turning up their noses when they actually still think well of each other?

True, Miss Arcadia Walker hadn't found her ideal mate in Seth Stanfort, but probably she hadn't bumped into him anywhere else either. Nobody had risked his life to rescue her as she craved. As for her ex-husband, he had fond memories of her intelligence and colorful personality, and his only regret was that he'd married her.

So after exchanging these initial remarks, which made no reference to their life together two months earlier, Mr. Stanfort placed himself at Miss Walker's disposal. Nobody knew they'd been man and wife, and nobody would have guessed. They were simply two friends of the opposite sex who'd met up by a stroke of luck at latitude seventy-three degrees north.

Arcadia gladly accepted Stanfort's offer, and they said no more about the cosmic phenomenon that would soon be taking place.

The news brought by the *Oregon* had a gigantic impact. Not only would the wait be shorter—barely even a hundred hours—it seemed to lend total credence to the astronomers' calculations. And after that morning when they'd more or less confirmed the fall of the shooting star, there was no further reason to doubt that it would happen in this part of Greenland.

"If only it hits the island!" thought Dean Forsyth.

"And not somewhere else!" thought Dr. Hudelson.

As you can see, both of them—along with Mr. de Schack, naturally—were worried about the exact same thing.

In fact they were now of one mind.

The days of August 1 and 2 were uneventful. Unfortunately the weather started taking a turn for the worse: it was getting noticeably colder, and an early winter seemed likely. The mountains along the shoreline were white with snow, and when the wind blew down the coast, it was so harsh and biting that people hurried to hide out in the ships' lounges. So it wouldn't do to dawdle in these latitudes, and once they'd seen what they came for, our curiosity seekers would be more than willing to head south again.

No doubt the delegate from Denmark would have to stay behind by himself and guard the treasure till his government could engineer its removal. And who knows if our two rivals, stubbornly hoping to shore up their claims, might not decide to keep him company? This was a real worry for Francis Gordon, the prospect of a long winter in such harsh conditions. And he thought about poor Jenny, her mother, her sister, and other loved ones who were counting the hours till the travelers returned.

During the night of August 2–3, a major storm blew up over the island. Twenty hours earlier the Boston astronomer had confirmed that the shooting star was definitely passing overhead and was going slower and slower along its orbit. But the state of the skies had kept him from making out its distance above the earth. And the storm was so violent, our good curiosity seekers kept wondering if it wasn't about to "carry the meteor to hell and back."

It was impossible to stay outdoors, and the cottages in Upernavik didn't have room for so many people. So the travelers were forced to remain on their ships, and it was lucky the gusts blew from the east, because if they'd come off the water, every one of those vessels would have been torn from its moorings.

The whole day of August 3, the weather gave no sign of calming down, and that night it got so rough, the captains of both the *Mozik* and the *Oregon* actually began to fear for their ships. It was literally impossible to go from the one to the other, even though they were anchored only three hundred feet apart.*

But during the night of August 3–4, the storm appeared to be dying down. If it let up in a few hours, all the passengers would be certain to take advantage of the fact and head back ashore. August 4—wasn't that the exact date when the meteor was supposed to fall?

And sure enough, at 7 a.m. that day there was a sort of dull boom, and it was so loud that the whole island shook.

Then one of the locals ran up to the house where Mr. de Schack was staying, and he had great news.

The shooting star had just landed on a cape at the northwest end of Upernavik Island.

16. Which, though the purchaser may read it and weep, the author needs to write for the sake of historical accuracy and proper recording in the annals of astronomy

True, since Noah's flood we've had quite a few pieces of news that have caused uproars in the world, but none had greater impact—literal and figurative—than that meteor falling on Upernavik Island. Actually America and Europe only heard about it a little later—a cruise ship put to sea immediately, but it took her a couple of days to convey the news to the first semaphore station in Quebec, from which it instantly shot around the world.

But here in Upernavik it barely took a minute to spread the word all over the island and to the dozen or so ships anchored nearby.

Their passengers disembarked in a flash. With Omicron at their heels, Forsyth and Dr. Hudelson were the first ones ashore, two fathers dying to see a newborn child whose paternity both were claiming. Of course Francis Gordon went along too, ready to step in if needed. In all honesty Messrs. Forsyth and Hudelson were now much angrier with the government of Denmark than with each other. Hadn't that government refused to recognize their rights as discoverers?

Concerning Mr. Seth Stanfort, as soon as he was ashore he went looking for Miss Arcadia Walker, whom he hadn't seen during those three days of bad weather. Given their current status as good friends, wouldn't they naturally want to inspect the shooting star together?

"It's fallen at last, Mr. Stanfort!" Miss Walker said when they met up.

"At last!" he echoed.

"Finally!" the whole crowd kept repeating, as they proceeded to the cape at the northwest end of the island.

But two individuals had a fifteen-minute head start on all the curiosity seekers: Mr. de Schack and the Boston astronomer had instantly rushed over from the government quarters where they'd been staying since their arrival.

"That dratted delegate will get there first and lay claim to the shooting star!" Forsyth muttered.

"And keep it for himself," Dr. Hudelson mumbled.

"Who knows if he'll be able to keep it?" Francis commented, offering no explanation for this remark.

"But that won't stop us from asserting our rights!" Mr. Dean Forsyth insisted.

"Absolutely not!" Dr. Stanley Hudelson concurred.*

To the boundless satisfaction of the young man who was both the former's nephew and the latter's one-time future son-in-law, the two rivals had clearly forgotten their personal conflicts; they were consumed with a mutual hatred for the claims of King Christian and his two million Scandinavian subjects.

Thanks to a lucky chain of events, the weather had undergone a complete change between 3 and 4 a.m. As the wind had subsided to the south, the storm died down. If the sun rose only a couple of degrees above the horizon—over which it still swept in its daily arc—at least its rays poked through the few remaining clouds. No more precipitation, no more gusts of wind, just fair weather, calm skies, and a temperature of forty-six to forty-eight degrees Fahrenheit.*

And among all these passengers from Europe and America, you could find a few with enough "Greenland savvy" to conclude: "No doubt about it, the meteor actually disturbed the atmosphere as it approached; its nearness to the earth had a major effect. But now it's on the ground, and we've got decent weather again."

It was a good couple of miles* from government headquarters to that cape in the northwest, and everybody had to go on foot. Upernavik hadn't gotten around to providing such luxuries as transportation. But it wasn't a hard walk, because the pebbly ground stayed fairly level and only changed significantly along the coastline. There the landscape featured a few cliffs that dropped straight down to the sea.

It was on one of these cliffs that the shooting star had come to rest, too far away to be seen from the town proper.

At the head of the crowd was the local who'd been the first with the big news; close behind him were Messrs. Forsyth, Hudelson, Omicron, de Schack, and the Boston astronomer.

Francis Gordon was a little farther behind, still keeping an eye on the doctor and his uncle, deliberately leaving the two men to themselves, yet impatient to see what effect the meteor would have on them when they saw it . . . their meteor.

Besides, Francis was strolling in the company of Mr. Seth Stanfort and Miss Arcadia Walker. The two ex-spouses hadn't forgotten their married days in Whaston, so they were well aware of the rift between the two families and its aftermath. Both of them felt genuine concern for Francis's tricky situation and his efforts to bring things to a happy conclusion.

"It'll all work out," Arcadia kept repeating.

"I hope so," Francis replied.

"But maybe it would have been better if this meteor had gone to Davy Jones' locker," Stanfort commented.

"Yes, for everybody!" Miss Walker added, with reason on her side. Then she said again, "Don't lose heart, Mr. Gordon, it'll all work out. A few hardships, problems, and anxieties are to be expected before a wedding. When getting married is too easy, there's an actual risk of the marriage going sour. Wouldn't you agree, Mr. Stanfort?"

"No question, Miss Walker, and we ourselves are a prime example! We were on horseback, remember, and we didn't even bother to dismount when that justice of the peace married us. He was a decent old guy and didn't seem at all surprised, the sign of a wise man! Yes, that's how we did it—we tied the knot in no time . . ."

"Only to untie it six weeks later," Arcadia replied with a smile. "Which goes to show, Mr. Gordon, that if you don't marry Miss Jenny on horseback, you'll stand a slightly better chance of achieving happiness!"*

Needless to say, in the midst of this exodus of passengers, this horde of curiosity seekers, Seth, Arcadia, and Francis had to be the only ones conversing about something besides the meteor. They were waxing philosophical à la Judge Proth himself.

Everybody moved briskly along. There wasn't any path to follow, just flatland filled with scrawny shrubs and with numerous birds that kept flying off as their Upernavik habitat was continually disturbed.

In half an hour they'd covered nearly two miles and only had about three thousand feet to go.* However the shooting star was still out of sight at the far end of the cliff. But nobody doubted this was the spot it had occupied all morning. The Greenlander couldn't have been wrong on that score. He'd been at the scene, barely a third of a mile away,* when the meteor hit the ground.* He'd heard the racket it made—as had plenty of other people, no matter how far off they were.

And another phenomenon had occurred that was already causing concern and that seemed just as remarkable. The air was starting to get warmer. No doubt about it, in the vicinity of this cape at the northwest end of the island, thermometers were reading several degrees higher than they had back in town. The difference was quite noticeable, and the heat became more and more intense the closer you got to the landing site.

"Maybe that shooting star not only affected the weather in these parts, it also improved the whole climate," Stanfort said with a grin.

"Which would be a lucky break for the natives," Miss Walker replied, grinning back.

"Most likely that ball of gold is still white-hot," Francis commented, "and the heat it gives off can be felt inside a certain radius . . ."

"Good point!" Stanfort exclaimed. "Does that mean we have to wait till it cools down?"

"It might have cooled a lot faster if it had missed the island completely," Francis answered, returning to an idea that made Dr. Hudelson and his uncle gnash their teeth.

But the two rivals were out of earshot. Along with Omicron they were in the lead; already mopping their foreheads, they were literally running neck and neck.

What's more, Mr. de Schack and the astronomer Mr. Wharf were perspiring just as profusely, as were the whole crowd and all the Greenlanders who'd come along for this once-in-a-lifetime ride.

Less than a quarter of a mile away,* past a curve in the cliff, the meteor basked in all its radiant glory, while a thousand eyes popped out of their heads.

But who knows? Maybe that radiance would prove to be too much to bear . . . or even approach.

Finally their local guide came to a stop, some ways short of the cape itself. He obviously couldn't go any farther.

Forsyth, Hudelson, and Omicron caught up with him in an instant and stood at his side. After them came Mr. de Schack, Mr. Wharf, Seth Stanfort, Arcadia Walker, and Francis Gordon, followed by all the curiosity seekers the various vessels had shipped to this part of Baffin Bay.

No, it wasn't possible to go any farther—or closer, to be exact—and the shooting star was still barely a quarter of a mile off.

It was the very same globe of gold that had gotten caught in the earth's gravitational pull and had been traveling through the skies for the past four months. It was no longer as brilliant as it had been while orbiting through outer space. But its brightness was still more than human eyes could stand. Its temperature, like the temperature of that fiery rock that had fallen to the earth in 1768, must have been close to the melting point;* even though it had cooled as it slowed down, it had automatically heated up again as it entered the denser atmosphere closer to the earth's surface. If this amazing meteor had been literally untouchable while going along its trajectory in space, it didn't seem a bit more touchable now that it was on the ground.

That part of the coastline was shaped like a sort of plateau, one of those rock formations known in local parlance as *unaleks*. Rising about thirty feet above the level of the water, it sloped toward the sea. The meteor lay close to the edge of the plateau.* If it had fallen some yards to the left, it would have plunged into the waves at the foot of the cliff.

"Yes!" Francis couldn't help saying. "Fifty feet farther and it would have gone to the bottom!"

"Beyond all reach," Arcadia Walker added.

"But Mr. de Schack doesn't have to worry about that," Seth Stanfort noted, "and he'll do what it takes to pack it off to King Christian!"

Which, sooner or later, was just what was scheduled to happen. It was a question of time, nothing more. All they had to do was wait for the meteor to cool off, and with the Arctic winter on its way, they wouldn't be waiting long.

Mr. Dean Forsyth and Dr. Stanley Hudelson stood stock-still, practically in a trance at the sight of that dazzling mass of gold. Both of them had tried to inch closer but had to shrink back, and ditto for impatient little Omicron, who came within twenty-five feet of turning into roast beef.* Even at a quarter of a mile away, the temperature had climbed to 140 degrees Fahrenheit,* and the meteor gave off so much heat, the air was unbreathable.

"At last . . . there it is . . . it made it to the island . . . it didn't go into the sea! It isn't lost to the world . . . lucky old Denmark will get to take it home! All we have to do is wait . . . so let's!"

Which is what the curiosity seekers kept saying over and over, while that suffocating heat kept them on the other side of the curve in the cliff.

Fine, they would wait . . . but for how long? They were above the seventy-third parallel, and in a few weeks the polar winter was due to dump a succession of ice storms, blizzards, and sixty-below temperatures on these parts,* so this was a good question. But the shooting star wouldn't take a month or two to cool off, would it? Yes, when imbued with such intense heat, some masses of metal *do* burn a long while—which is often the case with meteorites and other space rocks whose dimensions are infinitely smaller.

Three hours went by and nobody would have dreamed of leaving the place. They were determined to wait till they could go up to the meteor. But this definitely wasn't about to happen that day or the next, so unless they fetched provisions and camped out in the area, they would have to go back to their ships.

"Mr. Stanfort," Arcadia said, "do you think that piece of white-hot rock is going to cool down in just a matter of hours?"

"Not hours or even days, Miss Walker."

"All right, I'm going back to the *Oregon*, then I'll return this afternoon."

"We may as well walk together," Stanfort proposed, "since I'm heading back to the *Moʒik*. It's about time for lunch, I believe . . ."

"My thoughts exactly," Miss Arcadia answered, "and if it's all the same to Mr. Gordon . . ."

"It is, Miss Walker," the young fellow answered, "but what about Dr. Hudelson and my uncle? Would they be up for going with us? Somehow I doubt it . . ." He went over to Dean Forsyth. "Would you like to come along, uncle?"

Forsyth didn't answer him, took a dozen steps forward, then had to back away hurriedly, as if he'd blundered too close to an open furnace.

Right behind him, Dr. Hudelson retreated just as promptly.

"You see, uncle? You see, doctor?" Francis went on, "Now's the time to go back to the ship! Hell's bells, nobody's going to swipe your shooting star! You've been feasting your eyes on it long enough, how about another kind of feast?"

Francis couldn't get a word out of either man and gave up. So Mr. Seth Stanfort and Miss Arcadia Walker headed back to town without him, followed by several hundred other tourists whose nutritional requirements were persuading them to return to their respective vessels.

As for Messrs. Forsyth, Hudelson, and Gordon, they didn't come back till evening, weak with hunger and now willing to put off their next vigil till the following day.

Bright and early at 7 a.m. on August 5, passengers, settlers, and natives went back to their observation posts, Forsyth and the doctor leading the way.

Needless to say, the meteor was still lying there on the plateau, still giving off an enormous amount of heat. Its temperature didn't seem to have gone down at all during the night. A burning smell hung in the air. If it had been October instead of August, there wouldn't have been a trace of snow on the ground within four or five hundred yards of the meteor.*

However, the most impatient, most bullheaded individuals—no need to name them—were able to get fifty feet closer, yet if they'd gone another fifty feet, the scalding air would have wiped them out.*

But among the impatient ones cited above were neither Mr. Seth Stanfort, Miss Arcadia Walker, nor even Denmark's delegate to the international commission. Mr. de Schack felt that his countrymen had no need to worry about their eight hundred billion. It was as safe as if it were in the national treasury. True, they couldn't currently lay their hands on it, but whether it took a couple of months or the whole polar winter, they could rest assured that this white-hot mass would eventually cool off, then all 1,389,000 tons of it would be shipped to Europe. And at around eleven hundred tons per ship,* it would take at least twelve hundred vessels to transport the whole works to Copenhagen or other Danish ports.

However—and this comment came that same morning from Francis Gordon, who shared it with Seth Stanfort, who in turn passed it along to Arcadia Walker—it seemed that the shooting star had slightly changed position on the rocky surface where it had been lying since the day before. Had it slid toward the ocean a bit? Was the ground giving way little by little under the meteor's tremendous weight? Could this factor ultimately cause it to fall into the sea?

"That would be a strange way for such a momentous affair to end!" Arcadia Walker noted.

"It wouldn't be the happiest ending you could think of," Stanfort agreed.

"But it would definitely be for the best," Francis insisted.

Now then, the thing young Gordon had just noticed, i.e., the meteor's gradual slide toward the cliff edge, was soon obvious to everybody else as well. No doubt about it, the terrain was starting to give way bit by bit, and if this tendency continued, that smoldering golden ball would end up rolling off the edge of the plateau and into the ocean depths.

A wholesale wave of anger and chagrin rose up against that underqualified plateau, so unworthy of the marvelous meteor. If only the shooting star had fallen inland—or better yet, on the solid basaltic cliffs of Greenland proper—there wouldn't have been the slightest danger of its being lost to greedy humanity.

But yes, the meteor *was* sliding, and it was maybe only a matter of hours, or even minutes, till the plateau would suddenly collapse under its enormous load!

Nor was there any way to avert this catastrophe, any way to keep the meteor from sliding, any way to prop up that inadequate plateau till the shooting star could be carted off!

Something like a shriek of horror burst from the lungs of Mr. de Schack when he recognized the impending calamity. Goodbye to any chance of making Denmark a nation of billionaires! Goodbye to any prospect of turning all of King Christian's subjects into wealthy men! Goodbye to any likelihood of buying Schleswig-Holstein back from the Germans!

As regards Mr. Forsyth and Dr. Hudelson, when they saw that the initial swaying motion was about to change into a rolling one, Francis Gordon feared for their actual sanity. They stretched out their arms in desperation! They cried out for help as if they actually believed there was somebody who could!

"My meteor!" called the one.

"My meteor!" yelled the other.

"Our meteor!" hollered both of them,* just as a sharper movement nudged that ball of gold closer to the drop-off.

Along with Omicron they dashed right into the scalding air. They'd gone a good eighty yards* before Stanfort and Francis could get to them. Realizing they were about to drop in their tracks, they'd held onto each other, then flopped on the ground and lay still.

Francis Gordon instantly rushed out to them. Seth Stanfort was right behind him. And when she saw the risk he was taking, Arcadia Walker must have been afraid that her ex-husband was in grave peril, because she blurted out: "Seth! Seth!"

Since the air was unbreathable, Stanfort, Francis, and a couple other courageous onlookers had to crouch close to the ground, creeping along while pressing handkerchiefs over their mouths. Finally they all made it to Forsyth and the doctor. They picked up the two rivals and carried them as well as they could without running the risk of being parboiled.

As for Omicron, who lay a few yards farther on, you might say that he already was!

Luckily these three victims of their own impulsiveness had been rescued in time. They received prompt attention and soon returned to consciousness—only, unfortunately, to see all their hopes dashed to pieces.

It was exactly 8:47 a.m. Edging above the horizon, the sun came into full view.

The shooting star continued its slow slide, either because of the slope itself or because the surface kept gradually giving way under the meteor's weight. It was inching nearer and nearer to the brink of the plateau, a cliffside that dropped straight down into the ocean.

Now in a state past describing, the whole crowd started to wail. "It's going to fall . . . it's going to fall in!"

These horrified words dropped from the lips of everybody except Francis Gordon, who seemed distinctly undisturbed.

Suddenly the golden ball stopped moving. Oh, how devoutly everybody hoped it wouldn't roll any farther, that it wouldn't go over the cliff edge, since the slope there wasn't as steep! Yes, maybe there was a chance it would now stay put! Then it would gradually cool off. And it would be possible to go nearer. And the Danish representative would finally lay hands on his cosmic treasure. And Messrs. Forsyth and Hudelson would be able to hug and kiss it. And precautions would be taken to protect it from harm while a thousand ships made their way to Upernavik to pick up their golden cargoes.

"Well, Mr. Stanfort, is the shooting star finally all right?"

As if in answer to this question from Miss Walker, who was down by the shore, there was a hideous cracking sound. The rocks suddenly gave way, and the meteor plunged into the sea.

And if the riotous clamor from the crowd didn't echo up and down the coast, it's because that clamor was instantly drowned out by the sound of an explosion louder than thousands of thunderclaps roaring across the skies.

This sound passed like an airborne tidal wave over the surface of the island, and it had such force that it knocked every single onlooker to the ground.

Like so many other space rocks or meteorites entering the earth's atmosphere, the shooting star had just exploded. Simultaneously, thanks to the meteor's high temperature, swirls of steam were rising from the water.

As it plummeted into the depths, the meteor likewise raised an enormous wave that crashed against the shore, then fell back with overwhelming fury.

Unfortunately, when this wave washed ashore, the sudden mass of water caught Miss Arcadia Walker, knocked her down, and dragged her away.

It looked like she was beyond help, but Seth Stanfort dived in anyhow, risking his life to save her; and chances were excellent that there would be two victims instead of one!

Stanfort managed to reach the young woman just as she was being dragged under, and by hanging onto a rock he was able to withstand the backwash from that gigantic wave . . .

Then Francis and a couple of bystanders ran down and pulled them to higher ground.

Stanfort was still conscious, but Miss Walker didn't move. They immediately attended to her and soon brought her around; she took her ex-husband's hand, then spoke to him as follows: "From the moment I needed rescuing, my darling Seth, it was obvious who my rescuer was meant to be!"

But the marvelous meteor, not as lucky as Miss Arcadia, hadn't been able to dodge its dismal fate. It had plunged into the sea, and even if, by some herculean effort, it could have been dredged up from the ocean at the foot of the cliff, this possibility was no longer in the cards.

Because, in short, its nucleus was what had exploded. It had burst into smithereens and was scattered across the waves, so when Mr. de Schack, Dean Forsyth, and Dr. Hudelson went looking for fragments along the shore, they didn't find a solitary thing; out of that amazing eight-hundred-billion-dollar meteor, not a crumb was left.*

17. The final chapter, which records the latest developments in this totally fictitious narrative, after which Mr. John Proth, Whaston's justice of the peace, gets the last word

Their inquisitiveness now satisfied, all those thousands of curiosity seekers had nothing left to do but go home.

But maybe they *weren't* satisfied. Had it been worth all the hardships at sea, all the expense of traveling to the polar basin, merely to see the meteor for a few hours on that crumbling plateau and not get any closer than four hundred yards? Oh, if only it hadn't plunged into the depths, if only that precious gift from the heavens had been preserved! What a dismal ending to an affair that had knocked the whole world for a loop, particularly for Great Britain, the United States, Russia, Norway, Afghanistan, Nicaragua, Costa Rica, and above all Denmark! As for the experts, they'd been right all along. That globe of gold had landed in territory belonging to a Danish colony. And now it was gone, and not a grain of it was left on that seashore at the northwest tip of Upernavik Island.

Were there any grounds for thinking another trillion-dollar meteor might show up on the earth's horizon? There weren't. The same thing would hardly be likely to happen twice. Possibly there were other space rocks out there that were made of gold, but the odds were so slim that any of them would ever be caught in the earth's gravitational pull, nobody would have bet a red cent.*

And in general this was a good thing. Putting eight hundred billion dollars' worth of gold in circulation would have totally devalued this metal, so cherished by those who have it, so despised by those who don't. No, there wasn't any reason to mourn the loss of that meteor, since it would have caused colossal problems in the world money market—unless Denmark had possessed the good sense to stick it in a glass case like an exhibit in some planetarium, then had refused ever to let it out in the form of ducats, crowns,* or other Danish coins.

But the various interested parties had every right to feel cheated by this dismal outcome. How gloomily Mr. Dean Forsyth and Dr. Stanley Hudelson looked around the area where their shooting star had exploded! And how vainly they searched for leftover pieces on the sand. Not a particle of that cosmic gold was left, not even enough for a tiepin or a cufflink, assuming Mr. de Schack's homeland didn't have an automatic claim on it.

But in their mutual disappointment, it seemed that the two rivals had finally gotten over their jealousy, to Francis's great delight and the sincere relief of Seth Stanfort and Arcadia Walker. And why should those two old friends have kept on with their blood feud? Since the meteor no longer existed, there was no point in squabbling over who it should be named after.

So their only option was to say goodbye to Greenland and "go home empty-handed," to use the appropriate hunting lingo, returning to the lower latitudes of America, Asia, and Europe. Before six weeks were out, Baffin Bay and Davis Strait would be frozen over, and all the ships now moored off Upernavik would be boxed in for eight months. And not a single one of their passengers felt enthusiastic about wintering in the High Arctic.

Oh, if only that shooting star still existed, if only there was still a need to guard that ball of gold till warm weather returned, then certainly Mr. de Schack—and maybe Messrs. Forsyth and Hudelson—would have braved the rigors of a polar winter. But since the meteor had exchanged its aerial habitat for an aquatic one, there was no reason to hang around any longer.

On the morning of August 7, every one of those British, American,

Danish, French, German, and Russian vessels weighed anchor, took advantage of a favorable wind from the northeast and sailed through the chain of islands below Upernavik. Since they were high-speed steamers rather than sailboats, their propellers quickly took them down to the strait.

Needless to say, Forsyth, Omicron, Dr. Hudelson, and Francis Gordon were aboard the *Moẓik* in their usual cabins; however it *does* need to be said that Miss Arcadia Walker was also on board, as was Mr. Seth Stanfort. Mr. de Schack had departed on a Danish vessel bound for Copenhagen, freeing up his cabin for a certain lady passenger who wanted to get back to America fast.

Crossing through Davis Strait wasn't too awful for those with easily troubled stomachs. The *Moẓik* hugged the Greenland coastline, which protected her from winds off the open sea, so the passengers had an easy time of it till she passed Cape Farewell the evening of August 15.

But from then on, the rolling and pitching were soon claiming a host of new victims. And how many of them heartily regretted the compulsive curiosity that had led them to sign on for this utterly worthless and acutely uncomfortable voyage.

So Messrs. Forsyth and Hudelson were renewing members of the wretched community of the seasick, and Francis Gordon hovered over them constantly.

As regards Seth Stanfort and Arcadia Walker, they were old hands and immune to travel sickness, so they passed the time chatting pleasantly. About the past? The future? Good question. Francis often took part in their conversations, and he could see this divorced couple still had feelings for each other.

When the first semaphore station came in view on the American coastline, the *Moẓik* immediately signaled her identity, her next port of call, and the outcome of that whole expedition to the northern seas.

So it was this steamship that furnished the first news of the meteor, how it had fallen on Upernavik Island, and how it had plunged into the depths of Baffin Bay.

Naturally this news was disseminated with dazzling speed, naturally it raced along the telegraph lines of Europe and the United States in a few hours, naturally there was a wave of emotion over the dismal, almost ridiculous end of this shooting star that had winched up everybody's curiosity and greed. No doubt it would be an exaggeration to say that there was a period of public mourning, and yet in all America not even the shameless *Whaston Punch* had the nerve to poke fun at this scientific setback.

On August 27, after a cruise with plenty of east winds and lots of discomfort for most of her passengers, the *Moȝik* dropped anchor at the port of Charleston.

It isn't far from South Carolina to Virginia, and railroads are plentiful in the United States. So as early as the next day, August 28, Mr. Dean Forsyth, Omicron, and Dr. Stanley Hudelson were back in Whaston and ready to man their respective watchtowers on Elizabeth Street and Morris Street.

Their households had been expecting them ever since the *Moȝik*'s impending arrival had been announced by the U.S. semaphores. Mrs. Hudelson and her two daughters were at the station when the Charleston train dropped our three travelers off. And honestly, they must have been deeply touched by the welcome they received. Neither Forsyth nor the doctor batted an eye when Francis wrapped his arms around his fiancée and wife-to-be, nor when he gave Mrs. Hudelson a cordial hug. As for madcap Miss Loo, there she was, collaring Forsyth and saying: "So it's all over and done with, right?"

And yes, it *was* over and done with. As the ancient Romans liked to remark in their cozy old Latin tongue, *sublata causa, tollitur effectus*—if you get rid of the cause, you'll get rid of the effect. Which is just what the local newspapers pointed out, not excepting the *Whaston Punch*, which published a delightfully sassy article about the return of the two former rivals.

All that's left to mention is that on September 5, the bells of St. Andrew's pealed out noisily above this Virginia town. And in front of a congregation made up of parents, leading citizens, and friends of the two families, Father O'Garth presided over the wedding of Francis Gordon and Jenny Hudelson, after they'd finally weathered all the complications created by that unreasonable meteor showing up on the town horizon.

And you can be sure that a dewy-eyed Mrs. Mitz was there at the ceremony, likewise Miss Loo, ravishing in a new gown that had been ready for over two months.

Furthermore, just as things had turned out well for the Forsyth and Hudelson families, they also took a favorable turn for Mr. Seth Stanfort and Miss Arcadia Walker.

This time they weren't on horseback, nor did they stand single file to hand over their paperwork in Judge Proth's home. No, they were walking arm in arm. And when the magistrate did his duty and remarried these two ex-spouses who'd been divorced only a few weeks, they bowed courteously to him.

"Thank you, Judge Proth," Mrs. Stanfort said.

"And goodbye," Mr. Stanfort added.

Yet when the philosophical fellow was back in his garden, he turned to his old housekeeper: "Maybe I shouldn't have answered 'Goodbye' to them," he remarked, "but 'I'll be seeing you!'"*

⇒ THE END

NOTES ON THE TEXT

With these annotations we hope to enhance your enjoyment of Verne's *The Meteor Hunt*. First of all, we offer context, background information that was probably better known to Verne's original audience than to us today. For example, what does he mean when alluding casually to Stiegler, Parry, or Aliboron? We also provide a running commentary on his characters, plot, and the messages he intends; these notes especially should warm us up for our broader discussion, in our afterword, of Verne's literary maneuvers. Then there's the matter of updating his science. Since he arouses our interest in scientific questions, it's natural for us to wonder what today's answers are. In our text, too, we have converted Verne's metric-system measurements of weight and distance (kilograms, kilometers) to their Anglo-American equivalents (pounds, miles), but if you want them in their original form, you'll find them here. The same goes for his monetary figures. Finally, for the scholar especially, we include below textual information about Verne's original manuscript (MS), the Société Jules Verne edition (SJV) of 1986, and the Archipel reissue of 2002. As explained in our foreword, these editions are the splendid work of Olivier Dumas, president of the Société Jules Verne. In other words, these notes are an extension of our foreword and text, and a transition to our afterword.

CHAPTER I

1 *characteristic hardheaded Yankee*. Right off Verne trumpets one of his chief social themes: How each nation's history can create distinctive national characteristics. He's always especially interested in the United

States as a new type of society most likely to produce a new type of personality. So we've been alerted now to watch his characters reveal what his world sees as typical American traits. Characters from other countries won't be exempt from such generalizations. As a Romantic, Verne champions nationalism; as an heir to the Age of Reason, he strives for generalization. And sociopolitical concerns are almost as important to him as are his scientific notions and his need to joke.

3 *world's champion gamblers*. See what we mean?

4 *untroubled existence of a bachelor*. There was a time, some forty years before he wrote this book, when Verne found the bachelor's life *very* troubling. Here he foreshadows another of his social concerns: the nature, advantages, and disadvantages of marriage, with his usual ambivalent swing from misogynist wisecrack to androgynous conceptions.

5 *because she was female*. The ambivalent swing in its misogyny phase.

7 *the wedding's off*. Verne is fascinated by characters who—for better or for worse—are obsessed with clock time (as distinguished from Bergson's psychological time). Most famous, of course, is Phileas Fogg, who calculates exactly how he can go *Around the World in Eighty Days* and then heroically improvises as chance, change, and the unexpected all stand in his way. One of Verne's earliest stories, "Master Zacharius," features a clockmaker who views the mainspring as analogous to the human soul. The prototype for such arithmetical living—from Zacharius to Fogg to Stanfort—is Verne's own father, Pierre. He knew the exact number of steps it took him to go to his office; on vacation he had a telescope trained on the clock of a nearby church steeple so that he could regulate his family's day precisely. On this as in most matters, Jules himself feels ambivalent, now revering time-fanatics, now satirizing them.

9 *money with . . . shrewdness*. When Proth "shifted his attention to the woman," he could indeed see for himself all that Verne reports in this paragraph. But our author continues with a second paragraph about her, almost nothing of which Proth could have known on his own. In other words, Verne is still working in the premodernist mode in which an author could blithely mix points of view—a character's and the author's—without fear of jarring the reader. Consider chapter 8 of *From the Earth to the Moon*. Barbicane is digesting his first impressions of Ar-

dan when somehow they drift off into things only Verne could know. Verne here continues a favorite practice of Fenimore Cooper, one of the Romanticists he was brought up on.

9 *said . . . of Mr. Stanfort.* The net effect of this transition is to make Arcadia the equal of Seth, yet another example of Verne's swinging from misogynist wisecrack to androgynous conceptions. That Arcadia's spirited independence could derive in part from her wealth is irrelevant. What's pertinent is that Verne can admire it *in a woman.* As we'll soon see, his admiration for female freedom (à la America) is not limited by economic considerations.

9 *March 27.* As Dumas observes, Verne's MS mistakenly gives the date here as October 29, forgetting that the novel's second paragraph says March 27. The SJV text corrects this slip, and our translation follows suit.

10 *Stanfort answered.* Curiously, the Archipel text (p. 23) reads *répondit Whaston.* Since Dumas doesn't attach a note here, this may be a production fluff rather than a slip in the MS.

10 *required fees.* It's doubtful that marriage licenses made out in Massachusetts and New Jersey would be valid in Virginia. Verne is enjoying his own license here as a writer of romantic comedy.

11 *get married as . . . divorced!* In his valuable preface to his 2002 Archipel edition of *La Chasse au météore,* Dumas sees Proth as "very likely a spokesman for the author."

As in some other works, like his *The Mighty Orinoco,* Verne launches his story with comic action involving only minor characters. We shall not meet the aristocratic couple again for many chapters. Nevertheless, they've served to introduce a major theme: Verne's view of American mores—e.g., their hardheaded punctuality, tendency to gambling, casual flexibility in a sacred ceremony, and enjoyment of individualism.

CHAPTER 2

12 *April 3.* According to Dumas, the MS gives November 3, the whole chapter being laid in early winter—a discrepancy ironed out subsequently by Michel and Hetzel fils.

13 *Harvard.* Verne's MS leaves the university name blank. Dumas is certain that Harvard is indicated, and our translation follows him.

13 *extinct species of servant.* Verne seems nostalgic here for the kind of master-servant relationship he portrayed in earlier novels. In *Five Weeks in a Balloon*, Dr. Ferguson's servant, Joe—and in *20,000 Leagues under the Sea*, Professor Aronnax's Conseil—unquestioningly risks his life for his master. In the latter especially Verne handles with great skill the psychological complexities that can develop in such associations. The professor, for example, comes to yearn for greater informality in his relations with Conseil, while that servant, for all his loyalty, wants to keep some distance from his boss. Mrs. Mitz, we soon see, is a variation on this so-called "dying breed" in that she represents the loyal opposition.

In his classic *The Political and Social Ideas of Jules Verne*, Jean Chesneaux argues well that Verne's "species of servant" can exist only in a middle-class setting, and that's the only setting in which Verne feels really comfortable.

14 *Omicron . . . Whiff.* The joke is that in the Greek alphabet, omicron is the small lowercase *o*, while omega is the capital uppercase *O*. Even in English the contrast is visible in the words "micro" and "mega." Watch Omicron for another example of Verne's handling of the master-servant relationship, especially its effect on Omicron's dignity. That his "moniker might well have been Omega" hints that Omicron has been undervalued.

In Verne's original, Omicron's "real name" is Tom Wif. The Grant Richards edition—a translation by Frederick Lawton of Michel's text—changes this to "Wife." Much as Verne loved risqué allusions, we feel he had no intention of making such a gross one here. But transliterating Wif into Whiff does satisfy a need to anglicize the name, and the suggestion of slight, brief gusts seems inoffensively relevant.

15 *some shooting star.* Verne often favors the term *bolide*, an exceptionally bright, explosive meteor also known as a "fireball."

20 *first week of April.* The MS says the end of October. As Dumas points out, Verne repeatedly misdates events in this chapter, giving October as the month and citing the onset of winter. This is the sort of inconsistency that editors and publishers appropriately correct. Michel and Hetzel fils did so, and our translation does likewise.

21 *Stanley Hudelson.* Forsyth's hated rival is the subject of another amus-

ing discrepancy in Verne's MS. Dr. Hudelson's first name is alternately given as "Stanley" and "Sydney." Since he's called the former more frequently than the latter (by a score of 22 to 7, according to our tally), we call him Stanley throughout.

CHAPTER 3

23 *not just astronomers*. This line can be understood to mean "Everybody (including Jules Verne) should have such a wife." For in his own mind, at least, his wife wasn't "a model partner." She was allegedly incapable of tolerating "her husband's foibles" or of encouraging him in his work. But note that the description of Mrs. Hudelson conforms to the old patriarchal model of a wife. Apparently she happily subordinates herself to her husband's every whim. She isn't an equal. We're reminded here of how Judge Proth—considered to be the author's spokesman or "chorus character"—marveled at how easy it is to get divorced in America.

25 *interesting theories*. Though Verne is being playful, modern criminologists take many of these theories seriously, since crime rates routinely show a spike during the warm-weather months: "over a hot summer, irritation caused by the heat has been cited by psychologists as a factor in the seasonal rise in violent crime" (Emma Brockes and Oliver Burkeman, "Blame it on the Sunshine," *The Guardian*, May 30, 2001).

26 *fifty-one stars*. Is this one of Verne's typically sarcastic remarks about American imperialism? Actually, at the time he was working on *The Meteor Hunt* (1901), he should have said *forty-five stars*. Utah had been admitted as the forty-fifth state in 1896. We have strong clues as to Verne's message in raising it to fifty-one. For example, in his futuristic novel *Propeller Island* (1895), Verne has described Old Glory as sporting *sixty-seven stars*! Reason? The United States had "annexed Canada right up to the Polar Sea, the provinces of Mexico, Honduras, Nicaragua, and Costa Rica right down to the Panama Canal." This was not incredible to Verne readers familiar with the doctrine of Manifest Destiny. The United States had already invaded Canada twice; absorbed Texas after its war with Mexico (a new star); defeated Mexico, converting some of its richest territories into six new states (six more stars); and now and then occupied other Latin American countries. And just before Verne

set pen to *The Meteor Hunt*, the United States had defeated the Spanish navy and annexed the Philippines and Cuba. According to Chesneaux, at the end of the nineteenth century "the minds of men" were preoccupied with such questions as "the destiny of the United States, for so long a mirage and already a danger" (*Social and Political Ideas of Jules Verne*, p. 21). So shooting stars weren't the only ones on Verne's mind.

26 *below twenty degrees Fahrenheit*. Verne: "seven or eight degrees below zero centigrade."

27 *been there*. As Dumas notes, the MS at this point shows the word *transporté* lined through and not replaced.

31 *April 3*. Here Verne straightens out some of his chronological difficulties. He has revised the inconsistent dates himself, as Dumas notes.

CHAPTER 4

34 *April 9*. At this point Verne's MS offers another piece of absentmindedness: he adds the year 1901, forgetting that his policy elsewhere has been to conceal the actual time and place of these events.

34 *27 Morris Street*. The SJV text reads "17 Morris Street," conflicting with the house number given in chapter 3.

CHAPTER 5

37 *friendly wave . . . Walker*. With just a few phrases, Verne deftly establishes a telling contrast. After giving us advance details of a religious wedding, he reminds us (literally, in passing) of the judge's recent secular ceremony.

39 *treetops*. Dumas notes that the MS leaves out the French qualifier for "tree," leaving *les têtes d'* [the tops of . . .] to be filled in later. Such writer's shorthand is safe. What else is likely to form "a vault of greenery overhead"?

40 *chilly relations*. Verne is now intertwining four plot strands: the relationship between the horsepeople; the judge's relation to his town; the astronomers' discovery and its consequences; and the romance between one astronomer's daughter and another's nephew. All four keep us in suspense, the first out of sight, the others more visible.

40 *fifty days . . . May 31*. Verne's MS gives "forty-five days" and "May 25,"

in conflict with the dating he gives in chapter 3 and chapter 7.

41 *Mt. Chimborazo.* Located in Ecuador, to be precise.

41 *the Alleghenies.* They stretch some five hundred miles from Pennsylvania to West Virginia, but not, as Verne suggests, as far as Georgia and Alabama.

41 *five or six thousand feet.* Verne: "fifteen or eighteen hundred meters."

CHAPTER 6

46 *twentieth century astronomy.* This opening paragraph is a splendid example of Verne's command of epideixis: deliberate, self-indulgent, show-offy attention to rhetoric. Here he uses the phrase "If ever" five times to introduce sentences that seem parallel but are actually variant in structure. Four sentences gradually zoom in from continent to nation to state to city, the fifth zooming out to a grand overview. This is ceremonial oratory with a musical-comedy rhythm and an ironic twist. And what irony! Tucked in the middle of this grand verbal structure is still another dig ("fifty-one states") at America's expansionism. Lovers of exhibitionist epideixis should see what Verne can whip up from mere facts about an ocean in his opening paragraph of part II, chapter 8 in *20,000 Leagues under the Sea.*

49 *old Aliboron.* In other words, each of our rival astronomers is stubborn as a mule. Verne alludes to Jean de la Fontaine's *Fables* (1668–1694) in which the great poet gives an obstinate jackass the name of Aliboron, from an Old French term designating a stupid person. Each of Fontaine's 230 fables is a short tale in verse about animals who, acting like men, serve to comment on human traits.

49 *Potentially visible.* But if you're in the country on your average dark night, far away from city lights and haze, you're lucky to spot five meteors per hour. You might see most of them for just a second or two. They light up only as they pass through—or burn up in—the earth's atmosphere. On rare occasions, meteors come in "showers," in bursts of up to fifty per hour. But more on those when Verne gets to them in chapter 8.

50 *American equivalents of Larousse.* Probably the best was *The American Cyclopædia* (New York: Appleton, 1871–1875). WJM uses many of its beautiful illustrations—of everything from a Dahlgren gun to Baltimore

as seen from Federal Hill—to add period flavor to *The Annotated Jules Verne: From the Earth to the Moon* (New York: Crowell, 1978; New York: Gramercy/Random House, 1995).

50 *these meteorites.* This is a good place to remind ourselves of the difference between meteors and meteorites. The "shooting stars" Verne has been discussing are meteors; those that hit the earth become meteorites.

51 *loving care in Mecca.* Not all experts agree that the Black Stone is of meteoric origin. It's built into the east wall of the Kaaba, the central shrine of Islam, within the Great Mosque of Mecca in Saudi Arabia. Because it has been touched and kissed over the centuries by millions of Muslim pilgrims, who regard it as their most sacred object, it has fragmented into three large and several smaller pieces, now held together by a silver band. An Islamic legend holds that it was white when given to Adam and has become blackened by absorbing the pilgrims' sins.

51 *Ensisheim.* This celebrated meteorite is believed to be the earliest *witnessed* fall in the Western world. Near noon on November 16, 1492, a young boy saw a large stone plummet from the sky into a wheat field near Ensisheim in France. He summoned townsfolk, some of whom looked on it as a supernatural sign. Many began to chip off souvenirs until, much later, the authorities saved the remainder for science and local fame. A 120-pound chunk is currently displayed in a glass case in the town hall. Fragments are exhibited all over the world, notably in the Arthur Ross Hall of Meteorites in New York's American Museum of Natural History. Some bits are still on sale, for example at http://www.naturesource.com.

51 *Seres in Macedonia.* Verne writes *Larini en Macédoine*. Seres seems to be indicated, since it was the site of a meteorite fall in June 1818.

51 *iron slag.* The SJV text gives *écume de fer*, but this may be a slip for *écume de mer*—sepiolite, also known as meerschaum, a white clayish mineral of hydrous magnesium silicate that's used in manufacturing the bowls of some tobacco pipes.

52 *nearly seven miles.* Verne: "eleven kilometers."

52 *our eyes.* This indicates that the description is a direct quote, yet the SJV text omits quotation marks around this passage. We've added them.

52 *25 miles.* Verne: "forty kilometers."

53 *12½ miles*. Verne: "five leagues." In Verne's usage here, one league equals four kilometers.

53 *1,500 pounds . . . 13,000 pounds*. Verne, respectively: "700 kilograms" and "6,000 kilograms."

53 *30,000 pounds . . . 41,000 pounds*. Verne, respectively: "14,000 kilograms" and "19,000 kilograms."

53 *Durango*. Twice spelled "Duranzo" in Verne's MS, but Dumas is sure that Durango is meant.

54 *astronomers in Pittsburgh and Cincinnati*. The SJV text reads *les astronomes de l'Ohio et de Cincinnati*. Since Dumas makes no comment, this may be a production slip.

CHAPTER 7

58 *bottomless supply of gasoline*. Aside from the neat joke, there are two possible readings of the last clause. One is that here, the Prophet of Science fails. If nothing else would date this book, this clause would. Verne is aware that since Edwin L. Drake discovered oil in Pennsylvania in 1859, America certainly appeared to have a "bottomless supply." But Verne doesn't foresee that the lone automobile expected in chapter 1 (a vehicle powered by refined oil) would multiply so fast! And that not too far into the twentieth century, America's gigantic oil companies would seek to supplement their native supply with Saudi Arabian imports. That soon the real question would become: Does even the whole world have "such a bottomless supply of gasoline"? Or, an alternative reading: Here the sarcastic Prophet knowingly ridicules those who believe the supply is bottomless. This would accord with the Verne we know as a successful forecaster, the creator of the Captain Nemo who warned us about overdrafts on Nature's bounty.

65 *Cerberus*. But the watchdog of the infernal regions—to whom Verne is comparing Mrs. Mitz—*was* male and had at least three ferocious heads (according to Homer and Virgil) or as many as fifty (Hesiod). Only heroes like Hercules and Orpheus could cope with such a monster, so Dean Forsyth also suffers from the analogy.

CHAPTER 8

68 *Stiegler. . . globetrotters*. Although the MS says "Ziegler," Dumas notes

that Verne is alluding to Gaston Stiegler, globetrotter and author of *Around the World in 63 Days* (Paris: Lacène, 1901). Among the "other globetrotters," Verne is alluding, of course, to Nelly Bly (byline of Elizabeth Cochran) who circumnavigated the earth in seventy-two days in 1889-1890 and wrote it all up for the *New York World*. Her stories included a colorful, gracious account of her visit to the Vernes in Amiens, a side trip made at the risk of missing a connection and losing several days! On January 26, 1890, a first-page sidebar story about Bly's visit with Verne was topped with headlines like: *The French Romancer in Ecstasy Over the Achievement of 'The World's' Voyager* and *His Phileas Fogg Outdone*. Why has Verne mentioned Stiegler by name and not Bly? "Other globetrotters" is a humorous way of referring to somebody who doesn't *need* to be named: "You know who!"

69 *frequency . . . meteor showers.* Unlike the great Leonid Meteor Shower of 1833—which incidentally was visible to all of North America—many smaller showers can be counted on to make annual reappearances, that is, when the earth passes through certain swarms of particles that intersect its orbit. These showers are named after the constellations they appear to come from: the Lyrids (about April 21) from Lyra; the Perseids (August 12?), Perseus; Orionids (October 20?), Orion; the Taurids (November 4?), Taurus; Leonids (November 16), Leo; Geminids (December 13?), Gemini. Some of these "rain" up to fifty meteors per hour. Usually the most spectacular are the Showers of Perseus, which may deliver more than one hundred shooting stars in one hour.

70 *some 125 miles.* As Dumas observes, the MS features several figure slips in this vicinity. Here Verne gives the equivalent of sixteen to eighteen miles ("twenty-six to thirty kilometers"), which is contradicted by the two paragraphs immediately following.

70 *March 14, 1863.* The SJV text gives 1864, exactly two months before the Castillon meteor. This seems to be a slip: chapter 11 gives the year as 1863.

70 *40 miles per second, in other words, 2,400 miles per minute, or over 140,000 miles per hour.* Verne: "65 kilometers per second, hence 3,900 kilometers per minute, hence 5,800 leagues per hour." In the SJV text the figure given for leagues seems to be a slip for the round figure 58,000.

70 *a little better than 1,000 miles per hour.* This corrects yet another figure

slip. Verne initially puts the meteor's speed at "400 to 410 kilometers per hour," or about 250 to 255 miles per hour. In the very next paragraph he increases this speed to the more plausible 420 leagues (i.e., 1,680 kilometers) per hour, or 1,044 mph. Our translation favors this last figure.

70 *the Dhaulagiri and the Chomo Lhari.* Dumas notes that the MS spells these "Dawalagiri" and "Chamalari." He goes on to cite the former's elevation as 26,811 feet (8,172 meters) and the latter's as 23,996 feet (7,314 meters), while noting that Mt. Everest is higher than both at 29,028 feet (8,848 meters).

70 *33,000 feet.* Verne: 10,000 meters.

70 *faster than 1,000 miles per hour.* As noted above, Verne's second figure for the meteor's speed is 420 leagues (i.e., 1,680 kilometers) per hour, which, if not rounded down, converts to 1,044 miles per hour.

70 *about 125 miles above the earth's surface.* Verne: "200 kilometers."

70 *125 miles up.* Verne: "50 leagues" (i.e., 200 kilometers).

71 *1,500 to 2,000 feet across.* Verne: "five or six hundred meters."

71 *eleven miles up.* Verne: "eighteen kilometers."

73 *coma.* A luminous cloud of dust and gases.

76 *going out by herself.* Such female behavior was unthinkable in France at the time of the action—so Olivier Dumas emphasizes in his Preface to his 2002 French edition. It's to Verne's credit that he, so often dubbed a "misogynist," can expansively admire the American girl's "complete freedom." One of Michel Verne's most audacious distortions occurs here: in his semiforged edition he deletes this passage as he indeed cuts many of his father's refreshing reactions to American mores. Note that here Jules's ambivalence about women has swung again toward belief in androgyny and equality of the sexes. So far he has praised Loo's mother for her conformity to the patriarchal ideal and now admires Loo herself for being the antithesis. This whole situation, of a clash between cultures, reminds us of the novella *Daisy Miller,* by Verne's near contemporary, Henry James (1843–1916).

CHAPTER 9

79 *366 days of the sidereal year.* Today usually cited as 365 days, 6 hours, 9 minutes, and 9½ seconds.

80 *bowie knives . . . revolvers.* Like many Europeans, Verne saw the bowie knife as symbolizing an American penchant for ready violence. Ten to fifteen inches long, more than an inch wide, it is single-edged except for its double-edged point. According to *The American Cyclopædia* (1871), Texas Army Colonel James Bowie popularized it (!) by using it in a duel with "terrible effect." It's not clear whether this dagger is named after the colonel or its putative inventor, his brother Rezin Bowie. Verne sometimes sees this weapon as the American male's vade mecum. During a meeting of the Baltimore Gun Club (chapter 1, *From the Earth to the Moon*), Tom Hunter is "hacking the arm of his chair with his Bowie knife." As acceptable as chewing tobacco! Later in the same novel, Verne writes a dramatic version of the savage "Kentucky duel," settled by an allegedly more humane Frenchman: Ardan.

82 *Some thirty miles.* Verne: "fifty kilometers."

82 *remains in a solid state.* This is a big problem that should, right off, make this "news item" *bad* news. For, as metals go, gold has a relatively low melting point—a mere 1,948° Fahrenheit or even lower. Now, isn't the meteor's temperature rising because of the friction it encounters in resistance from the earth's air? As a matter of fact, how has it been able to survive so long in our atmosphere? Meteors composed of other elements obviously have a better chance: iron doesn't melt until it hits 2,795° Fahrenheit, and carbon 6,422°! That's why some of those ferrous or carbonaceous meteors can drop down even farther into denser air and sometimes even reach the earth and qualify as meteorites. So what future does Verne's "shooting star" really have? Do any of his experts in Boston and elsewhere really know how high a meteor's melting point must be for it to be making this trip? Does their science yet have all the data needed to grasp this situation? We'll find out.

CHAPTER 10

85 *a whole century . . . to count to a billion.* This assertion seems a little exaggerated. The same question has been posed more recently on Drexel University's prestigious Math Forum located at http://mathforum.org/library/drmath/view/58739.html, where it receives the following answer: "Counting non-stop, at one number a second, it would take you

31 years, 251 days, 7 hours, 46 minutes, and 39 seconds to count to 1 billion." But maybe Proth is just being his usual realistic self: what human could count non-stop for 31 years or even 31 hours? How about breaks for sleep, meals, and the restroom?

By the way, here and elsewhere Verne uses the word *milliard*, French for one thousand millions, which is what most Americans now define as a billion. In his day, throughout much of Europe, "billion" was the word for one *million* millions. Today, with American finance packing a worldwide influence, American usage (a billion is one thousand millions) is becoming standard.

90 *famous Walter Wragge*. Verne spells his surname "Vragg."

90 *some three to three and one-half miles up*. Verne: "five to six thousand meters."

91 *A hot air balloon . . . crowd*. With just a few scattered phrases, Verne catches the gracefulness and caprices of a balloon in flight. Writing in 1901, he must have been thinking back over his fifty years of close association with lighter-than-air craft. It was in 1851 that he published his first balloon story. Then he started to hang out with one of the most remarkable persons of his day—Gaspard-Felix Tournachon (1820–1910), better known to history as Nadar, a truly great photographer and pioneer balloonist. He and Verne worked together on what turned out to be one of the greatest publicity campaigns ever. First Nadar helped Verne sell his novel *Five Weeks in a Balloon*, which in 1863 became an instant bestseller in both the adult and juvenile markets. And Nadar exhibited, in the center of the Champ-de-Mars, his balloon *Le Géant*, a huge silvery pear from which hung a two-story wicker basket. Of course Verne's novel, the talk of the town, helped focus attention on Nadar's first flight on October 4, 1863. Thousands of Parisians crowded the field to watch Nadar and his celebrity passengers rise over Paris and drift to the east. That night they wined and dined aloft and descended in Meaux, twenty-five miles away. And of course, Nadar's flights increased Verne's sales—a perfect symbiotic interaction.

While writing about Wragge in 1901, Verne must also have mused over Nadar's taking the first-ever aerial photographs, from a balloon 260 feet above the Bievre Valley, and Nadar's setting up a balloon postal system to get French messages out of Paris when it was surrounded by Prussian troops in 1870. Verne's fondest associations, though, must have been of the day he was working on *From the Earth to the Moon* and modeled his character Ardan (who saves the American militarists from themselves) after his bluff, giant friend Nadar.

92 *piece of heroism.* When we first met them, Seth and Arcadia acted like very unconventional people. And now, in a masterful bit of comedy, Verne has them reverting to traditional values. Seth no longer wants a woman as independent as himself; Arcadia wants a protector, a man more heroic than herself. That is, in certain ways, neither of them now wants an equal for a mate. Is Verne just spoofing egalitarianism? This time his swing of ambivalence is away from androgyny. One way or the other, this passage proves to be one of his best pieces of vaudeville dialogue.

93 *untied than tied.* Verne now echoes what Judge Proth said as the punchline of chapter 1, reinforcing our feeling that Proth is Verne's spokesman (or "chorus character").

96 *philosophically . . . garden.* Verne is making it clear that we might see Proth as Candide at middle age. In Voltaire's novel *Candide* the eponymous hero (and classic naïf) and his philosophy tutor, Pangloss (all glosses!) are hounded by disasters from one country to another. At the end they settle down on a farm. Pangloss, a disciple of Leibnitz, still insists that all's for the best in this best of all possible worlds. The now-wiser Candide simply answers: "We must cultivate our garden."

What does Voltaire's ending mean? Work is more rewarding than abstract speculation? Work is our antidote to our unhappy lot? Return to the simple life—it gives us better perspective? We should start over—"drop out"—and attempt only what we can really comprehend and control?

Now we can understand better what Verne meant, in chapter 1, when he called Proth "a man of no ambition." It was a compliment! Limiting himself to what he can do best, saving himself time for reflection, he is admired by the townspeople for his balance, tolerance, and fairness.

CHAPTER 11

98 *price of sunglasses.* Dumas notes that the MS omits the qualifier for

"sun," and that Michel's rewrite misconstrues this substantive as "optical glasses."

99 *barely twenty miles*. Verne: "some thirty kilometers."

99 *about thirty feet across*. Verne: "ten meters."

99 *over forty-one hundred tons . . . over eleven thousand tons*. Verne, respectively: "3,763 metric tons" and "10,083 metric tons."

99 *more than six billion dollars*. Verne: "thirty-one billion francs." Our renderings translate Verne's francs into American currency using the conversion rate of five francs to a dollar, a rate consistent through most of the nineteenth century and into the early twentieth, according to *Gold and Silver Standards* at http://www.cyberussr.com/hcunn/gold-std.html.

However Verne's MS—mirrored by the SJV text—immediately makes an additional comment, and since our translation favors conversions for the benefit of U.S. readers, we've chosen to present this comment as an endnote: "As you can see, the *Whaston Daily Standard* was up with the latest trends and was working out its calculations using the metric system. Because back then Americans had already started to adopt this system, and instead of dollars and yards were using francs and meters." Alas, this Vernian prediction went wide of the mark. Needless to say, francs haven't replaced dollars, and aside from scientists comparatively few American readers are fluent in metric weights and measures. In fact The U.S. Metric Association at http://lamar.colostate.edu/~hillger/ notes that only three countries have still not adopted the metric system, Liberia, Burma, and the United States: in short, "among countries with nonmetric usage the U.S. is the *only significant holdout*."

101 *over 1,350 feet . . . over 1,600 feet*. Verne, respectively: "420 meters" and "500 meters."

101 *300 feet*. Verne: "a hundred meters."

101 *over 4,100,000 tons . . . over 11,000,000 tons*. Verne, respectively: "3,763,585 metric tons" and "10,083,488, metric tons."

101 *over six trillion two hundred and fifty billion dollars*. Verne: "31 trillion 260 billion francs."

101 *divvied up . . . human race*. Kate raises a question that not even the United Nations has an answer for today. If a golden meteor could even exist

and hit the planet, is it a *planetary* property? Is all humanity involved? We're conditioned, by our economic system, to think that natural resources—oil, gold, silver—belong to the persons on whose property they're discovered, after having been there all the time. But suppose a natural resource from outer space is newly added to the property? It's not hard to realize that in some Utopias, the meteorite would become the people's. Kate, the simple housekeeper, has posed a Utopian notion. What will the population of Verne's world think of this?

101 *forty-two hundred dollars per person.* Verne: "21,000 francs."

102 *broke as . . . before.* This sounds like the old argument management used to pose against reducing the number of hours in the workweek. People would go "drinking and partying." Employers were doing society a favor by keeping workers tied down to a job and out of trouble. Actually—after the workweek was reduced from sixty to forty hours—most people used their new freedom for *productive* leisure (reading, movies, education), which helped create new industries and new jobs. Here our Voltairean judge slips up in his wisdom, using what "many people" might do against what the majority would do.

102 *thirty and one-half inches.* Verne: "777 millimeters."

103 *the U.S. Naval Observatory.* Its website may be found at http://www.usno.navy.mil, where it describes itself as "one of the oldest scientific agencies in the country. Established in 1830 as the Depot of Charts and Instruments, its primary mission was to care for the U.S. Navy's chronometers, charts, and other navigational equipment." Vernians have a special affection for the USNO. Matthew Maury, who was placed in command of the Depot in 1842, is one of the idols of the characters in *20,000 Leagues.* Captain Nemo and Professor Aronnax often discuss Maury's *Physical Geography of the Sea* (1855), the first classic work of modern oceanography.

103 *exactly 164 feet.* Verne: "fifty meters."

104 *1,389,393 tons.* Verne: "1,260,436 metric tons."

104 *over 781 billion dollars.* Verne: "3 trillion 907 billion francs."

104 *about $530.* Verne: "2,650 francs." Needless to say, the purchasing power of these dollars would be many times greater in the twenty-first century.

105 *challenging . . . to a duel.* The American penchant for formal dueling has

died out just a decade before Verne writes this passage. His fear that the two astronomers might resort to swords or pistols actually shows us how high both men have risen in public esteem. For in the heyday of prearranged combat between two persons, only aristocrats, military officers, and congressmen and other politicians were expected to "defend their honor" by issuing or accepting written challenges—and they would disdain fighting their social inferiors!

Between 1798 and the Civil War, for example, the U.S. Navy lost two-thirds as many officers in formal duels as in combat with national enemies! Even many major politicians who opposed dueling in principle (Alexander Hamilton, Henry Clay, Sam Houston) felt required to accept challenges, because ignoring them might darken their political future. Hamilton paid the price in New Jersey on the same grounds where one of his sons also died in a duel.

Most American duels, however, were fought below the Mason-Dixon Line. New Orleans—famous for its grove of "dueling oaks"—probably enjoyed more displays of ritualized murder than any other American city.

As Verne well knew, dueling might have reached its peak in America but had its origins in Europe. During the reign (1760–1820) of King George III, at least 172 duels were staged in England. France's hundreds of well-choreographed duels included at least one *fought over Paris in balloons*! And it was well known that many German students aspired to sport scarred cheeks. But it's hard to imagine our two "normally civil" astronomers going that far. (For more information on this bloody subject, see the Duelling Oaks Web site at http://www.duellingoaks. com/oaks and also Ross Drake's excellent article in *Smithsonian*, March 2004.)

106 *one thousand miles per hour*. Verne: 28 kilometers per minute. See note for p. 70 "a little better than 1,000 miles per hour."

106 *an extra powerful cannon . . . French novelist*. As Dumas notes, Verne is waggishly plugging two of his earlier novels about Yankee ingenuity, *From the Earth to the Moon* and *Topsy Turvy*.

107 *519,000 tons*. Verne: "471,000 metric tons."

108 *fall to the earth*. A splendid cliffhanger chapter close, for Verne's day at

least. In our notes for chapter 9, though, we pointed out that a golden meteor couldn't remain in a solid state if it dropped very far into our atmosphere. For the melting point of gold is too low for it to survive the friction of our air and reach the earth. We also asked whether Verne's scientists knew how high a meteor's melting point has to be for it to make that trip. Obviously they didn't. So from now on, for readers today, the problem can simply be rephrased: What if a meteor composed of a substance of overwhelming economic value *could* hit our planet?

CHAPTER 12

109 *New York Herald.* The *Herald* was founded in 1835, absorbed by the *New York Tribune* in 1924, and in between figured prominently in Verne's "American" fiction: the Baltimore Gun Club (*From the Earth to the Moon, Around the Moon*) sold this newspaper the full story of its lunar journey; Professor Aronnax (*20,000 Leagues under the Sea*) published in its pages his view that the "enormous thing" terrorizing ships worldwide was a giant narwhale; Gideon Spilett (*The Mysterious Island*) was a war correspondent on the *Herald* staff; and its investigative reporters probed the sinister doings of Dr. Schultze in the Pacific northwest (*The Begum's Millions*). In 1885 Verne actually did a little business with this paper, when *Herald* editor Gordon Bennett commissioned him to write a futuristic short story about America. The *Herald-Tribune* put out its last American issue in 1966 but survives today in an international edition published in Paris.

115 *Solomon . . . two mothers.* Verne invokes a nearly perfect comparison. Certainly, on that historic day somewhere around 968 BC, Solomon's court must have hushed up fast as everybody strained to hear the wise king's decision. One of the two women had claimed that the other had lost her own new baby during the night and had substituted her dead infant for the new baby of the plaintiff. While the audience held its breath, Solomon decided on an extreme tactic to see if the real mother could prove herself. He ordered that the infant in the defendant's arms be sliced in two and divided between the "two mothers." As Solomon expected, the plaintiff proved herself by offering to give the baby to the false mother rather than see it die. But the case goes on! Some pun-

dits claim Solomon's tactic wouldn't necessarily have worked so well. Mightn't the false mother realize she had to act like the real one, and make the same offer? Just search the web using keywords like "Solomon, two mothers" and you'll find that even game theory becomes invoked.

116 *divided up between you.* Our author slyly continues to exploit his "two mothers" analogy by echoing Solomon's solution.

117 *phonograph player.* Instead of *appareil phonographique*, the sJV text gives *photographique*, apparently a typo.

118 *enormity.* After bowie-knife duels and "American-style shootouts," Verne now adds a notorious type of mob action to his catalogue of U.S. horrors.

118 *irreparable rift.* Verne admired the music of German composer Richard Wagner (1813–1883), whose comic opera set in Renaissance Germany, *The Master Singers of Nuremberg* (1868), easily could have furnished a model for the rambunctious scene just concluded. In the opera's second act, its two squabbling savants set off an outrageous street riot and all Nuremberg goes crazy, much as we've seen just now with Verne's Whaston.

CHAPTER 13

120 *twenty-five miles . . . eighteen miles.* Verne, respectively: "forty kilometers" and "thirty kilometers." In a footnote Dumas suggests that these figures are slips. Actually Verne has had repeated difficulties tracking the meteor's distance from the earth. In chapter 7 he seems to give that distance as 125 miles overhead (200 kilometers, or 50 leagues), which was an immediate correction of his initial estimate of 16 to 18 miles (26 to 30 kilometers). Verne's latest estimate prior to the present chapter occurs in chapter 9: there he gives the meteor's distance as 30 miles overhead (50 kilometers). Apparently this distance has been discreetly shrinking all along. By chapter 13 Verne has gone full circle and ended up back at his original estimate of 18 miles.

121 *Cybele . . . Attis.* The sJV text links Cybele with the Roman god Saturn, and so do many reference books. The ambiguity is understandable. Before Cybele—one of the many names of the Great Mother of the Gods—became a wife of Saturn, she had a notorious affair with

Attis (Attes, Atys), who had introduced her worship to Asia Minor.

122 *Antarctic . . . largely unexplored.* Verne had no idea how relevant Antarctica would become to his question of "Who owns the meteor? Why not divide it up?" Antarctica is the only continent without a native population and still the least populated. Its vulnerability to unilateral exploitation prompted twelve nations to sign, in 1959 in Washington, D.C., the Antarctic Treaty, which makes the continent a demilitarized zone preserved for scientific research: "Any activity relating to mineral resources, other than scientific research, shall be prohibited." Each signatory is required to file annual reports on its Antarctic activities; the United States does so through its National Science Foundation. As a matter of fact, in 1990 the U.S. Congress proposed creating an Antarctica World Park! Then, the following year, Keith Suter published his *Antarctica: Private Property or Public Heritage?* For the first word in Suter's title we just substitute *Meteor* and we have Verne's ownership theme succinctly restated.

123 *uninhabited and would stay that way.* But according to *The CIA World Factbook*, although Antarctica has "no indigenous inhabitants . . . approximately 27 nations, all signatory to the Antarctic Treaty, send personnel to perform seasonal (summer) and year-round research on the continent and in its surrounding oceans; the population of persons doing and supporting science [will vary] from approximately 4,000 in summer to 1,000 in winter."

123 *devoutly desired . . . South Pole.* Just a decade after Verne is writing this line, the Norwegian Roald Amundsen will reach the southern end of the earth's axis on December 14, 1911. And just a month after Amundsen's party leaves the pole, his rival, British Captain R. F. Scott, will make it too. But Scott's party will all perish on the return trip.

In 1926, flying in a dirigible with the Italian aeronautics engineer Umberto Nobile, Amundsen will pass over the North Pole (reputedly discovered by Robert Peary in 1909). In 1928 Nobile's airship will crash near Spitzbergen. Flying to rescue Nobile in a plane that also crashes, Amundsen will die in the Arctic at age 56.

In Verne's fictional world, though, his Captain Nemo claims to be the first to reach the South Pole. In part II, chapter 14 of *20,000 Leagues*

Nemo orates a long list of explorers who never made it: from Captain James Cook, who got as far as latitude 67° south in 1773, to Sir James Clark Ross, 78° in 1842. Then Nemo climaxes his speech: "And now, professor, on March 21, 1868, I myself, Captain Nemo, have reached the South Pole at 90°."

123 *Albemarle, Chatham, Norfolk.* Today Albemarle and Chatham are known as Isla Isabella and Isla San Cristobal. Verne's reference to Norfolk is puzzling since this island lies off Australia, over ten thousand miles away from the other two. Maybe Verne was thinking of Darwin's voyage aboard the *Beagle,* and the islands on her itinerary had gotten mixed up in his mind.

124 *three million dollars.* Verne: 15,000,000 francs.

124 *5,675 square miles.* Verne: 147 square myriameters.

124 *eight degrees.* Dumas notes that the number of degrees is left blank in the MS.

124 *French cruise ship to Suez.* According to the SJV transcription of Verne's MS, the vessel's embarkation point is left blank (*sur un paquebot à X . . .*). This is the second blank spot relating to Afghanistan—maybe Verne's extensive home library let him down and he hadn't gotten around to the outside research.

125 *haughty representative of a nation.* In Verne's hit-and-run talk of the "pigheaded" American, the "lordly" Briton, and other delegates, we hear echoes of his belief in "national characteristics" that we discussed in our very first note.

126 *close to eight hundred billion dollars.* Verne: "four trillion francs."

126 *never have to pay taxes again.* If not all the nations working together, at least one country plans to "divvy up" the way Kate imagined it could be done.

127 *a radius of eighty-two feet.* Verne: "25 meters."

130 *a fraction.* As Dumas notes, the MS seems to be unfinished here. It doesn't specify an exact figure but only supplies a blank number cubed: $(\ldots)^3$.

130 *their gold deposits.* Verne, of course, gives all sums in this paragraph in francs. See the note attached to p. 99 for our conversion policy; to arrive at Verne's original totals in francs, simply multiply the dollar amounts by five. But whether in dollars or francs, Verne's numbers don't entirely jibe. Was he simply giving rough estimates? Could some of the figures

contain typos? Are entries missing (such as totals for Spain or Scandinavia)? The cause of the discrepancies isn't clear.

CHAPTER 14

132 *1,650-ton ship*. Verne: "1,500 metric tons."

132 *belonging to Denmark*. In Verne's day, and until 1953 when it became a protectorate. Greenland attained home rule in 1979 and full self-government in 1981. But it is still described in the *Columbia Encyclopedia* as "an autonomous territory under the protection of the kingdom of Denmark."

133 *oversized island*. Actually, the largest island in the world.

133 *Parry, Nansen*. Sir William Edward Parry (1790–1855) led several searches for a Northwest Passage to the Orient, as well as efforts to reach the North Pole. Fridtjof Nansen (1861–1930) was a Norwegian explorer, oceanographer, and humanitarian who won the Nobel Peace Prize. He will figure again in the story.

133 *capital city of this Danish possession*. Upernavik, population 3,000, sits on Melville Bay on the northwest coast of Greenland. As Dumas points out, Verne is mistaken in calling it the country's capital city: "The current capital of Greenland is Nuuk (formerly Godthåb)."

134 *big names . . . in astronomy*. Like Hudelson and Forsyth, Sir William Herschel started out as an amateur astronomer, but unlike them, he became a full-time professional. After he discovered a new planet, later named Uranus, he was appointed King's Astronomer (1782). Dominique François Arago (1785–1853) wrote the classic *Astronomie Populaire* (1862). Urbaine Jean Leverrier (1811–1872) is considered to be codiscoverer (along with John Couch Adams) of the planet Neptune. Just as we can't mention Dr. Hudelson's work without giving some credit to Tom (Omicron) Whiff, we must acknowledge it was Leverrier's assistant, Johann Galle, who actually first saw Neptune—but right where his employer told him to look.

135 *shrewd . . . Danes*. Now it's their turn to suffer from Verne's belief in national characteristics. See our notes on this in chapters 1 and 13.

136 *twenty-six hundred nautical miles*. "or around 5,000 kilometers," the French adds. The alternative figures are typical of Verne's style throughout his career. Unless South Carolina hadn't gone metric, as, back in

chapter 11, the author's MS claims the rest of the United States had.

137 *Schleswig-Holstein.* Denmark had sold these duchies to Prussia in 1866.

137 *thirty-two billion dollars.* Verne: "160 billion francs."

138 *Canada's current capital.* Not true, as Dumas points out: "Queen Victoria made Ottawa the capital in 1858." But Taves in a private communication to FPW/WJM suggests: "Verne deliberately chose Toronto as the capital for the same reason he gave the U.S. flag 51 stars—a bit of forecast. Toronto was the nearest large Canadian city Verne had approached on his single North American visit, recounted in *A Floating City.* The memory of Niagara proved so durable that over two decades later he laid pivotal episodes there: the hero and heroine in *Family without a Name* go over the cataract in a fiery ship, while Robur flies out of Niagara into the air by transforming the *Terror* from a ship into an airplane. Given its proximity to the United States and Niagara, the promulgation of Toronto as the capital is hardly an accident or error."

139 *semaphores on shore.* A semaphore station is a building on shore with which a passing ship can communicate by visible means. For example, the semaphore apparatus may consist of a post with pivoted arms at the top. A signalman can indicate each letter of the alphabet by a different arrangement of the arms. Or he can use his own arms, maybe with small flags, as indicators. For a landlubber, the simplest analogy is the railroad semaphore we may see at the side of the tracks. It has just one arm with three possible positions: vertical means "clear"; horizontal, "stop"; inclined halfway, "caution."

141 *Lindenau.* Verne spells it "Lichtenau."

141 *radius of twelve to fifteen miles.* Verne: "five- or six-league radius."

143 *the mainland.* Verne writes "the American continent." Geologically, Greenland is part of the Canadian Shield and hence part of North America. It was on this basis that the United States—after the Nazi occupation of Denmark in 1940—invoked the Monroe Doctrine and established military bases in Greenland.

CHAPTER 15

144 *definitely didn't work.* But we know now, as wasn't widely known in Verne's day, that it *did* work. In 985 AD., after advertising his misnamed

discovery among Norsemen in Europe, Erik led some 400 people (in some 14 ships) to colonize Greenland. By 1100, as Vatican records show, the new settlers had enough believers to constitute a bishopric and build a cathedral. By the late twelfth century their number reached 10,000. But, for mysterious reasons, by 1500 the Norse Christian settlements died out. Had ice masses overwhelmed them? Were they wiped out by illnesses like tuberculosis brought in by the immigrants? Were they absorbed into the Inuit aboriginal culture? In any event, ruins of churches and monasteries of that period still survive. A second wave of European colonization didn't begin until 1721.

Despite Verne's stand-up comedy, Erik the Red *did* have red hair. He fathered Leif Ericsson, usually credited with having "discovered America," and he set up short-lived colonies west of Greenland.

144 *doesn't amount to much more than ten thousand.* It would have to be mainly from the second wave and the Inuits. In a July 2005 estimate, *The CIA World Factbook* puts Greenland's current population at 56,375.

144 *get within reach of it.* The main problem is that the entire interior of Greenland is covered with a great ice cap, "the inland ice."

145 *Whymper . . . Nansen.* The Englishman Edward Whymper (1840–1911), who in 1865 became the first person to climb the Matterhorn, surveyed the problems of scaling the Greenland ranges a second time in 1872. The Swede Adolf Erick, Baron Nordenskiöld (1832–1902), led his 1870 expedition 35 miles inland to an elevation of 2,200 feet, then walked 70 miles inland in 1883. Five years earlier, the Danish captain Jens Arnold Dietrich Jensen had gotten 45 miles inland to reach 5,400 feet. These three explorers penetrated from the west coast. But the Norwegian Fridtjof Nansen (1861–1930) tried it from the east. He made the first complete crossing of the inland ice, over the cap at 8,992 feet. He became the League of Nations High Commissioner for Refugees and won the Nobel Peace Prize in 1922.

145 *6,500 to 10,000 feet.* Verne: "two to three thousand meters."

145 *forty to eighty degrees below zero.* Verne: "−40° to −60° centigrade."

145 *twenty-six and one-half tons.* Verne: "24 metric tons."

145 *Lincoln Sea.* Verne identifies this body of water as *l'océan de Nares*, presumably because it laps the shores of Nares Land.

145 *sixty-four degrees Fahrenheit.* Verne: "18° centigrade."

146 *favor this corner of the world.* Dumas notes that in the MS, Verne originally wrote, then neglected to strike out: *are most willing to fall on* this corner of the world.

147 *twenty-five miles.* Verne: "10 leagues."

147 *three to six thousand feet.* Verne: "one or two thousand meters."

148 *red and white colors.* Dumas notes that Verne's MS leaves the colors blank.

148 *may amount to around twenty thousand.* Oddly, the opening paragraph of this chapter puts the population at half that.

148 *over twenty pounds.* Verne: "ten kilograms."

149 *New World colonies.* Including the Danish West Indies, some one hundred small islands east of Puerto Rico. The United States purchased them in 1917 for twenty-five million dollars because of their strategic position near the Panama Canal. The largest islands are St. Croix, St. Thomas, and St. John.

150 *didn't get above the mid-thirties.* Verne: "wasn't more than a few degrees above zero centigrade."

151 *seemed to be up there.* Dumas notes that "be up there," or some such wording, is missing in the MS but needed for sense.

151 *fifty-one stars . . . flag.* For Verne's purpose in exaggerating the number of stars in Old Glory, see our notes for chapters 3 and 6.

156 *three hundred feet.* Verne: "half a cable length."

CHAPTER 16

158 *our rights . . . concurred.* How subtly Verne has had each man shift from *my* to *our* rights, and from disagreeing to agreeing. It reminds us to pay detailed attention to his dialogue. Listen to Seth and Arcadia especially.

158 *forty-six to forty-eight degrees Fahrenheit.* Verne: "8° to 9° centigrade."

158 *a good couple of miles.* Verne: "one whole league."

160 *achieving happiness.* Arcadia is surely aware she's playing Pollyanna here. More important, she's talking not only to Francis but also to Seth. Verne has had more than comic reasons for developing the parallel plot of the Seth-Arcadia marriage. He wants to make the point that getting married should be a less impulsive and more felt-through experience. We cannot

escape the feeling that he is reflecting on his own hasty (almost desperate) decision to marry Honorine, for which mistake there was no such easy correction as Arcadia and Seth have had.

160 *nearly two miles . . . about three thousand feet.* Verne, respectively: "three-quarters of a league . . . 1,000 meters."

160 *barely a third of a mile.* Verne: "⅛ of a league."

160 *hit the ground.* Today scientists know that if he'd been that close to the actual impact, he would have died instantly.

161 *less than a quarter of a mile.* Verne: "500 paces."

161 *melting point.* As we now know, because of gold's low melting point, the meteor would have evaporated long before it could reach the ground.

162 *edge of the plateau.* Actually, the meteor's hitting the plateau at terminal speed should have dug a crater at least a mile across.

162 *twenty-five feet.* Verne: "ten paces."

162 *140 degrees Fahrenheit.* Verne: 60° centigrade.

162 *sixty-below temperatures.* Verne: "temperatures of −50° centigrade."

164 *four or five hundred yards.* Verne: "four or five hundred meters."

164 *fifty feet.* Verne: "twenty paces."

164 *eleven hundred tons.* Verne: "1,000 metric tons."

166 *hollered both of them.* Again, Verne stresses how adversity is drawing the rivals back together.

166 *a good eighty yards.* Verne: "a hundred paces."

168 *eight-hundred-billion-dollar meteor.* The SJV text values it at "four billion" francs, a slip for four *trillion* (see chapters 11 and 13).

CHAPTER 17

169 *a red cent.* The odds that a meteor of gold, with its low melting point, would make it through our atmosphere are even slimmer: invisible, actually.

170 *crowns.* According to Dumas, the MS has a word scratched out here, which he has replaced with "crowns."

173 *"be seeing you!"* But doesn't Verne leave us with the feeling that this time it's more likely to last? After all, the moral of this subplot has been that it's advisable for lovers to wait until they've had enough self-

understanding and mutual experience before they get married. Surely by now Seth and Arcadia have had more than enough of both. But Verne's handling of this strand of his story is just part of our larger discussion of his literary maneuvers in our afterword.

AFTERWORD

Working on *The Meteor Hunt* in his seventies, Verne demonstrated that he had lost none of his talent for *looking far ahead*—for prophecy. But it was his *looking back* on the sadness of his own life and on the human condition generally that provided him with much of his material. His bleak experiences and opinions also dictated his tone. He resorted to black humor to get through so much of the sadness, making us chuckle or laugh to save us from the full impact of human fallibility.

OMENS OF DISASTER

His prophecy in this novel is simply that we as a people are probably unprepared for perhaps the greatest catastrophe that could hit us and our habitat. As WJM/FPW said in their Naval Institute Press edition of *20,000 Leagues under the Sea*, "Verne's dreams—including some of his nightmares—will pop up in the news with greater regularity as astronomers fine-tune their tools for spotting and tracking killer comets and asteroids."

Just three years after Verne's death (1905), at 7:17 a.m. on June 30, 1908, a stony meteor, probably smaller than the one featured in *The Meteor Hunt*, exploded low in the air over Tunguska, Siberia. It burst with a force of about seventy Hiroshima-sized atom bombs, or one of today's larger H-bombs. Fortunately, this happened over a wild forest, over an area half the size of New York City, a forest that it devastated as it would have devastated the city itself. Reindeer herders and hunters camping 20 miles away were knocked unconscious. Windows shattered 40 miles away. People 110 miles south saw a mysterious, sun-bright fireball and heard roaring noises. Others 300 miles away saw fiery clouds on the horizon. And 600 miles distant from the explosion, scientists recorded seismic vibrations. But they couldn't assemble all the facts for another eighty-five years.

It wasn't until January 7, 1993, that the *New York Times* could run a full account under the headline: "Study Finds Asteroid Leveled Siberian Area." (So much is now known that William K. Hartmann has ventured a series of paintings of the event [see the Planetary Science Institute Web site, http://www.psi.edu/projects/siberia/siberia/html]). And in that same 1992-93 winter, the *Times* reported repeatedly on other situations similar to those Verne had prophesied in *Hector Servadac* and *The Meteor Hunt*: "Big Comet May Strike Earth in August 2126." A week later the paper described how "Scientists Ponder Saving Earth from a Comet," specifically, Comet Swift-Tuttle. Then as now scientists have been searching for spots in the solar system in which they could intercept Swift-Tuttle with nuclear rockets. (So you see, O Messrs. Forsyth and Hudelson, many scientists *do* share discoveries via that altruistic link, the hyphen.)

After that particular alert was canceled—or rather postponed until 3044—we then devoured a news story about a four-mile-wide stony dumbbell that had just whipped past us barely ten times the distance from us to the moon! And in 2004 The *Washington Post* informed us of another grim discovery: a six-mile-wide meteor that had crashed off Australia's coast 251 million years ago. Was this the reason that some seventy percent of land life died out at that time, along with ninety percent of the marine population?

Although Verne admitted that at the time his meteor hit the earth, science had nothing with which to stop it, clearly he was prophesying that science would need to develop something soon. Maybe that will be the reason the people of the earth finally unite in a common cause.

Prophecy, however, was only part of Verne's mission as a writer of scientific romance. The other part was to educate the lay public about science itself. In this novel that task has involved two sciences. In his lessons about astronomy Verne shakes us up over our naked vulnerability in space, where there are millions of asteroids and meteors whose paths often cross ours. The novel also excites us all over again about that elementary school subject, geography, driving us back to our maps and globes. We follow intently the reason why the S.S. *Moʒik*'s captain detours into the Gulf of St. Lawrence. And even for some allegedly sophisticated readers it's a surprise to discover that Greenland actually lies in Canada's back yard, is a part of North America, and that it's green only around the edges!

OBSESSIONS AND COMPULSIONS

A master of plotting, Verne paces his narrative according to the meteor's journey. Most of his characters' actions and reactions are direct or indirect responses to the shooting star's trajectory. An equally satisfying way of looking at the novel's structure is to see it as a fugue, a musical composition with four or more intertwining voices. First we hear the motif of the rich couple who are unripe for marriage but go ahead anyway. Then the statement about the two astronomers. Next the theme of the plan of Jenny and Francis to marry. These subjects follow a classical pattern of union, separation, reunion. Through these themes Verne threads a fourth, that of the judge's relationship with his housekeeper and his town, a more constant and stabilizing motif than the others. Verne develops these situations as steady, lively counterpoint.

To emphasize Verne's interest in the growth of personality, we can look at his characters in three distinct groups. There are those who are hopelessly obsessed: Mr. Forsyth, Dr. Hudelson, Omicron. There are those mildly obsessed and curable: Arcadia and Seth can learn to think and grow, thanks to the needs of love. And there are those who are already well-balanced thinkers, Francis and Loo, who hence love well and develop from there. Pursuing this line of thought, we may detect the traces of autobiography in *Meteor* that we have anticipated.

Intending to use these terms more in a literary than a scientific sense, we glean from the lexicons that an obsession is a persistent preoccupation with an irrational idea, attitude, or feeling. A compulsion is an irresistible impulse to repeat certain acts. Such preoccupations and urges can serve as a defense against anxiety from unresolved, maybe unconscious conflicts—adding up to obsessive-compulsive behavior.

In Verne's fiction we meet dozens of explorers, scientists, and madcap laymen who display such behavior. There's Phileas Fogg and his obsession with time, his ridiculously rigid daily routine; Captain Hatteras, who carries pole-seeking to the point of madness; the brain-locked astronomer Palmyrin Rosette, with his endless calculations; the manservant Conseil, trying to master an entire system of taxonomic classification by rote. Note, however, that these men carry out their irresistible impulses on large canvases—the Arctic, the seven seas, the whole world, even the whole solar system.

The Meteor Hunt also has its obsessive-compulsives: for instance, its two youngbloods running from themselves by perpetually roaming the globe, never having to "worry about what anybody else wanted," wistfully admitting that their values "don't prepare us very effectively for the obligations of marriage." But the novel's noisiest eccentrics are its two amateur astronomers, the bachelor Forsyth and the family man Hudelson. "Addicted to skywatching," these two hobbyists are "exclusively interested in discovering new stars and planets," yet, regarding each other as competitors, they get into "endless feuds."

What's amusing and distinctive about these over-the-top stargazers is that they act out their compulsions mainly on a domestic scale rather than on a vast heroic one. Their afflictions—compared with Fogg's and Hatteras's—are humble. They skywatch from their own rooftops in the chilly night air, missing meals, forgetting appointments, and getting bronchitis, sore eyes, runny noses. In this tale of "meteor madness," Verne's typically nutty protagonists go off the deep end in standard fashion, but—unusually for Verne—we see the homely, down-to-earth effects of their behavior on their middle-class families and neighbors.

The passing details in this novel are surprisingly realistic and homebound. Forsyth's housekeeper, Mrs. Mitz, sulks and scolds when he's late for lunch; Dr. Hudelson's wife and younger daughter routinely mollycoddle and manipulate him; their entire households are devastated when the competitors threaten the upcoming marriage of two members of their families. The anxiety, disappointment, and pain that result seem life-sized, believable, and domestic.

The two hapless skywatchers risk their decades-long friendship ("two days wouldn't have gone by without their . . . inviting each other over to dinner"); the bachelor Forsyth jeopardizes a forty-five-year working relationship with his housekeeper ("a couple of good-sized tears glistened in her eyes"); the married Dr. Hudelson utterly exasperates his sweet-natured wife (called "totally accepting" in chapter 3), so when he leaves town on an ocean voyage (chapter 14), she isn't "exactly heart-broken." During that voyage the two amateurs are so ruled by their unreasonable ideas and feelings that they don't deeply mind even being seasick. Finally, when their meteor has fallen to earth, both men are so driven to inspect the burning rock that they risk "turning into roast beef."

If behaviors like these can function as a defense against anxiety from unconscious conflicts, the question becomes: What conflicts? Does the bachelor Forsyth compensate for his celibacy by staying glued to his telescope, an obvious phallic symbol? Does the married Dr. Hudelson escape into space because he fears emotional entrapment as a lone male outnumbered by a wife and two daughters? Is sexual privation what drives both of them to obsessive overwork? Verne doesn't say, and could not, given that he's writing for family magazines in the pre-Freudian era. But of course the answer may relate more to the author's own life. For the fact that he's still toying with these questions at the end of his life says something about him and his work.

And there are signs of hope in this novel. Our first example of a curable obsessive who can grow and change is Arcadia. It's she who takes the initiative in giving marriage a second chance. Exploiting the idea of consoling Francis, she says, "Don't lose heart, Mr. Gordon, it'll all work out. A few hardships, problems, and anxieties are to be expected before a wedding. When getting married is too easy, there's an actual risk of the marriage going sour." This speech is obviously a result of some brave self-analysis (can we imagine Hudelson capable of such introspection?). Arcadia follows up with a subtle cue for her ex-husband—"Wouldn't you agree, Mr. Stanfort?"—who seizes the opportunity to confess his own misbehavior. The two obsessively independent travelers are learning how to become interdependent. They have become excompulsives, something the astronomers will never graduate to being.

Francis is, of course, the greatest contrast to the obsessive-compulsives, becoming a genuine foil for them. As Ophelia's brother Laertes, a man of action, stands against Hamlet's neurotic inaction, so the rational Francis stands against the mentally paralyzed stargazers. Partly to set Hudelson's mind at ease about leaving his daughter at home (and available to her forbidden lover), partly to see what he can do to untie the knots of the situation, Francis too makes the trip to Greenland. He takes every opportunity to ease the two rivals closer together, as with his subtle trick of moving their deck chairs nearer each day. And it's Francis who actually gets the snob de Schack to think of the forgotten astronomers and to agree that maybe they *do* deserve some of the fortune whizzing overhead.

This enables us now to return to the question of how much of *The Meteor Hunt* is autobiographical. Clearly Verne never could shake off the aura of his father Pierre, the obsessive time-fanatic who trained a telescope on a church clock and counted the steps he took from home to office. From Fogg to Hudelson, Pierre is a prototype for our author.

For the purposes of *Meteor*'s plot, Verne could easily have put Francis into any profession. But he chose the one for which he himself was training at the time that he suffered the Herminie trauma: the law. So are Verne and his early lost love the models for Francis and Jenny? Like Francis Gordon, Jules Verne had been forbidden by his beloved's father to see her. As Dumas put it when considering that this situation might be autobiographical, "Herminie's family . . . preferred the gold of a country squire to the hypothetical literary glory of the poet." Some students of Verne's life believe that the "unique siren" might also have been Herminie, returned to Verne later in life, this time to be taken away by the sterner father, Death. Is *Meteor* the medium in which our author imagines a happy ending for his affair(s) with Herminie?

Could these tragic events be the reasons—or some of them—why Verne himself became an obsessive-compulsive, a mad writer creating mad scientists, a workaholic defending himself from the effects of his frustrations in love and his anxieties over his miserable marriage? As Count Piero Gondolo della Riva put it, on a television show with WJM and other Verne fans, "It was impossible to live with him." His writing was his only escape from misery.

Surely Verne's own bitter experiences with women could explain his fretting ambivalence toward them in *The Meteor Hunt*. On the one hand, the judge lives "the untroubled existence of a bachelor," implying that married life is a troubled one. His housekeeper is nosy because "she's female," while out on the street stands a row of very nosy men. Hudelson is lucky to have "a model partner" in his wife Flora, but to earn that praise she has to be totally subservient, colorless, almost invisible. Adding that "everybody should have such a wife," the author implies he doesn't but should. Before Seth sees the light, he complains that raising American girls to be independent doesn't prepare them for "the obligations of marriage."

But on the other hand, Verne's own plotting leads Seth to the light. And our author himself obviously admires the independence of American women, especially when Loo steps out alone on a mission conceived by herself. She's of "a species that doesn't know the meaning of fear. They enjoy complete freedom, they come and go as they please," and Jules loves it. And he assigns some of the best thinking in the book to women: to Arcadia, not Seth; to Kate, not her boss; to Mrs. Mitz, not hers. Again, don't all these revolving contradictions sound like a male author suffering a turbulent and hopeless anxiety over his own unharmonized, unfulfilled relations with women, revealed in, but only partly relieved by, his writing?

Probably it was for more objective reasons that Verne expressed ambivalence for American characteristics. True, he can praise the way the United States has produced a new breed of women (for his time: some other nations have since caught up with or even passed America in that department). And his oeuvre sparkles with admiration for American technical and scientific prowess. But when he tries to typify your average American males he finds them hardheaded, pigheaded, "unbuttoned personalities," with their bowie knives, revolvers, shootouts, and lynchings, imperialists who imperil world peace with their violent tendencies. Chesneaux in his classic *Social and Political Ideas of Jules Verne* sees this as one of the less subtle political prophecies of the Prophet of Science (especially in a chapter titled "The American Mirage and the American Peril").

Yet when Verne focuses on specific American men, he finds many of them not raw flat types but three-dimensional human beings, individual thinkers like the gentle peacemakers Francis and Judge Proth.

SURFACE PLEASURES

But beyond its psychothematic concerns, the surface charms and pleasures of this novel are many. For instance, Verne arranges for his humble, local, domestic conflict to mushroom into a national issue, then into a global one. And while the tone of this progression is mockingly satirical, the event itself seems perfectly plausible and comprehensible. An international commission meets to determine how to portion out an eight-hundred-billion-dollar windfall and—what did we expect?—fails to reach any agreement. It's a choice example of mighty effects springing from tiny causes.

Or take Verne's dialogue. As usual, in *Meteor* he's such a master, we wish he would use it more often. Whether obsessive or thoughtful, his dramatis personae quickly characterize themselves in speech. "I've got a simple question for you, and all you have to do is answer yes or no." So Seth introduces himself as a no-nonsense, self-seeking go-getter. Proth's slower, circumspect, more contemplative statements practically label him as a well-respected judge. Loo's every word describes herself as bright, fresh, on-target, eager to amuse. Seth and Arcadia stage a superb duet as they agree on their grounds for divorce.

Speaking in his own voice, Verne poses throughout as the humorously inclined observer. Maybe the newspapers are attacking the astronomers because they let their subscriptions lapse? Will Galapagos be represented on the international commission by tortoises? Would Omicron (nicknamed after the small *o* in the Greek alphabet) deserve to be dubbed Omega (the big *O*) if he weren't such a pipsqueak? Is Greenland's name nothing more than an ironic wisecrack? We need only compare the titles of chapters 16 and 17 to appreciate the fact that the humorist never nods. Or think of entire scenes that are pure comedy: the couple on horseback asking if they need to dismount to get married; Omicron trying to get some recognition for his contributions to the teamwork without treading too heavily on Forsyth's greater need for recognition. Verne is a comic artist.

And it's also in his own voice that the author speaks in metaphors. We remember Loo most easily as a bird flitting here and there. "Figuratively speaking, [Mr. Stanfort and Miss Walker] would no longer be two ships convoying side by side, but a single top-quality vessel so well-rigged and so seaworthy it could sail any ocean." Then Verne shifts from this seaman's point of view to the music lover's when he wonders about the couple's failure in marriage: "Was there a wrong note in their wedding march?" (A dig, too, at how they'd foregone any such frills!) Verne sometimes even sees things as a homemaker when the situation suggests it: "'What!' Forsyth exclaimed, leaping up as if the seat cushion in his armchair had just poked him with a loose spring." When the weather improves, Verne sees the barometers as hard-working employees taking a vacation; near the end he even personifies a plateau as "underqualified." And islands dangle from Greenland like "a string of beads." Jules the boy poet excels in metaphor even as an old man.

And so now, a hundred years after Jules Verne's death in 1905, we're able to cancel out his son's travesty and give Anglophone readers one more benefit of Verne's own original scientific and sociopolitical prophecy, his scorn of greed and competition, and his superb ability to build a story, create new people, and teach us to enjoy language.

APPENDIX

Michel Verne as Editor and Rewriter

In the fifteen years immediately following Jules Verne's death in 1905, eight more *Voyages extraordinaires* appeared over his byline. These posthumous novels were accepted as authentic until 1978, when the Italian scholar Count Piero Gondolo della Riva discovered the original manuscripts and revealed that the posthumously published versions were partial or total counterfeits engineered by Verne's son Michel.

Even Brian Taves, a leading Michel apologist, acknowledges that the facts aren't in dispute. "Michel substantively altered all the works posthumously published under his father's name, in both minor and major ways, even originating two of the books himself," Taves states in a private communication to FPW/WJM. Yet controversy still surrounds Michel's motives and his ethical/moral standing in this deception: Many scholars denounce him outright, others want to spread the blame over additional family members, including Papa Jules himself. We see these issues as beyond the scope of this volume, so we'll confine ourselves to indicating *The Meteor Hunt*'s early publication history and to describing and assessing what Michel Verne actually did in preparing this novel for print.

As edited by Michel, *La Chasse au météore* appeared first as a serial in *Le Journal* from March 5 through April 10, 1908. On April 30 Hetzel fils published the full novel in both a luxury edition (illustrated by George Roux) and a twofer (coupled with *The Danube Pilot*, also edited by Michel). The following November, British publisher Grant

Richards issued a translation of Michel's text by Frederick Lawton, who entitled it *The Chase of the Golden Meteor*. Though couched in Edwardian English and skimping on occasional details, this rendering still gives a fair idea of Michel's handiwork, and it's this version that the University of Nebraska reissued in 1998.

In contrast to his father's MS, which features seventeen chapters, the son's version offers twenty-one—which is merely the most obvious of Michel's several thousand modifications, large and small, of his father's work. In drafting this comparison of Jules Verne's original with Michel Verne's rewrite, we've used the 2002 Archipel reissue of the first (the basis of the translation before you) and the Rencontre reprint (coupled with *Travel Scholarships*) of the second.

For the first seven chapters the two versions generally resemble each other, though Michel's revisions start with the very first paragraph, little touch-ups that mostly seem inconsequential, and also unnecessary. Among other trivial adjustments in this opening chapter, Michel adds a joke about Whaston's regrettable absence from the maps, gives Seth Stanfort "a face-elongating beard," and for some reason changes Proth from justice of the peace to plain judge. Forging ahead, he often fusses with the most innocuous details and wordings—as in this apparently pointless rephrasing during the discussion of space rocks in chapter 6:

> *Jules Verne*: comparing them to other rocks, one finds they have the same composition and contain nearly a third of all the elements.

> *Michel Verne*: their composition is no different from other rocks familiar to us, and overall they contain nearly a third of all the elements.

As the novel continues, so do the needless changes. In chapters 9 and 11, Jules Verne has the Boston Observatory determine the meteor's composition and the U.S. Naval Observatory the size of its nucleus, but his son reassigns these tasks to the observatories in Paris and Greenwich. Sometimes, too, Michel's tinkerings result in foolish errors, such as his slip in chapter 17 (chapter 15 in the original). There his father describes Greenland as *cette vaste region hyperboréenne* ["that huge High Arctic region"], which his son then mangles as *cette* verte *region hyperboréenne* ["that *green* High Arctic region"]. Michel's attempts at humor can also cause problems: for example, in chapter 3 his father extols the sweet-natured Mrs. Hudelson with a genial aside ("Everybody should have such a wife"), then Michel has to gild the lily with an acrid, antifeminist add-on ("Unfortunately they only exist in novels"). In the same vein he overhauls the feisty servant Mrs. Mitz, making her spew streams of clunky malapropisms: "astrocomical" when she means "astronomical," "absurditory" instead of "observatory," "spoiled eggs" for "boiled eggs," and similar groaners.

Beginning with chapter 8, however, the son no longer restricts his editing to minor fiddlings with detail: his changes are structural and significant. Michel consistently tones down Jules's observations on American mores, deletes his father's sly references in chapter 11 to his prior American novels, and omits the whole revealing passage where little Loo visits the enemy's lair in the role of mediator.

As for what remains, Michel inverts, rearranges, cuts, combines, substitutes, and—most crucially—fabricates major episodes, an additional storyline, and even new dramatis personae. Though his father's original locale and leading characters are *entirely* North American, Michel pulverizes this unity of place by abruptly shifting the narrative to Paris and dragging in a fresh cast of principals from left field: the scatterbrained inventor Xirdal, his pal Leroux, the cynical financier Lecoeur, and a meddling housekeeper called the Widow Thibaut. Michel jockeys these newcomers through a tomfool subplot sharply different in tone and believability from the storyline surrounding it: motivated by avarice, Xirdal purchases a tract of land, then forces the multibillion-dollar meteor to fall on it and thereby become his property; he carries out this scheme by inventing a mysterious apparatus powered by the made-up mineral Xirdalum, whose "neuter-heliocoidal" rays can "repel any object." In contrast to the decently researched science in his father's *Voyages extraordinaires*, Michel's technical explanations are gobbledygook, the slapstick complications that follow simply silly: the housekeeper Thibaut periodically tidies Xirdal's parlor, keeps repositioning the ray machine, and causes the meteor to change its trajectory repeatedly. What's more, Michel even reworks events in Jules's original that *aren't* connected with the meteor: in Michel's version the young aristocrats Seth and Arcadia become estranged because, out of the blue, they take opposite sides in the Forsyth-Hudelson conflict. Even less plausibly, Seth then arrives at the divorce proceedings by hitching a ride—somehow—on a hot air balloon engaged in studying the meteor.

Out the window, needless to say, goes the splendid surprise at the end of chapter 11 in Jules Verne's original.

From the hundreds of gratuitous rephrasings, to the cheap malapropisms foisted on Mrs. Mitz, to the jarring intrusion of the cartoonish Xirdal and his fictitious ray machine, Michel's alterations have the ultimate effect of coarsening, cluttering, and diminishing his father's work. Where the elder Verne is mischievous, plausible, deft, and cogent, his son is raucous, outlandish, blatant, and busy. It's almost as if Michel looked over his father's achievements, asked himself how he could best add to them, and then trotted out the old formula "If it's worth doing, it's worth overdoing."

ANNOTATED BIBLIOGRAPHY

Listed here are books, articles, and websites that are referred to in our critical commentaries or offer further information on topics we've discussed.

PRINT AND FILM

Allott, Kenneth. *Jules Verne*. London: Crescent, 1940; New York: Macmillan, 1941.

In the first Verne biography written in English, the scholarly Allott places Verne in the context of nineteenth-century thought. But he relies blindly on Marguerite Allotte's frequently inaccurate work (see below) and overlooks some of Verne's influence on science itself.

Allotte de la Fuye, Marguerite. *Jules Verne, sa vie, son oeuvre* [His life, his work]. Paris: Hachette, 1928. Translated as *Jules Verne* by Erik de Mauny (London: Staples, 1954; New York: Coward-McCann, 1956).

In a private communication to FPW/WJM, Taves sums it up: "Her exaggerations and errors are hardly well-meaning, but outright deceptions even more outlandish than Michel's alterations to the novels." Allotte is the source of many legends about Verne—e.g., his sailing off at age eleven as a cabin boy, and his command of English—which have derailed many a writer on Verne. She started endless speculation about Verne's "unique siren" by barely mentioning her.

Brockes, Emma, and Oliver Burkman. "Blame it on the Sunshine." *The Guardian*, May 30, 2001.

A view of the weather's influence on crime, similar to Dr. Hudelson's.

Butcher, William. *Verne's Journey to the Centre of the Self.* Foreword by Ray Bradbury. New York: St. Martins, 1990.

The United Kingdom's foremost Verne scholar and translator gives us a sympathetic and original study of Verne's spatial and temporal themes. In discussing the question of authorship of the posthumous novels, Butcher cautions that "we can still not rule out the possibility of spoken or written material by Jules Verne being a source." The fact remains that Michel, in effect, denies this in articles in *Le Figaro* and *Le Temps* on May 2 and 3, 1905, respectively.

La Chasse au météore. French television film, 1966. Director: Roger Iglesias; producer, Claude Santelli.

Chelebourg, Christian. "Le Blanc et le noir—amour et mort dans les *Voyages extraordinaires*" [White and black—Love and death in the "Extraordinary voyages"]. *Bulletin de la Société Jules Verne* no. 77, 1st quarter, 1986.

He brilliantly analyzes "the Herminie complex."

Chesneaux, Jean. *Une Lecture politique de Jules Verne.* Paris: Librairie François Maspero, 1971. Translated as *The Political and Social Ideas of Jules Verne* by Thomas Wikely (London: Thames & Hudson, 1972).

Chesneaux's is the classic work on the subject. However, he writes before Gondolo della Riva made his definitive discoveries about the posthumous novels. Hence Chesneaux's conclusions about them—including *The Meteor Hunt*—and about Michel Verne unfortunately tilt in the wrong direction.

Drake, Ross. "Duel!" *Smithsonian* (March 2004).

Overview of U.S. dueling from the revolutionary era to its decline after the Civil War.

Dumas, Olivier. "La Choc de Gallia choque Hetzel" [Comet Gallia's impact shocks Hetzel] and "Le premier dénouement *d'Hector Servadac*" [The first ending to *Hector Servadac*]. *Bulletin de la Société Jules Verne* no. 75, 3rd quarter, 1985.

————. "Preface: Le Savant chassé de *La Chasse*" [Preface: Chasing the scientist from *La Chasse*]. *La Chasse au météore (Version originale).* Paris: Société Jules Verne, 1986.

In his preface to the Society's limited edition, Dumas wants to chase

Michel's scientist Xirdal from the story: i.e., to go back to Verne's original text. He tells why, much the same way as in his next preface.

———. "Preface." *La Chasse au météore*. Paris: L'Archipel, 2002.

In a new introduction for the commercial edition, Dumas retells the story of how "Michel Verne, the writer's son, rewrote the works left by his father, changing their very nature."

———. "Le Maudite soif de l'or dans l'oeuvre de Jules Verne" [The cursed thirst for gold in the works of Jules Verne]. *Revue Jules Verne* (Amiens) no. 2, 1997.

Evans, Arthur B. *Jules Verne Rediscovered: Didacticism and the Scientific Novel*. New York: Greenwood, 1988.

After the mistranslation scandals were exposed, a new study was needed to inform Americans about the intellectual stature of the real Verne. Evans discusses America's popular misconceptions about Verne, then analyzes the educational purpose of the *Voyages*, their ideological subtexts (especially the positivist and romanticist visions), and Verne's didactic methodology.

Gondolo della Riva, Piero. "À propos des oeuvres posthumes de Jules Verne" [On the posthumous works of Jules Verne]. *Europe* (Nov./Dec. 1978).

One of the articles that changed our understanding of Verne's last works, his intellectual development in his final years, and his son's role in shaping his father's reputation.

James, Henry. *Daisy Miller*. Edited by Geoffrey Moore. New York: Penguin, 1984.

James's 1878 novella features a contrast between cultures like the one Verne alludes to.

Jules-Verne, Jean. *Jules Verne, a Biography*. Translated and adapted by Roger Greaves. New York: Taplinger, 1976. Translation of *Jules Verne* (Paris: Librairie Hachette, 1973).

Jean Jules-Verne gives a valuable account of his grandfather's life, including many poignant personal memories. But he's unconvincing in his view of "the unique siren." And his work is marred near the end with disinformation about the posthumous novels: as Taves asserts in a private communication to FPW/WJM, "He carried on the family charade" that Michel merely edited them.

Lottman, Herbert R. *Jules Verne: An Exploratory Biography*. New York: St. Martin's, 1996.

Lottman sifts fact from family myths, especially on the question of Michel's treatment of his father's works.

Margot, Jean-Michel. *Jules Verne et son temps* [Jules Verne and his times]. Amiens: Encrage, 2004.

A well-edited collection of writings by French critics (e.g., Emile Zola, Théophile Gautier) about Jules Verne and his work (1863–1905). Margot is president of the North American Jules Verne Society.

Miller, Walter James. "The Rehabilitation of Jules Verne in America: From Boy's Author to Adult's Author—1960–2003." *Extraordinary Voyages* (December 2003).

Published version of speech WJM gave at the Library of Congress, July 23, 2003.

————. *The Annotated Jules Verne: 20,000 Leagues under the Sea*. New York: Crowell, 1976.

To show the damage done to Verne's reputation by "the standard translation," WJM corrects and annotates Mercier Lewis's version; translates and annotates the twenty-three percent of Verne's text that Lewis had omitted, including crucial technical, philosophical, and political passages; discusses the overall textual problems in his "Foreword: A New Look at Jules Verne"; and sums up the results in his "Afterword: Jules Verne Rehabilitated." The afterword is reprinted in Sharon K. Hall, ed., *Twentieth Century Literary Criticism*, volume 6 (Detroit: Gale, 1982).

————. *The Annotated Jules Verne: From the Earth to the Moon*. New York: Crowell, 1978; New York: Gramercy/Random House, 1995.

Both editions contain WJM's new translation; a foreword on "Verne as a Political Writer" and "Verne as Private, Public, and Literary Selves"; annotations on technical, historical, and literary matters; and afterword on "Revaluation of *From the Earth to the Moon*"; appendices on how Verne calculated escape velocity (by David Woodruff and WJM; and on how the early translators damaged Verne's reputation. In the 1995 edition, WJM tops his foreword with news that "in the twenty-first century NASA will use a modified form of Verne's Space Gun to blast off payloads into Outer Space—at one-fortieth the cost of rocket liftoff."

Miller, Walter James, and Frederick Paul Walter. *Jules Verne's 20,000 Leagues under the Sea*. Annapolis MD: United States Naval Institute, 1993.

Newly translated and annotated. Nemo's life story is completed in an appendix, including a new translation of chapter 16, Part III, *The Mysterious Island*. WJM/FPW review the history of the textual problems in Verne publishing. According to Brian Taves (in Taves and Michaluk, "Corrections and Additions to *The Jules Verne Encyclopedia*"), "this should serve as the definitive English-language translation."

Roth, Edward. *The Baltimore Gun Club*. Philadelphia: King & Baird, 1874.

Roth "freely translated" and adapted *From the Earth to the Moon* for his own purposes, actually as a forum for his grievances against the women's rights movement, congressmen, the Philadelphia High School, and the Orion Debating Society of Catharine Street, Philadelphia. He gives us the impression that Verne wrote the novel in the first person. Roth quotes verses that he claims Verne wrote for an address to the Polytechnic College of Philadelphia. Roth's "translations" are typical of the wild exploitation of Verne's reputation that gave America a mainly incorrect picture of Verne and his work. Dover Publications, then in New York City, kept Roth's *The Space Novels of Jules Verne* in print until about 1980. They then honorably withdrew them after WJM's *Annotated Jules Verne* edition exposed them in "Appendix B: Some Notes for Purists on Verne's Translators." Not all publishers have been so ethical about Verne's 1870s Anglophone "translations."

Taves, Brian. "Review: Jules Verne, *The Chase of the Golden Meteor* (Lincoln: University of Nebraska, 1998)." *Extrapolation* (Summer 1998).

The Library of Congress expert on Verne complains that the translator mangled the meaning of the French text and that "there is no recognition of the obvious question of the true authorship of the novel."

———. "The Novels and Rediscovered Films of Michel (Jules) Verne." *Journal of Film Preservation* 62 (April 2001).

Taves, Brian, and Stephen Michaluk Jr. *The Jules Verne Encyclopedia*. Lanham MD: Scarecrow, 1996.

The core of the book is Michaluk's 100-page compilation of data about American and British editions of Verne's works. Eight other chapters include Taves' critique of "Hollywood's Jules Verne" and his "Jules Verne:

An Interpretation"; Ray Cartier's "Philatelic Tributes to Jules Verne"; and Edward Baxter's translation of Verne's short story "The Humbug: The American Way of Life."

Thomas, T. L. "The Watery Wonders of Captain Nemo." *Galaxy* (December 1961).

A malicious attack on Verne that signaled the low point of his reputation in America. Practically all of the errors (of omission and commission) that Thomas attributed to Verne himself were the handiwork of the translator, Mercier Lewis. These were listed and discussed in the 1965 Washington Square Press edition. The only error that seemed truly Verne's (about his scuba gear) was later proven by FPW to be yet another serious mistranslation (see the Naval Institute's *20,000 Leagues under the Sea*). Thomas's judgments were typical of those critics who didn't bother to check Verne's original French but carelessly trusted the Anglo-American translators.

"Verne, Jules." *La Chasse au météore*. Paris: Hetzel, 1908.

The semiforgery by Michel Verne. An honest edition would have listed him as coauthor and explained the changes and additions made to his father's original.

————. *The Chase of the Golden Meteor*. Translated by Frederick Lawton. London: Grant Richards, 1909.

Uneven translation of Michel's semiforgery.

————. *The Chase of the Golden Meteor*. Introduction by Gregory A. Benford. Lincoln: University of Nebraska, 1998.

A reprint of the 1909 edition that omits the translator's name. Benford's otherwise relevant assessment has one flaw: he didn't know he was working with a text not wholly Jules Verne's.

Verne, Jules. *Hector Servadac*. Paris: Hetzel, 1877.

Verne's first story about a heavenly body colliding with the earth. His original draft of chapter 20, the ending, was rejected by his publisher. Verne used its thesis as the basis for his own original version of *The Meteor Hunt*.

————. *La Chasse au météore (Version originale)*. Preface by Olivier Dumas. Paris: Société Jules Verne, 1986.

Limited edition, first printing from Jules Verne's original manuscript, the basis for the 2002 Archipel edition and of this University of Nebraska translation.

————. *La Chasse au météore*. New preface by Olivier Dumas. Paris: L'Archipel, 2002.

A commercial edition based on Dumas' 1986 text.

————. *The Mighty Orinoco*. Translated by Stanford Luce, edited by Arthur B. Evans, with introduction and notes by Walter James Miller. Middletown, CT: Wesleyan University Press, 2002.

The first-ever English version of Verne's *Le superbe Orénoque* (Paris: Hetzel, 1898). It was the first of Verne's novels to be suppressed in English, largely for political reasons. It helps destroy two hoary myths about Verne: that he rarely wrote about women and love, and that he seldom portrayed the working class. The question often raised in our critical commentaries of *The Meteor Hunt*—why Verne seems to swing from misogyny to androgyny—becomes almost irrelevant in *Orinoco*. Here he explores and dramatizes the basic androgyny of human personality.

————. *20,000 Leagues under the Sea*. Translated by Anthony Bonner. New York: Bantam, 1962.

According to Taves, "the first significant modern improvement over the Mercier translation, although flaws remained." These were corrected by FPW in a 2003 reissue. Bonner could have claimed a first, exposing the corruption of Mercier and the whole textual problem with English editions, but he wrote no preface. The job was left for the 1965 Washington Square Press edition.

————. *20,000 Leagues under the Sea*. Translated and with a preface by Walter James Miller; afterword by Damon Knight; illustrations by Walter Brooks. New York: Washington Square Press, 1965.

The preface, entitled "Jules Verne in America," is called "a dramatic introduction" by Taves and is credited with launching the rehabilitation of Verne in the Anglophone world.

————. *20,000 Leagues under the Sea*. Translated and with a foreword by Mendor Thomas Brunetti. New York: Signet Classics, 1969.

The second edition, published in 2001 includes an afterword by Walter James Miller, who discusses the early problems of rescuing Verne for the English-speaking world.

————. *Journey through the Impossible*. Translated by Edward Baxter; introduction by Jean-Michel Margot; artwork by Roger Leyonmark. Amherst NY: Prometheus, 2003.

This book typifies the renaissance of Verne in the Anglophone community. A production of the North American Jules Verne Society, it's the first-ever edition of *Impossible* in any language. Margot includes two long reviews of the original 1882 Paris production—one by a *New York Times* reporter—and annotates the entire edition. In this, his only true science-fiction work for the stage, Verne features situations and characters from three of his novels and one of his short stories.

Voltaire. *Candide*. Translated and with an introduction by John Butt. New York: Penguin, 1947.

From Judge Proth's frequent attention to his garden, we gather that Verne wants us to see the connection between *The Meteor Hunt* and Voltaire's classic novel, written in 1758 as an attack on the Leibnitz doctrine that "this is the best of all possible worlds."

ONLINE

http://lamar.colstate.edu/~hillger/ U.S. Metric Association Web site.

http://mathforum.org/library/drmath/view.58739.html. Drexel University's Math Forum Web site, which poses the same riddle found in chapter 10 of *The Meteor Hunt*: How long would it take to count to a billion?

http://www.cia.cov/cia/publications/factbook/. The CIA's *The World Factbook*, a comprehensive, up-to-the-minute source of unclassified information about every nation on earth.

http://www.cyberussr.com/hcunn/gold-std.html. Hugo S. Cunninham's Web site giving gold and silver standards, including historical conversion rates for major world currencies.

http://www.duellingoaks.com. Duelling Oaks Web site, devoted to New Orleans' famous grove—which they still spell with two l's.

http://www.naturesource.com. Offers space rocks for sale, including fragments of the Ensisheim meteorite.

http://www.psi.edu/projects/Siberia/Siberia/html/. Planetary Science Institute Web site, showcasing William K. Hartman's paintings and account of the 1908 meteor explosion over Siberia.

http://www.usno.navy.mil. U.S. Naval Observatory Web site.

IN THE BISON FRONTIERS OF IMAGINATION SERIES

Gullivar of Mars
By Edwin L. Arnold
Introduced by Richard A. Lupoff
Afterword by Gary Hoppenstand

A Journey in Other Worlds: A Romance of the Future
By John Jacob Astor
Introduced by S. M. Stirling

Queen of Atlantis
Pierre Benoit
Afterword by Hugo Frey

The Wonder
By J. D. Beresford
Introduced by Jack L. Chalker

Voices of Vision: Creators of Science Fiction and Fantasy Speak
By Jayme Lynn Blaschke

At the Earth's Core
By Edgar Rice Burroughs
Introduced by Gregory A. Benford
Afterword by Phillip R. Burger

Beyond Thirty
By Edgar Rice Burroughs
Introduced by David Brin
Essays by Phillip R. Burger and
Richard A. Lupoff

The Eternal Savage: Nu of the Niocene
By Edgar Rice Burroughs
Introduced by Tom Deitz

The Land That Time Forgot
By Edgar Rice Burroughs
Introduced by Mike Resnick

Lost on Venus
By Edgar Rice Burroughs
Introduced by Kevin J. Anderson

The Moon Maid: Complete and Restored
By Edgar Rice Burroughs
Introduced by Terry Bisson

Pellucidar
By Edgar Rice Burroughs
Introduced by Jack McDevitt
Afterword by Phillip R. Burger

The Moon Pool
By A. Merritt
Introduced by Robert Silverberg

The Purple Cloud
By M. P. Shiel
Introduced by John Clute

The Skylark of Space
By E. E. "Doc" Smith
Introduced by Vernor Vinge

Skylark Three
By E. E. "Doc" Smith
Introduced by Jack Williamson

*The Nightmare and Other Tales
of Dark Fantasy*
By Francis Stevens
Edited and introduced by
Gary Hoppenstand

Tales of Wonder
By Mark Twain
Edited, introduced, and with
notes by David Ketterer

The Chase of the Golden Meteor
By Jules Verne
Introduced by Gregory A. Benford

The Meteor Hunt
By Jules Verne
Translated and edited by Frederick Paul
Walter and Walter James Miller

The Croquet Player
By H. G. Wells
Afterword by John Huntington

In the Days of the Comet
By H. G. Wells
Introduced by Ben Bova

The Last War: A World Set Free
By H. G. Wells
Introduced by Greg Bear

The Sleeper Awakes
By H. G. Wells
Introduced by J. Gregory Keyes
Afterword by Gareth Davies-Morris

The War in the Air
By H. G. Wells
Introduced by Dave Duncan

The Disappearance
By Philip Wylie
Introduced by Robert Silverberg

Gladiator
By Philip Wylie
Introduced by Janny Wurts

When Worlds Collide
By Philip Wylie and Edwin Balmer
Introduced by John Varley